Maine Line to Wembley

Nick Udall

Copyright © 2025 Nick Udall

All characters and events in this publication, other than those clearly in the public domain, are fictitious and any resemblance to real persons, living or dead, is purely coincidental.

ISBN: 978-1-918264-22-7

For beautiful Doreen and our little pal Vincent.

Chapter One

Wembley. It was the centenary final and my first visit to the famous old stadium. The season could have ended in disaster but Big Mal had gone, John Bond had arrived and it was full steam ahead. In May 1981 City were a club transformed; the fans buoyed with enthusiasm. Over thirty thousand Blues were heading for the capital and my grandad, his pals and I were going too. It made me feel proud to be a Manchester man and conscious that for me, university beckoned and I had a decision to make. For so long I had assumed that I would leave for pastures new but then I met Millie and the desire to remain and study at Owens was increasingly difficult to resist. This weekend, the most important in the football calendar, would help to define the rest of my life.

It started before tea on Friday. Jumping off the 192 at Ardwick Green, it was over the grass towards Wadeson Road and my grandad's house off Hanworth Close. Determined that I would follow in his footsteps, he had taken me to Maine Road from the age of eleven. Now, he had secured us tickets for the final. Grandad had seen City five times at the famous stadium but I swear that he was more excited at the prospect of going for a sixth, than I was my first. He had wanted to take me in 'seventy-six but my mother had put a stop to his plans. Now that I was eighteen and on the verge of going to university, fears for my safety seemed somewhat ridiculous.

Walking along the familiar row of identical three-bedroom houses, the insubstantial rail fences marking off the small front gardens, I approached grandad's front door and knocked. The Brunswick estate was just over a decade old but it was already looking tired. The Corporation had attempted a re-brand but the new name had never caught on. Unwilling to turn their backs on the past the tenants still considered themselves residents of Chorlton-on-Medlock. The new homes had failed to herald in a bright new future. Poverty and disillusion abounded, fuelled by the dark economic tenets of Thatcherism and the attendant rise of unemployment.

As the door began to open, I was set and ready. With an excited bound, Shep was upon me, paws on my coat, wagging and panting in equal measure. A black labradoodle he was six now but had lost none of his energy. When he was a pup, I had been given the chance to name him and loving Blue Peter there seemed no other choice. And he didn't disappoint; he was barmy. Grandad loved him too, even forgiving him for drinking from the toilet, rather than his bowl, when someone forgot to shut the bathroom door.

As I walked into the hall and through to the front room Shep followed, bounding on to the settee as I sat down.

"Get down Shep!"

Grandad's voice seemed unusually terse and Shep quickly obeyed. It seemed that something was bothering his master. Soon it all became clear.

"It's going to have to be chippy for tea."

"Why's that then?" I asked.

"Muriel's gone home again"

I wasn't surprised. Their relationship had experienced a series of mini-crises. They had met a couple of years ago and although ostensibly they were living together, with marriage on the horizon, Muriel had the good sense to keep hold of her flat as a refuge to which she could retreat when co-existence became unbearable. Dougie Fraser was a hard man to live with; irresponsible and inconsiderate. Growing up, I had often seen his antics as hilarious. Once he had driven six-inch nails into the bedroom walls, hung his clothes over the length of string he had tied between them and then congratulated himself on avoiding the cost of a wardrobe. Easy going and disorganised, Dougie could drive Muriel to distraction, especially when he pretended to be hard of hearing. It was a tactic that he employed whenever he wished to ignore her. Eventually she had insisted that he go for a hearing test, after which he returned with a hearing aid. Muriel's delight soon turned to disappointment as Dougie would either mislay it, say that it was 'playing-up' or claim that the batteries were flat. Cocooned in his supposedly silent world, Grandad chose to hear as much as he wanted. Today though, she had clearly had enough. Yet far from being concerned that her departure may carry the risk of losing her, Dougie's focus was solely on the inconvenience that her absence would cause. Who was going to run around after him and see to his needs? I liked Muriel and had sympathy for her but Grandad clearly took her affection and hard work for granted.

"What's happened?" I asked, in a tone that wisely implied no criticism of Dougie.

"She's just being daft; complaining and moaning like she does. A typical bloody woman!"

I nodded sympathetically. It was the best thing to do but I wasn't convinced that the matter was quite so straightforward. Grandad soon confirmed my suspicions.

"She's got a cob on because I forgot her birthday."

"Oh, no. Didn't you try to say you were sorry?"

I knew straight away that I should have held my tongue for he was looking at me with suspicion in his eyes; disapproval at my sympathy for Muriel. It seemed that my words confirmed to him that living out in the suburbs, alongside my middle-class neighbours, had made me soft. I was a young man who had lost touch with the reality of how matters should be between a man and a woman.

"Say I'm sorry?" he asked, with a shake of his head. "I told her straight. I've had far too much on at work and having to sort out getting to Wembley. These things are important and if she can't see that, then it's just too bad. You can have a birthday any time. Bloody hell, she's had enough of 'em!"

Poor Muriel. I know that I shouldn't have but I couldn't help laughing. It did have the advantage of raising me in his estimation, a look of approval on his face in reaction to my outburst.

"Well, yes grandad," I said quickly. "Now that you put it like that."

"She said I loved the dog more than her," he continued. "That I always made a fuss of him and never forgot to take him out or feed him."

I shook my head in sympathy and raised my eyes in disbelief.

"But do you know what, Rick? She's right. I do love our Shep more than her, don't I boy?"

Hearing his name, Shep sidled up to his master, his body waggling in excitement.

Desperately, I struggled to stifle my laughter. Grandad was deadly serious and this was no time for levity. He was in a philosophical mood and about to impart some words of wisdom.

"It's like this Rick, our Shep's my best pal. Never complains. Always there to greet me when I come home and he'll see off anyone who tries to break in or attack me. He'll be faithful to the end. Now if you can find a woman out there that can show you anywhere near the same amount of loyalty, well I'll show my arse on Ardwick Green."

I nodded, an indication that I acknowledged his insight. It was the sensible thing to do. I loved all his little quirks, even to the extent of accepting that to him, I would always be Rick. I'd been christened Michael and almost straightaway Dougie, much to the chagrin of my mother, insisted on shortening it to Mick. Somehow, over the course of time and the fact that in my early years I saw nothing of him, Grandad began to refer to me as Rick. The name stuck and I was never inclined to correct him.

"Anyway, you need to get off to the chippy. I'm starving. Can you believe it? She cleared off without even making me a sandwich."

Reaching into his pocket, grandad pulled out his wallet and handed me a couple of pound notes.

"Fish, chips and peas for me Rick and whatever you're having. And go to the Chinese chippy at the bottom of Stockport Road. From what I've heard, the ones who've taken over Brunswick Street are no better than the old lot."

As I set off along Wadeson Road, I thought about my grandad. It had been our shared love of City that had brought us so close together. My dad, busy building up his business, had not been inclined to take me to Maine Road and my mother, swayed by the sensational stories of football hooliganism, would not allow me to go on my own. It was only after Dougie was back in our lives that she relented and allowed him to take me to the games. That was when I was eleven and my mother, Dougie's only daughter Anne, felt the need to finally reach out to him. Whether she felt guilty for not seeing him since the death of her mother, or feared creating a poor impression among the wives of father's business associates, if they found out how she had ignored him, I had no way of knowing. Importantly, as I got older, I was able to stay with him at weekends and in the holidays. It was an introduction to a world that was so different to the one I inhabited with my parents.

Dougie Fraser had been born in 1914 on Cresswell Street in Chorlton-on-Medlock. His grandfather was a highland Scot but his own roots were planted firmly in Manchester and I never heard him express any particular interest in his Scottish heritage. This didn't however, stop his closest friends from ribbing him about the matter. Apprenticed as a painter and paper hanger at fourteen, it was a trade he had followed ever since. Independently minded, Dougie had worked for himself almost as soon as he was able. Skilled at his work and charging reasonable rates, he was never short of customers. With more than a passing resemblance to Humphrey Bogart, he was also popular with the ladies and my mother was convinced that neither marriage nor the birth of his daughter had stopped him from carrying-on with other women when given the opportunity. In the War, Dougie had served in the navy and had many chilling stories to tell. Like how his crew had machine-gunned U boat survivors waiting to be rescued from the sea. Shocked at his revelation I questioned how he felt about it.

"They did it to us, so we did it to them," he replied.

"Do you still feel the same way now?"

He shrugged his shoulders.

"It was the War. Different times."

He had drawn a line underneath it and I understood why. The War had taken six years of his life and he would not allow it to impact negatively on him again.

"As kids growing up in the twenties, we saw so many broken men, their minds still living in the trenches. Those who couldn't cope were finished; no use to their families or themselves. Pals from the navy have gone the same way too. Not me. What's done is done. It was us or them and I'd have done anything to survive." I appreciated his honesty and understood why he never seemed to slow down. Surviving the best efforts of the Kriegsmarine to finish him off and given another chance at life, Dougie was determined to enjoy it, regardless of the negative judgements of others.

Chapter Two

Having returned with the chips, Grandad and I sat down at the table in the middle room where he had put out a couple of mats, plates, knives and forks, along with the salt and vinegar. Surprisingly, he'd saved me the job of buttering some bread; the clearest indication that he needn't have gone hungry that afternoon and could easily have made himself a sandwich. Yet that would have deprived him of the satisfaction of grumbling about how inconsiderate Muriel had been.

"Leave them in the paper Rick. The plates are cold. I've not warmed them up."

Nodding I placed the wrapped meals on the plates.

Almost immediately I could feel Shep's tail wagging furiously against my legs. Food was on offer and he was determined not to miss out.

"Boody hell Shep, give the lad a chance!" exclaimed Dougie.

Unwrapping his tea, he offered his pal a couple of chips. Wolfing them down, Shep sat down beside him, lifting his head towards his master. His ears pricked and his eyes wide and expectant, he waited for more.

"No, that's enough," said Dougie, sharply. "You've not long had your Winalot. Don't be bloody greedy."

Dougie talked to Shep on the assumption that he could understand every word he said. Perhaps he could for his pal soon got up and disappointedly slunk off into the front room.

"Are you going to make us a brew then?" asked grandad. "I normally have one with my tea."

Getting up, I walked into the kitchen and filled the kettle. I had the impression that this weekend I would be expected to fill in for Muriel.

"These chips are nice," shouted grandad. "Good job you didn't open yours right away, or they would have gone cold."

Taking in the drinks, I sat down. Unlike grandad's meal, mine was barely warm, a fact he was no doubt aware of as he sat back in his chair lazily drawing on a Benson.

"Your dad's not going tomorrow then?"

"No."

"Couldn't he get in the royal box with his pal Swales?"

Dougie laughed. He liked my dad; well, sort of. He recognised that John Taylor had given his daughter and grandson a secure and comfortable life but he couldn't help having a dig. After all, John ran his own company and was firmly across the divide; on the side of 'them' not 'us.' Furthermore, Dad's connections to members of City's boardroom didn't sit too well with him. He was already suspicious of those who ran the club and wasn't impressed that his son-in-law had done business with them.

"I suspect he'll be having a round of golf tomorrow rather than watching the game on Grandstand," I ventured.

Dougie sighed and shook his head.

"Yes, lad. A part-time supporter. He's not like us, is he?"

"No, I'm afraid he isn't."

"How's your mam?" asked Dougie. "Is she keeping well?"

"Yes. Why don't you come down to see her?"

"No. It's too much messing about."

"We're only in Sale. It's not the ends of the Earth."

"I know, but I can't just drop in, can I? Your mam expects me to make an appointment. That might be all right for her posh friends, but it's no good to me. That's what you get from mixing with the middle-classes. Everything's so bloody formal. No nipping in and out of each other's houses like we do round here. That's because we're not false and don't have things we want to hide from one another."

He was right. Mother certainly didn't want him turning up when she had any of her own friends at the house. Dougie never hesitated to call 'a spade a spade,' no matter who was present. The thought of the embarrassment that this could cause was terrifying to her. Dougie knew that his daughter would rather visit him back in Chorlton-on-Medlock and as sparingly as possible. Nevertheless, he wasn't concerned. Through a shared love of City, he had connected with his grandson and I was the only part of his family that he needed.

"What are you doing tonight grandad?" I asked, changing the subject.

"I'm meeting Vic in the 'King Billy,' so you've no need to stop in with me. Anyway, I suppose you'll be wanting to see that lass of yours."

"Yes. Millie's expecting me to go round after tea."

Grandad smiled

"I thought so. You've got it bad, haven't you?"

His comment hit the mark, but it still caught me unawares and I struggled for an answer. Dougie laughed.

"Well, I don't blame you. She's a nice girl Rick; friendly too. She always lets on when she sees me and there's not many lasses her age would. You'll have to keep on your toes though. All the lads'll be running round after her. I'd tell you to make sure that you treat her right but I've no doubt you do anyway."

It was surprising to hear Dougie's comments. He rarely paid compliments to anyone, especially not young women. Advising me to treat her with respect didn't correspond to the cavalier way in which he dealt with the women in his life. I knew that he would never consider any feelings of remorse towards them or acknowledge that he had made mistakes that he didn't want me to repeat. Dougie didn't care when women left him, for he would always find someone else to come along, share his bed and do his cooking and cleaning. No matter how old he was getting, they always did. 'Take me as you find me or leave me alone,' was the tenet that governed his life. I was pleased he had recognised that I was different; that my relationship with Millie was so important to me. Not once did he ridicule my feelings for her.

I got to know Millie just before Christmas. Wearing a short, black leather jacket, blue top, beige pants and heels, she walked quickly and with purpose; light on her feet and graceful. Millie was exceptionally pretty and had a stunning figure, yet that tight jacket gave her an edge; tough and independent. Passing, she had given me a smile; one that I returned. Twice more I had passed her and again she had smiled. Unsure of myself I was unable to speak, for it was hard to believe that she could possibly be interested in someone like me. It therefore fell to Millie to make the introductions and she did so one Friday tea-time when I emerged from the newsagents on Brunswick Street as she was coming in.

"Hello," she said, "we must stop meeting like this."

She laughed, her green eyes sparkling as her soft lips parted into a welcoming smile.

"I'm Millie. Your Dougie's grandson, aren't you?"

Her words had taken me by surprise and although thrilled that she had spoken to me, I hesitated, only able to smile weakly at her in return.

Shaking her head, her long hair gently curling around the sides of her face, she laughed once more.

"Well, are you?"

"Yes, I am."

"I suppose you have a name, don't you?"

"Yes, of course."

I was captivated. Millie was truly beautiful. So natural. The freshest of complexions, with only a hint of makeup around her gorgeous green eyes.

"Well, are you going to tell me?" she asked. "Or am I supposed to guess?"

"It's Michael."

"Dougie said that you live in Sale and that you'll be off to university to study history in September. Is that right?"

"Yes, fingers crossed. I sit my exams in June."

"I don't envy you. When I was revising for my 'O' Levels it seemed to go on forever."

"Yes, it does, but I'll have to do it to get the grades for my offers."

"Where do you want to go?

"I haven't made a final decision yet but I suspect it will be Birmingham. I liked it there when I went for the interview."

"Not Manchester then?"

"Well, they have given me an offer but I can't help thinking that it's the safe option. I'll be too close to home and it won't force me to become independent. I want to experience living in a different city in another part of the country."

"But you can always do that later. Perhaps you just need to find something that'll make you want to stay in Manchester. Something that you won't be able to find anywhere else."

Millie fixed me with her alluring eyes and a smile that was cheeky and suggestive. I wasn't exactly sure what she meant but I couldn't deny that I felt a thrill of excitement. For a moment I dared to think that perhaps, through her, I would gain experiences that went well beyond the bounds of mere academic learning. Quickly however, she turned to more practical matters.

"Dougie said you don't know anyone on the estate yet, so I thought you could come over and meet some of my friends. I'll expect you after tea, around seven."

Giving me her address, she said goodbye and entered the newsagents. As I walked back to Dougie's, my head was in a spin. I was surprised that she had spoken to my grandad about me but I realised that given her generous nature, she was offering me the hand of friendship. Millie had made an indelible impression upon me. She was beautiful and enchanting and I already wanted more from her than just friendship. That however, was something that lay in the future.

Chapter Three

Over the following weeks I found out that Millie was eighteen and had lived on the estate for ten years. Her father had deserted his family when she was a baby and her mother had left when she was thirteen. Millie's elder sister Jeanette and her husband Terry had taken over the tenancy and moved into the house with their sons Craig and Gary, ensuring that Millie wasn't taken into care. Attending Central for Girls, Millie had done exceptionally well in her 'O' Levels but had no desire to stay on at school. Independently minded, she was keen to secure a good job and a steady wage with which to support herself and had therefore taken a position with Lloyds Bank.

It didn't take me long to discover that Millie Arkwright had a playful sense of humour and having recognised my rather serious demeanour, wasn't averse to teasing 'the posh lad from Sale.' Yet almost immediately she made it clear that she wouldn't allow any of her friends to cast aspersions on my sheltered and privileged background. I could see that most of them were surprised at her interest in me, for certainly we seemed to have little in common. On the surface, that view seemed to have validity. It was clear that Millie had little interest in history, a fact I learned early when she was dismissive of my efforts to engage her in conversation about her family name and her possible connection to Richard Arkwright, father of the factory system. "Was he really? How interesting," she had said and then burst into laughter, leaving me red faced with embarrassment. Nevertheless, she was supportive of my desire to go to university and took pride in telling others about my academic ambitions.

After that first visit to Millie's, I was completely captivated by her. Now I was spending every weekend at Dougie's, not only those when City were playing at home. It must have been obvious to Millie how eager I was to be with her but she never indicated any reluctance to see me. Yet, wrestling with my uncertainty, I was unable to make the connection; that perhaps she was developing similar feelings for me. Never one to take a risk, I felt it better to leave matters as they were. I would share Millie with her friends, although continuing to desire more intimate moments together. Deep down I knew that if I asked her to go out with me and she refused, that everything would end. I would have no alternative but to walk away, for how would I be able to stand by and see her in the arms of another? Of course, it had become obvious to Millie that I had fallen in love with her and fortunately for me, she was determined to do something about it.

The catalyst that finally brought us together came with my first visit to the 'Cyprus Tavern' and an encounter with Millie's ex-boyfriend, Scott. Located on Princess Street, the 'Cyprus' was just a short walk from the estate and so a popular late-night destination for dancing and drinking among the younger residents. It did have a bit of a reputation for trouble too and although it was a warning that I didn't need, I was told to be careful not to antagonise the bouncers. Millie loved dancing and it was surprising that she hadn't taken me there before. This evening, it was her friend Dawn's eighteenth birthday and it was decided that we should all go to the club to celebrate. Dawn and Millie had first started going when they were sixteen. Dressed-up, they didn't appear underage and as attractive young women, the bouncers were eager to welcome them through the door. Working at a clothes shop in the underground market, Dawn prided herself on wearing the most up to date fashions and seemed to have almost as many outfits as she did boyfriends. Having just finished with her latest, she had announced that it was her intention to cop down at the Cyprus. With a bubbly personality and being particularly well endowed, she was never short of attention. When it was suggested that she may get tired of men obsessing over her breasts, she simply declared: "If you've got them, flaunt them."

The club's entrance was dingy and unassuming. Inside it seemed relatively small, a series of arches attempting to give some character to the room. There seemed little space to dance, given the number of tables along the walls and the long, well-stocked bar to one side. Finding a table, we sat down. Flashing lights penetrated the gloom and the bass from the speakers boomed and throbbed as the regulars moved eagerly to the beat. It was loud and difficult to talk, but no-one cared, for they were there to dance. And Millie was a magnificent dancer, soon on her feet and moving seductively to the rhythm. Holding out her hand, she attempted to entice me on to the floor. I hesitated, knowing that when it came to dancing, I had two left feet but Millie just smiled.

"It's alright," she said. "Just enjoy it and do your best."

I tried, but despite her encouragement, I still felt foolish. Stiff and wooden, I must have looked ridiculous. As we sat back down, Millie laughed and shook her head.

"Well, you aren't John Travolta, are you?"

Before I could reply, Millie stood up and approached a tall, young guy who had been heading towards our table. Checking his progress, the two of them were soon deep in conversation. It was clear that Millie knew him and that the exchange had taken a more serious turn. The lad moved to the side, looking around Millie and towards us. In the flashing lights it was possible to see the anger on his face and Millie place her hands forcibly against his chest. It appeared that she was trying to calm him down. Having no idea who he was and beginning to become concerned, I moved back in my chair and started to get up. Straight away I felt a hand on my knee. It was Dawn.

"No Michael. Stay where you are. Millie's fine."

"But he looks angry. I should help her."

"There's no need. She can handle him."

I later realised that Dawn, just like Millie, was trying to protect me.

Looking at the lad, it did seem as if he had started to calm down. Slightly reassured, I asked Dawn who he was.

"It's Scott Lloyd, a lad we know off the estate."

"Well, he's certainly not happy about something."

"It's nothing serious. He's just had a bit too much to drink."

Dawn's confidence seemed well founded as the lad moved off and Millie sat back down on the other side of her friend. She then spoke quietly to Dawn who nodded.

"Is everything alright?" I asked.

"Yes," replied Millie. "It's fine."

"I'll go and find Dave," said Dawn, getting up.

Dave McClellan lived next door to Millie and like Dawn, had gone to school at Nicholls. A year older, he had for a time been Dawn's boyfriend. A City fanatic, he regularly travelled away, often getting into scrapes with opposition fans. A sheet metal worker, Dave was feared by the other lads on the estate. Given that I had always found him friendly, I found it hard to understand his reputation. He certainly loved to dance and never found himself short of partners. Ten minutes later, he and Dawn returned. Nodding at me, he turned to Millie.

"You and Michael can get off now. I've had a word."

"Come on Michael," said Millie. "Time we were getting back."

"Oh, you don't want to stay any longer?"

"No, I've danced enough for one night."

It was a surprising answer, for she hadn't been on the dance floor that long. I was certain that Millie was keeping something from me and that it involved Scott Lloyd. As we walked out of the 'Cyprus' and down Princess Street, I asked her about him.

"That lad you were talking to, he appeared to be angry. Was there a problem?"

"No, not anymore. We went out together but he was too possessive. I finished with him just before I met you."

"If you don't mind me asking, why was he behaving like that?"

She looked at me approvingly, pleased I had recognised that I couldn't just pry into her affairs.

"It's because he was jealous at seeing us together. He knows that you've been coming to the house and he thinks that you're the reason I stopped going out with him."

"But that's not true."

"Well, he's gormless, isn't he?"

"He must be," I replied. "I'm sorry I didn't help you. I didn't know what was going on and Dawn told me to stay where I was; that you'd be fine."

"Yes, she knew that I wouldn't want you to get involved."

"But will that be an end to it? He lives on the estate. What happens if he tries to cause you any more trouble?"

"He won't. I can handle him and besides, Dave's had a word and so there won't be any more nonsense. You can be sure of that," replied Millie, chuckling softly.

Despite her assurances, I still felt uneasy.

"I'm sorry Millie."

"Why?"

"Because I've let you down. I should have dealt with him. After all, I was the one he was angry with."

Millie stopped, taking hold of my arm.

"And what would you have done? Thrown your weight around; or tried to."

She was unhappy with me, but I didn't know why. I looked at her rather sheepishly.

"I can get any man who hits first and thinks later. You should know better. You don't have to prove anything to me and I wouldn't respect you for acting like an idiot and getting involved with Scott."

"Yet you and Dawn asked Dave to sort him out."

"That's different. Dave's off the estate. It's his world, not yours and besides Dave's heart's in the right place and I know that a warning from him will be enough."

Millie's words were pleasing. She had told me off but made it clear that she liked me just the way I was. I would never be tough like Dave but it didn't matter. The soft, sheltered lad from Sale was fine by her.

"And as far as Scott's concerned, I've told him straight. I'll go out with whoever I want, so he'd better get used to seeing the two of us together."

I was shocked. Had I heard right?

"Going out together?"

"Yes," replied Millie. "Is that a problem?"

Her voice was sharp; the tone clipped. She stared at me sternly.

"Well, is it?"

"No. No. Of course not. No problem at all."

I was stumbling over my words. My dream had become reality but I had imagined the moment of its realisation to be so different. Instead of wonder, there was shock. But that was Millie, wonderfully unique, gorgeous and in control.

Seeing my reaction, she laughed and gave me one of her cheeky smiles.

Turning into Grosvenor Street, Millie took hold of my hand, her fingers softly entwined around mine. Walking quietly together, my mind was struggling to accept that we truly were a couple, for Millie had revealed her feelings so suddenly and unexpectedly. It was hard to accept my good fortune and I started to fear that she would soon reconsider what she had said and change her mind. Reaching her front door, we stopped to say goodnight.

"Well, aren't you going to kiss me?" asked Millie.

There was nothing I wanted more but still, I hesitated.

"It's all right. I won't bite," she said, laughing.

Slightly embarrassed, I felt nervous. I had never kissed a girl properly before and I was desperate not to disappoint. Almost breathless, my heart began to pound. I had never known such a sense of anticipation. It felt electric but I remained uncertain. Understanding, Millie leant forward, put her arms around me and pressed her lips softly against mine. Suddenly it seemed so natural, my lips responding in return. It was our first intimate moment and one that I would always treasure.

When finally, we parted, I walked slowly back to Dougie's. I needed time to reflect on what had happened. It had been the most important night of my life and I was determined that I would remember every single detail. I never wanted to forget. I had admired Millie from afar, before becoming her friend and now I was certain that I had fallen in love. Already, I was thinking differently; no longer in terms of I, but of we. Now, the question of where I would be at the end of the summer, was no longer as straightforward as it once had seemed.

Chapter Four

On the eve of City's visit to Wembley, my eagerness to see Millie underlined the fact that the health of our relationship had become my main priority. Much as I was looking forward to tomorrow's final, I knew that I would find defeat far easier to accept than the prospect of Millie's rejection.   Had Dave known how I felt he would have been unimpressed, but there it was. At first, Millie had teased me, suggesting that I was suffering from infatuation. My professions of love were simply inspired by the excitement of innocence and inexperience. As the weeks passed however, my feelings had been confirmed. With Millie, I could find no fault. Everything about her confirmed that she was wonderful and she appeared even more beautiful every time I saw her.

Tonight, I would join Millie on baby-sitting duty; keeping an eye on her nephews, Craig and Gary, whilst her sister Jeanette and husband Terry enjoyed a rare night out. The latter worked as a driver for Pickfords Removers. The job was handy as the depot was nearby on Grosvenor Street but demanding as Terry was sent all over the country and so had to spend many nights away. Employed by a large and successful company, Terry was fortunate that in the difficult economic climate his job was secure. Nevertheless, it was hard graft and the wages, though reasonable, didn't allow Jeanette to save quickly enough to realise her ambition of moving off the estate and buying a house of their own in the leafy suburbs. Once there, she felt certain that her boys would escape the dangers of being sucked into a life of juvenile crime and delinquency that seemed likely to destroy the prospects of so many of their contemporaries.

As usual I entered the garden by the back gate, walked to the door and knocked. Millie opened it and stood there smiling, a hair brush in her hand and invited me into the kitchen. My eyes lit up; it was the first time that I had seen Millie in a skirt. The hem reached just below her knees, allowing me to admire her slim, delicate ankles and beautiful, well-formed calves. A stunning sight, I breathed in sharply, struggling to control my emotions.

Wearing her heels, skirt and blouse, Millie looked the height of sophistication. Not failing to notice my reaction she smiled.

"I've not had chance to get changed from work," she explained. "I've been busy helping Jeanette with her hair."

"Oh."

"So, you like me like this then?"

"You've got legs."

Still mesmerised by the sight of them, it was all I could think of saying. Almost immediately, I felt stupid.

"Of course," replied Millie, laughing.

"I mean, you can't see them when you're wearing pants."

"Can't you? Why not?"

"You know what I mean."

"Ah, I understand. What you're saying is that you can't see my bare legs through the material. Well now you can have a good look, can't you?"

Millie paused, smiling mischievously. She was clearly enjoying my embarrassment.

"Anyway," she continued. "I don't think they're much to look at. I've got footballer's legs."

"Oh no, they're beautiful," I replied, unable to hide my admiration.

Hearing laughter from behind her, I realised that we were not alone.

Standing to one side, Millie invited me into the kitchen. Jeanette was sat on a chair, a hair dryer, rollers and pins on the worktop beside her. Millie had been helping to set her hair. Stepping inside, I waited whilst Millie took a mirror and held it in front of her sister. Bobbing her head up and down, Jeanette turned her face to the sides.

"Yes, that's very nice. Thanks."

"That's all right."

"Do you like it, Michael?" asked Jeanette.

An unexpected question, I hesitated.

"You've made him feel uncomfortable. He doesn't know what to say."

Millie smiled and they both started laughing. Just like her sister, Jeanette wasn't averse to making fun of me.

"Are the boys in?" I asked, eager to change the subject.

"Not yet, they'll need to come in soon though," replied Millie.

"Yes, I like them in for half-six," added Jeanette.

The weather had warmed up now and the days were getting longer, excellent for the boys who got to play out after school but stressful for their mam who couldn't help worrying about them.

"They're only in the park, they'll be all right," remarked Millie.

"Well, just so long as they don't wander off. With all these cars racing round the estate and the cops chasing after them, some innocent kid's bound to get knocked down."

"I'm sure Craig and Gary will do as they're told and stay in the park."

"I hope they do but you can't tell. The other day I heard them talking about some of their friends going to the banana pond at UMIST. It frightened the life out of me. They crossed the Mancunian Way to get there. I told them that they weren't allowed to go and if they did, their dad would give them a good hiding."

"I'm sure they wouldn't," said Millie.

"Well, our Craig's got sense but you know what Gary's like. Too easily led."

Millie nodded.

"Yes, that's true but like you said, Craig's responsible. He'll look out for Gary."

"I try not to let the lads see that I'm worried about them. Terry tells me that sometimes I'm overprotective and it's not doing them any favours."

"That's right," came a voice from the next room.

Moving to the doorway I looked in and saw Terry at the table. Small, but powerfully built, his muscular frame the legacy of years of heavy lifting. With fiery red hair and a firm set jaw, he looked like a man you had no wish to cross, yet his soft eyes and gentle smile marked him as a loving husband and father. Already wearing his best jacket and tie, he had been ready for some time. In front of him was the Evening News, open at the sports page.

"Looks like your lot are going to be able to put out a strong side tomorrow."

Terry paused and nodded, he was a 'Red' and I was well-aware of what was coming.

"That's a shame. Then again, you're not going to have any excuses when you get beat, are you?"

Terry smiled wickedly. He would be made-up if it all went wrong for us tomorrow.

"Well," I replied, "We can't give you as big a laugh as you did us when Alan Sunderland got that last minute winner for Arsenal in 'seventy-nine. I remember you were all celebrating so much after coming back from two down, that you didn't see him put the ball in the net. Priceless. Talk about being brought down to Earth with a bang."

Terry winced. It was a great put-down and one I had been working on. There was nothing worse than being caught out by a rival's quip and not being able to think of a witty or acerbic rejoinder. Always remember; forewarned is forearmed.

"You can stop that you two," warned Jeanette. "We're off out. There'll be no arguments tonight. Men and their football. They get on my nerves!"

"There won't be any, love. Laddo knows I'm right," said Terry, laughing.

"Millie, can you and Michael go and fetch the kids whilst I get ready."

"Yes, of course."

Walking towards the park, I asked Millie about the car chases mentioned by Jeanette.

"Some of the older lads are going into town and breaking into cars," she replied. "Then they drive them back to the estate and race round the streets, hoping that the cops will chase them."

"Aren't they bothered about getting caught?"

"They don't think they will. It's easy to abandon the car, nip down the walks and alleys and into one of their friends' houses before the cops can get them."

"I see."

"Anyway, they don't care," continued Millie. "It's likely that they'll only get a slap on the wrist if they're caught and if they've been up before the magistrates, it makes them look tough. Gives them a reputation among the other lads."

"I don't see why when they could end up causing a crash or knocking someone down."

"But they don't think like you, Michael."

"Well, someone must know who they are. Like Jeanette said, it could be a young child who gets run over. Why don't they tell the police?"

"Everyone knows who they are but if you tell the cops, then you'll be lucky if you only get your windows put in."

"But how will they know who told them?"

"Because the cops need witnesses and if you give them your name and address, they come to your house. If they do, these lads find out and then you're a target."

"What you're saying is that the criminal element is effectively running the estate."

"In a way but it's not as simple as that. The police aren't trusted because all too often they don't treat people with respect."

"Why?"

"Because we live on a council estate and so they assume that most of us are villains."

"But that's nonsense."

"Of course it is, but unlike you, few coppers are fair-minded."

"Don't people complain?"

Millie laughed and shook her head.

"And who's going to take any notice? People are poor here; working-class. We don't count."

I nodded. For a moment I felt foolish. I was looking at matters from my safe, middle-class perspective, where notions of honesty and decency and 'doing the right thing' seemed so straightforward. But here, life was tough. To get by, it was necessary to accept that there were fewer moral certainties. It was why Millie had far more maturity than I; a pragmatism born out of experience. Not for her the idealism of a sheltered youth.

"I suppose that's why Jeanette wants to move away."

"Yes. At first, she was happy here. The houses are nice but then she realised it wasn't like where she'd been living in Denton. There, people looked out for one another. Everyone took an interest in the kids; made sure they didn't misbehave. Here it's different. People have been thrown together from all over and there's little sense of community. Parents won't accept their kids being told off by strangers and as the bad ones have got older, they do as they like and now many people have become afraid of them. Jeanette's worried that our Craig and Gary will turn out the same."

Reaching the park, we soon found Craig and Gary playing football with their pals. It was pleasing to see Gary throwing himself around; a young kid unafraid of the bigger lads and never shirking a challenge as he showed his determination to keep the ball out of the temporary net that was marked out by a couple of hastily laid jumpers.

"Craig, Gary, time for in," said Millie.

Her words brought the action to a shuddering halt.

"Oh no! Do we have to?"

Gary's pained expression reflected a deep sense of injustice.

"Yes. Your mam and dad are off out."

"But we can't stop now," said Craig, "we need to score a winner."

He was right. This game was as important to the kids in the park as tomorrow's was to the players of City and Spurs. There wasn't a field in the land that didn't represent Wembley to those who played on it. I wanted to back them up but just like the boys, I knew that it was pointless. Millie was in charge.

"Well, you'll just have to settle on a draw."

"But it's not fair," replied Craig.

"Well, it's not raining."

Millie smiled but the pulled lips persisted. The boys either hadn't got the joke or were unimpressed. Keen to cheer them up, I stepped in.

"I saw some good saves when we were walking over Gary. From a distance I thought I was watching Big Joe."

"Huh, he's rubbish," observed Craig. "Our kid's already better than him."

"Yeah, I'm going to be like Gary Bailey," said his brother, proudly.

"Fair enough," I said, being diplomatic. "He's a decent enough keeper."

The boys were Reds; Terry had made sure of it. Never mind, they were nice kids. Who they supported depended on family. It wasn't their fault but I resisted the temptation to feel sorry for them.

I had seen a lot of the boys since meeting Millie. Always full of energy, they would greet you with a beaming smile, faces full of freckles and ginger hair. Unlike most siblings, they rarely argued and they went everywhere together. They soon accepted me, especially as we played football together. Telling them that it would soon be time to turn to cricket, I was shocked to discover that they had rarely played. Outrageous as it was, I had to accept that to the boys, Old Trafford meant United and not Lancashire. I suppose it wasn't surprising. Here on the estate, close to the heart of the city, where were the neatly mown squares and carefully prepared wickets? The game seemed alien; one for the green and wealthy suburbs.

Millie was pleased at how well the boys and I were getting on. It had even prompted her to offer some careers advice.

"I've been watching you with Craig and Gary," she said. "You're as barmy as they are."

"Oh?"

"Yes."

For a moment I was concerned. Was she unimpressed?

"I don't mind. It's nice to see that you aren't always so serious."

I nodded, happy that she approved.

"But it isn't just Craig and Gary," she continued, "their friends like you too."

"Do they?"

"Yes. You must have noticed."

"Well, I suppose so."

"They can see that you take an interest in them; that you're genuine. Kids aren't easily fooled, you know."

"No. I'm sure they're not."

"I know that you haven't thought much about what you want to do when you finish university but I think you'd make a good teacher."

I was surprised.

"It's not something I could ever see myself doing," I replied.

"I don't see why not. You understand kids and you're fair and decent. It's what schools need. There are far too many nasty and vindictive teachers."

"Well yes, there are, but I can't see me as someone to replace them."

"But Michael, think about it. You could be just like Ken Barlow."

Surprised, I looked at her closely. She seemed so sincere. Then in a flash she burst into laughter. Once again Millie had been pulling my leg, although her original suggestion that I should consider becoming a teacher had been made in all seriousness.

"I knew the thought of all Ken's affairs would get you interested."

"No, it didn't."

"You went very quiet thinking about it though, didn't you?"

I hadn't thought any such thing but Millie had still made me feel embarrassed; a fact that she was clearly enjoying.

"Anyway, I definitely wouldn't be a teacher," I insisted. "I couldn't bear the thought of inhabiting the same world as some of the old curmudgeons on the staff at my school."

"Well, if you say so," she replied, a cheeky grin on her face.

Shaking my head, I smiled. Millie liked to tease but in the gentlest possible way. A ray of sunshine brightening up my life.

Chapter Five

After we had left the park and walked past the end maisonette on Hursthead Walk, Millie turned left.

"I'll need to get some milk from Giovanni's in case Dawn, Dave and Mark drop in."

Craig and Gary, unusually silent as they trudged back home, perked up.

"Can we have some toffees?"

Millie stopped and looked at them.

"And what do you say?" she asked, sternly.

"Please," mumbled the boys, lowering their eyes to the floor.

I smiled. They, like me, recognised that Millie was the boss.

"That's better. You can have twenty pence each and no more."

"Thanks Auntie Millie."

Given Millie's relative youth, it sounded a strange form of address. I always thought of aunties as middle-aged or elderly women carrying handbags and wearing big hats and long dresses. I suppose from the boys' perspective, Millie naturally seemed much older and wiser and besides Jeanette, keen on instilling respect, insisted that it was what they must call her.

Giovanni ran the only shop on the estate this side of Brunswick Street. He was Italian, having arrived in Manchester with his wife Silvia and young son, many years ago. No one knew from where in Italy he originated and just why he had decided to move to Manchester and Giovanni always stayed tight-lipped over the matter. The long, faded scar down the left side of his face fuelled speculation that it was a mark of retribution. Given his links with Italy, a rumour grew apace that his reticence to talk was because he was in hiding; on the run from the Mafia.

Giovanni didn't give the impression of being a wise guy for he was always pleasant and much to Silvia's annoyance, particularly attentive to any young woman who happened to take his eye. He did seem to have one link to the Mafia however, for anyone foolish enough to provide him with regular custom, could certainly be considered a victim of extortion.

"He doesn't sell much," Millie had explained. "Most people only buy bread and milk. He charges the earth on everything else and gets by on the sales he makes when people need something when Kwik Save's shut."

Giovanni was one of the small and select band of shopkeepers in Manchester who opened on Christmas Day. He never took a day off and the festive season provided one of the biggest opportunities of the year. Having stocked up on cheap Chinese batteries from the cash and carry, he would sell them on at four times the price of Duracell, confident in the knowledge that parents would have forgotten that for most toys, batteries were not included. Galling as it was to pay such inflated prices, only Giovanni could save them from suffering the heart-rending disappointment and complaints of children unable to operate their long-awaited presents.

Approaching Giovanni's, the door opened and we saw Mary. She walked towards us tightly clutching a Warburtons loaf and a bottle of sterilised milk. Slightly older than Jeanette, she had three kids and lived in the house at the end of Millie's row. Mary always gave the impression that after waking up in the morning she couldn't be bothered to get properly dressed. As usual she was wearing slippers, her footwear of choice and a long, old coat that reached almost to the ground. It was natural to assume that the latter was concealing a nightdress or pyjamas. Wearing a head scarf, Mary had her hair in rollers.

"Are you going out tonight?" asked Millie.

"No, tomorrow night. Colin's boss has paid for a gang of us to go to the Golden Garter. A meal and everything."

"That sounds good. Who's on?"

"Tony Christie."

I nodded, trying to hide my lack of enthusiasm. Sure, the guy was a great singer but he was hardly rock 'n' roll.

"Didn't you have to turn up in formal evening wear when they first opened?" asked Millie.

"I don't know," replied Mary, "but I'm making sure I look the part."

We watched as Mary walked off home.

"Mary's always friendly," I remarked, "but I find it hard to ever imagine her looking the part."

"You're wrong there," said Millie. "Mary could surprise you."

I shook my head and smiled, thinking that Millie was pulling my leg.

"But she never seems to care about how she looks. For one thing, when she goes to Giovanni's, she always wears her slippers."

"Why not? It's not very far to walk."

"But you'd never go out without your shoes on and she often has her rollers in and that big old coat on too."

"Lots of women go to the shops with a head scarf covering their rollers. They're not like the women in Sale, you know. They can't afford cleaning ladies to do the house work for them, whilst they spend the afternoon in James and Peter's on King Street getting an expensive hairdo."

"I'm sorry. I didn't mean to sound condescending."

"I know you didn't," replied Millie, "but you've still got a lot to learn about people round here."

I was pleased that I hadn't upset her. She was right of course. Having known Millie and her friends for a relatively short period of time, I hadn't gained enough insight into how different their expectations were to mine.

"If you weren't off to Wembley and could see Mary when she went out tomorrow night, you'd be amazed," continued Millie. "She looks lovely when her hair's done and she's got her make-up on. You wouldn't know her but then again," she continued with a wicked smile, "I've no doubt that you'd want to."

Millie observed me closely and rolled her eyes in amusement. She was teasing; alluding to the fact, as she put it, that it took hardly anything to get me 'all hot and bothered.' It was true. She often had to calm me down when we started to kiss and cuddle, tutting and shaking her head, whilst telling me that I was over-sexed. Recalling such occasions, I could feel myself going red, a situation that Millie was eager to exploit.

"Yes, definitely. There's no doubt that I'd have to keep my eye on you."

Her quiet words were loaded with meaning. Her soft voice sweet and seductive. Once again, I didn't know what to say. Millie had my emotions in the palm of her hand and she knew it. It was impossible to disguise, even had I wanted to, the depth of my feelings for her but I trusted her too. Millie would never try to hurt me. Laughing gently, she put her arm around me and smiled.

From the time that Millie had stopped to speak to Mary, the boys had stood quietly to one side. Promised some toffees, they weren't going to risk upsetting their aunt by trying to rush her into Giovanni's. Too young to understand our conversation, they found it hard to appreciate what it was that their aunt found so amusing. Craig and Gary thus endured a boring and frustrating wait until Millie finally indicated her readiness to move.

"Come on, Michael. We'd best go and get the kids some toffees."

The shop was dimly lit and unwelcoming. A musty mixture of rotting vegetables and weak disinfectant assaulted the senses. The latter was a legacy of cleaning up the mess left by the old Alsatian that Giovanni had sleeping in the shop to discourage break-ins at night. During opening hours, the dog was kept in the back room, on standby in case of trouble and as we made our way in, it seemed likely that he may be needed. Silvia, alone at the counter, was finding it difficult to deal with an irate customer who was angry that the shop was trying to profit at her expense.

"These eggs. I'm not having them. They're not fit to eat. I want my money back."

The young woman pushed the box of half a dozen eggs across the counter towards Silvia who glanced at her dismissively.

"You no buy those here."

It was an ill-judged response, that merely stoked the ire of a customer who, although small in stature, was clearly tough and determined.

"I thought you might try that one."

Pausing, she turned to address a young lad.

"Jimmy."

"Yes Mam."

"She's the one you bought them off, isn't she?"

The lad nodded. I recognised him as one of Craig's friends.

Becoming concerned, Silvia reached out and opened the eggs. Running her fingers across them she tacitly accepted the fact that she had sold them.

"No. These eggs are good. Nothing wrong."

"Yes, there is. Get a pan of water and you can see them floating."

"No. They good," insisted Silvia.

"How do you know, if you don't try?"

Silvia shrugged her shoulders, refusing to co-operate.

"If you won't do it, then you can just give me the money back. Now!"

There was more than a hint of menace in the young woman's voice. She felt that she had waited long enough. Rather foolishly, Silvia ignored the warning, still believing that she could avoid a refund.

"No money back. Eggs are good."

"You'll either give me my money back, or I'll take it out of your face!"

It was the point of no return as the other customers waited; fascinated to see how matters would be resolved. It was a situation that I found disturbing, yet when I looked around me no one else seemed to regard the incident as unusual. Both children and adults were taking it all in their stride, as was Millie who seemed not at all surprised by the violent threat made by the young woman. With matters hanging in the balance the door behind the counter suddenly opened. Giovanni, working in the back and alerted by the sounds of heated conversation, had come out to see what was going on. Observing the anger on the young woman's face and the fear in Silvia's eyes, he acted quickly.

"Marianne. What's the matter?" he asked.

"Either she gives me the money back for these rotten eggs or I'll take it out of her face. I'm not joking. I mean it."

Giovanni didn't need to be told. Normally pleasant and agreeable, Marianne's mood could change very quickly, especially if she felt she was being taken advantage of. Unafraid of standing up to the bullies, Marianne was respected and to a degree feared, by other women on the estate.

"I'm sorry Marianne. If you say they're bad, of course I'll take them back. Forty pence, wasn't it?"

"Fifty, more like!"

"Oh, yes. Of course. Sorry."

Marianne shook her head, fully aware that Giovanni just couldn't resist an opportunity to claw back some of his losses.

Handing her the money, Giovanni continued to try and smooth things over.

"You know me, Marianne. If you or anyone else isn't satisfied, I'm always willing to offer a refund. I can't think what's happened. It must be Silvia. She didn't understand what you were saying."

"Huh. I'm sure!"

It was a possibility but none of the customers believed that it was true. Silvia never felt comfortable living in England and had therefore never made a serious effort to become as proficient in the language as her husband. Having retreated along the counter and relieved at having avoided a beating, Silvia was unhappy that Giovanni was being far too accommodating to her would-be assailant. Distrustful of her philandering husband, she suspected that Marianne could be one of his fancy women. Feeling a sense of humiliation, she directed a tirade of Italian towards her husband and stormed off into the back room. Watching her depart, Marianne tapped her finger on the top of the egg box.

"And don't put these back on the shelves for some other poor so-and-so to buy."

"Oh no, of course not," replied Giovanni, attempting to sound shocked by her suggestion. "I'll take them in the back and put them in the bin."

I looked at the faces of the other customers. Their expressions told me that no one believed that Giovanni would do any such thing. After he closed-up, all expected that he would bring them out and put them back on the shelf.

The kids having chosen their toffees and armed with our bread and milk we left Giovanni's and started to make our way home.

"That shocked you back in the shop. Didn't it?" asked Millie. "It's not what you're used to, is it?"

"No," I replied. "I haven't experienced anything like it. I've seen men acting aggressively but never a woman."

"So, you don't approve of what Marianne did then?"

"Well, it did seem a bit extreme, saying that she'd take it out of her face. After all, it was only fifty pence."

"And she would have done," confirmed Millie, "if she hadn't got her money back."

"Really?"

"Yes. Certainly."

"It wasn't just a threat then?"

"No. Of course not."

"Oh."

"You need to understand. Marianne's on her own with three kids. Her husband cleared off and left them, just like my dad did with us. She's got to stand up for herself. That business in Giovanni's reminds everyone to leave her family alone."

"I see."

"Do you, Michael? I'm not sure that you do."

"Why?"

"Because you romanticise about what it's like round here and so you ignore the unpleasant realities."

"But what reason would I have for doing that?"

Millie stopped. Chuckling softly, she shook her head.

"Oh, Michael. It's so obvious that you feel guilty about where you're from. You never stop going on about the smug complacency and self-satisfaction of the middle-classes. Because of that you're desperate to believe that people here are more worthy of your consideration."

She paused and looked at me closely before continuing.

"You need to open your eyes and see what it really means to live here. There are lots of decent people but there are many who aren't. It can be savage and brutal and sometimes you have no choice but to fight. You should be pleased that it isn't like that where you are and you shouldn't feel guilty about it. Our Jeanette isn't alone. There's many on the estate who wouldn't think twice about moving if they got the chance. They don't have any illusions about their life here."

Millie was right. I was in denial. When I visited grandad and saw Millie and her friends, there was plenty of time for levity. They lived amongst a community where people could be warm and friendly but a darker mood was always bubbling beneath the surface; outbreaks of violence never far away. Millie's words had reminded me of just how intelligent she was. My academic journey would no doubt provide me with some impressive qualifications but Millie possessed the sharpest of minds; a depth of perception that I could never hope to match. Through the experience of growing up in this tough environment she would always be cleverer and more pragmatic than I.

Chapter Six

Back at the house Jeanette was waiting in the kitchen. She was relieved to see us.

"I was starting to get worried. I thought they might have wandered off."

"No mam," explained Craig, "we got held up in Giovanni's. Silvia was trying to rob Marianne."

"Rob Marianne?"

"Yes Mam," added Gary. "She sold her these rotten eggs and do you know what? She wasn't going to give her the money back."

"That's not surprising."

"Marianne said she'd take it out of her face but Giovanni came and gave her the money," continued Craig.

"Yes," said Gary, with more than a hint of disappointment. "We didn't end up seeing anything."

"And be thankful that you didn't. I've told you before, it's not clever to go around causing trouble."

"But Mam. Marianne wasn't."

"That's not the point and anyway, what have you been told?"

Craig bowed his head. It was clear from the tone of her voice that his mam was far from pleased.

"Well?" asked Jeanette.

Craig was silent, unsure of what he was supposed to say.

"That little boys should be seen and not heard, especially after six o'clock."

Jeanette shook her head and sighed. Fortunately for Craig, there were more pressing matters to attend to.

"Terry's mate will be here soon to pick us up and I'm still not dressed."

"Go on then," said Millie, "get on with it. You don't want to have him hanging around and end up getting there late."

Jeanette went upstairs and Millie turned to her nephews.

"You two best keep out of your mam's way. Come on, we'll go and sit in the front room and watch the telly."

The lads were more than happy, because it was Friday evening and it wouldn't be long before 'The Incredible Hulk' came on. It was one of their favourite programmes although having read the original Marvel comics, I wasn't quite as enthusiastic about how it had been adapted for television. Before the Green Goliath could appear however, Jeanette had returned from upstairs to make her own dramatic entrance.

"Well, do I look alright?" she asked.

Turning towards her, you couldn't help but be impressed.

"That dress is beautiful. Where did you get it?" asked Millie.

"Dawn helped me pick it out. It was from a batch she had in at work last week."

"It's a lovely shade of purple."

"Yes, it's called Orchid."

"It fits you lovely," said Millie. "It's not an open wrap over dress, is it?"

"No. It's closed. I'm not that daring. I wouldn't take a chance on the tie coming undone and it falling apart."

"No, you wouldn't want to give everyone an eyeful, would you?" asked Millie, laughing.

"Certainly not."

The dress, reaching just below her knees, was tied around the waist highlighting her   impressive figure. With her hair set and make-up on, matching heels and handbag, Jeanette seemed transformed. After all, she and Terry rarely went out and it was the first time I had ever seen her wearing other than her everyday clothes. I now understood perfectly the point that Millie had made about Mary. It was also a reminder of how lucky I was, for Millie always appeared captivating regardless of what she wore. Coming in to see what the fuss was about, Terry let out a long whistle.

"Well love," he remarked, his eyes full of admiration. "You look gorgeous. I can see that I'm going to have to keep an eye on the other blokes there tonight."

Jeanette smiled, clearly pleased at the compliments she was getting, especially off her husband. She and Terry were still very much in love. When not away working, Terry was content to spend his time with his wife, disinterested in taking up residence at the pub as did most of his contemporaries.

Putting his arms around her waist, Terry pulled his wife towards him and kissed her on the lips. Lingering but a short time, Jeanette pulled herself away.

"Careful. You're messing up my hair."

"Well, I don't know. I only wanted to show you how much you're appreciated."

Seeing the surprised expression on Terry's face, Millie began to laugh. It certainly was amusing but I was determined not to join in. Ready to go, Jeanette turned her attention to the boys.

"Craig, Gary. You're to go to bed when Auntie Millie tells you."

"We can watch the end of The Incredible Hulk though, can't we? asked Gary. "We do every Friday."

"Yes, of course."

"Mam," said Craig.

"Yes?"

"Can we stay up to watch 'The Professionals?'"

"No, it's too late and besides your auntie might have some of her friends coming and they don't want you two being a nuisance."

Just then, a knock came to the front door. Terry's mate had arrived to take them into town. Quickly, Jeanette gave out her final instructions.

"Millie, the boys had their tea early so they might get hungry and want a butty."

"I'm sure they'll let me know but I'll ask them anyway."

"And make sure they have a wash and clean their teeth before they get in bed."

"I will."

"And don't let them get away with washing their necks and behind their ears."

Over on the settee, I saw Gary glance over towards his brother and pull a face. He wasn't impressed at the thought of soap and water. Fortunately for him, his mam was too flustered to observe his reaction.

"Look, just get off and enjoy yourself," said Millie. "I'm quite capable of taking care of things."

"I know love. I'm sorry."

"Are you coming?" shouted Terry. "Everyone will have gone home before we get there!"

Finally, Jeanette was gone, the front door closed behind her and the rest of us breathed a sigh of relief.

"You'd think that she'd be eager to get out for a night," I observed.

"She is," said Millie, "but you're not a mother, are you?"

"Well, obviously not," I replied, somewhat surprised.

"It's not easy to stop worrying about your kids."

"Well, I can't say that my mother seems that concerned about me."

"Really? If that's the case, why wouldn't she let you go to Maine Road on your own?"

"Well, yes. Fair enough."

Asking Gary to move up, Millie settled down on the settee, whilst I sat in the chair next to Craig's across the room. There was to be no kissing and canoodling before the boys went to bed and given that some of Millie's friends would probably be turning up too, I accepted that tonight there would be little chance of any more intimate moments between us. Of course, the realisation of the fact meant that when I looked across at her on the settee, she looked more desirable than ever. With her stockinged legs drawn up beneath her, the folds of her skirt resting softly around them and her tailored blouse outlining her wonderful breasts, she looked magnificent; a mirage of loveliness seemingly floating in the air.

Unsurprisingly, I found The Incredible Hulk to be a difficult watch. It was hard to concentrate when Millie remained so near, yet so far. It was clear that she understood my frustration but her cheeky smiles were typical and I felt certain that the occasional smoothing of her skirt was her way of drawing my attention to the legs I so clearly admired.

"Are you enjoying the programme?" she had asked, in the first commercial break. "It's good, isn't it?"

Of course, she was being disingenuous. Millie regarded the idea of a man transformed into a giant, green monster by gamma radiation, as ridiculous but understanding my frustration at being unable to cuddle up to her on the settee, was taking the opportunity to tease me further.

"It's all right," I replied, somewhat unconvincingly.

"Yes, I'm sure there isn't anything else you'd rather be doing, is there?" she asked, a faint smile flitting across her lips.

Grimacing, I resisted the urge to reply. With the boys in the room, what could I say? Seeing my reaction, Millie burst out laughing.

"Oh, poor Michael. Is there something wrong?"

She had that beautiful serene look on her face. Her question seemingly so sweet and innocent. Craig and Gary, bored at watching the adverts, looked at me inquiringly, wondering if I was in some kind of difficulty.

"No, everything's fine," I insisted.

Thankfully, the Hulk returned and this time I fixed my eyes firmly on the screen, trying to watch the action unfold with as much enthusiasm as the boys. It was almost enough to stop my mind from wandering off into the fields of forbidden fantasies about Millie in that skirt. The show over, Millie swung her legs down gracefully to the floor.

"Are you hungry boys? Do you fancy a butty?"

"Oh. Yes please."

"There's cheese, potted meat, or corn beef. What do you fancy?"

The boys decided that they would prefer cheese with brown sauce and sat and waited at the table in the middle room whilst Millie got on with the task of preparing them. I joined her in the kitchen and was delegated the task of making two drinks of orange for the boys and a brew for ourselves. It was not long before we were all sat together. Millie had also provided a packet of McVitie's Chocolate Digestives. She had bought them herself as a rare treat for the boys. Jeanette considered them too expensive and so did not buy them. Custard creams and malted milk were the staples that Craig and Gary were used to and so their eyes lit up at the sight of the chocolate biscuits.

"You can have some but only when you've finished your butties," said Millie.

Craig and Gary nodded. I smiled. For one so young, Millie moved seamlessly into the role of mother. It was hardly surprising. Instrumental in helping Jeanette to bring up the boys, she had developed a mature understanding of how to deal with children.

Having finished their biscuits and drinks of orange, Craig and Gary began to express an interest in my arrangements for tomorrow. With money tight, their parents had never been able to afford a family holiday, although they had managed to take them on a couple of day trips to Blackpool. A visit to London and Wembley seemed to them like a trip into outer space.

"How are you getting there?" asked Craig.

"We're going on the train."

"From Piccadilly Station?" asked Gary.

"Yes. The train leaves at half past eight. It takes nearly three hours to get there and then you have to catch the underground to the stadium."

"No doubt you'll be stopping at a couple of pubs along the way, if I know Dougie," added Millie with a chuckle.

"It's a long way to go when you're going to lose," ventured Craig.

"You didn't say that to Helen when we saw her in the park earlier, did you?" asked Gary.

"Of course not. I wouldn't dare," replied his brother.

"Helen?" I asked.

"Yes, Helen who rings the bell at Maine Road," said Millie. "She lives on the estate."

I was surprised. Helen and her bell, ensconced behind the goal in the North Stand was City's most famous fan. She was loved by the players and big Joe Corrigan in particular, but when the opposition were receiving a sound beating and Helen was ringing it with enthusiasm, the away support would always be eager to suggest just where she could shove it.

"She won't be on the train," said Gary. "She always goes on one of the coaches."

"Anyway, it's time you were going to bed," said Millie.

"The Professionals will be starting soon," noted Gary.

"Yes, I'm sure it will."

Craig and Gary looked silently at Millie, imploring her to allow them to stay up a little longer. It was a forlorn hope.

"Come on, up we go," said Millie.

Her voice was cheerful but decisive; one that immediately crushed any possibility of opposition. Without a murmur of protest, the boys followed her out into the hallway and up the stairs proceeding to get washed and clean their teeth under their auntie's supervision.

Chapter Seven

With Millie upstairs putting the boys to bed, I cleared the table and washed the pots. As I was putting the cutlery back in the drawer there was a knock on the kitchen door. Once opened, I could see Dawn, Dave and his mate Mark King.

"Come in," I said. "Millie will be down in a minute, she's just seeing to the kids."

Going through to the front room, the lads settled down on the settee, whilst Dawn sat on the floor at Dave's feet. Smiling down towards her, it was obvious that he was enjoying the sensation of her breasts resting against his knee. Turning her face towards him, Dawn fluttered her eyelids, the hint of a smile on her lips. There was no doubt that despite it being some time since they had gone out together, there was still real chemistry between them.

"I wasn't sure if we'd see you, Dave. I thought you might be meeting up with some of the lads in town before the match tomorrow."

"I was going to and then I thought I might end up drinking too much, oversleep and miss the train in the morning."

"Oh, I see."

"Are you disappointed?" asked Dawn.

"Disappointed?"

"Yes, that we've come round."

"Of course not," I said, surprised.

"Are you sure? Aren't you annoyed that you haven't got Millie all to yourself with the kids in bed and Terry and Jeanette out for the night?"

Her face was expressionless; she seemed deadly serious. When Dave and Mark burst into laughter, I realised that she was having me on.

"I had you there, didn't I?" observed Dawn, a huge smile on her face.

The door from the hallway opened and Millie entered the room.

"Well, everyone seems in a good mood."

"Well, we are, but we're not sure about Michael," said Dave.

His comment triggered another burst of laughter. Millie, wondering what had brought on the general hilarity, looked around us for an explanation. Dawn was quick to provide one.

"Oh, we were just teasing him about having to put up with us, rather than being on his own with you. Poor old Michael," she said, turning towards me, "you've got to learn not to take everything so seriously."

Millie nodded. She understood that I needed time to adjust to how she and her friends related to one another. It was so different to what I was used to. Verbal sparring, giving as good as you got, with no subject or person left untouched. Witty rejoinders, self-deprecating humour; all to be taken in good grace. It was true Mancunian wit, part of life for the working-classes but difficult to find in the middle-class suburbs. 'Taking the mick' came with the territory in Chorlton-on-Medlock. Yet I still found it hard to become accustomed to it, especially when I found myself the target.

Moving towards the radiogram that was placed in front of the window, Millie raised the polished wooden lid.

"I'll put on some music," she said. "Olivia. Nice and soothing."

Millie loved disco and dancing but she was also particularly fond of Olivia Newton John. I suppose it was a sign of her maturity, for the songs she invariably returned to were those with more sophisticated lyrics; ones that delved into the nature of love and the failure of relationships. 'Changes,' 'I honestly Love You' and 'Love Song,' were some of her favourites. It had felt wonderful to sit with Millie on the settee listening to Olivia together. Not once did I feel any inclination to suggest that perhaps she may like to listen to one of my favourite bands. It was yet another sign that I had fallen in love, for listening to the right music didn't have quite the same importance as it once had.

As the needle went down on the record and the familiar strains of Olivia began to drift gently across the room, Millie sat down on the chair beside me and took hold of my hand. A simple act, I felt pleased and proud that she never hesitated to acknowledge our relationship in front of others.

"Do you like Olivia, Michael?" asked Dawn.

"Yes. She's all right."

"It's not what he usually listens to," remarked Millie.

"Interesting," said Dave. "What do you normally go for Michael?"

Millie had opened the door. Dave loved Northern Soul and Motown. I could feel him waiting to pounce, eager to poke fun at my musical tastes. Hoping to deny him the opportunity, I tried to skirt around the question.

"Oh, I like lots of things; no one in particular."

"You told me that you went to see Motorhead at the Apollo last year, so you must like them," said Millie.

She smiled at me with a twinkle in her eye, as the inevitable derisive laughter exploded around me.

"Oh no, Michael. I can't believe it," said Dave.

He and Mark jumped to their feet, air guitars at the ready and rocked back and forth, belting out a Lemmy-esque vocal.

"The Ace of Spades, da, da, da. Ace of Spades da da da."

"Are you into all that leather gear, Michael?" asked Dawn, laughing.

"It's all locked up in that special cupboard he's got at home," suggested Dave.

"Probably some whips and handcuffs in there too," added Mark.

"You'd better be careful Millie," warned Dawn. "Once he gets into that studded jacket, there's no telling what raging animal might be unleashed."

It was the second time that evening that my face was flushed with embarrassment. Millie's friends were merciless, but then I started to laugh. I couldn't help it. I had to acknowledge the humour contained within their observations, even if they were at my expense. Suddenly, I felt Millie squeeze my hand. Turning towards her I could see that she was pleased. It was almost as if I had passed a test. I had lowered my defences and shown that I could adapt. That I was able to understand the ways of her rumbustious friends. That however, was no guarantee that they would necessarily accept me. Coming from Sale and having wealthy parents, there was every chance that it would cause resentment. Furthermore, I had stayed on at school and not taken a job like the others had done and when Dawn asked me about my plans for university, Mark made it clear that he considered students to be privileged, spoiled and lazy.

"Well, there's one thing. When he gets there, he won't have much to do other than lie in bed all day. I rarely see any students up and about when I walk past the flats on Grosvenor Street on my way to work in the morning."

"There's nothing wrong with that," said Dawn. "They'll be tired after they've been clubbing all night. I'd do the same if I had the chance."

The observation was delivered without any hint of emotion but it was obvious to all but Mark that her words were designed to irritate him further.

"Oh, really" said Mark, dismissively. "And another thing. How come they get those new flats laid on for them."

"Because there's not enough private flats available and fewer landladies in Manchester prepared to take students. UMIST built them because they need to accommodate students from all over the country and the rest of the world too," explained Millie.

"I think we should be pleased that all these students want to come here. It makes you proud to be from Manchester, doesn't it?"

Dawn smiled. Once more she had baited the hook and Mark was eager to take it.

"No, it doesn't, not when they can't find any money for flats and houses for our own."

"But that's down to the Corporation. It's not the responsibility of UMIST or Owens," declared Millie.

Sensibly, I remained silent and resisted the temptation to get involved. I was unsure how Mark would react to my comments. After all, I would soon be joining the ranks of those he seemed so much to despise.

"Well," said Dawn, "I've got to say they've done an excellent job on the flats at Grosvenor House. The bedrooms are really nice and the bathrooms and kitchens have got all the mod cons."

"How do you know?" asked Mark, surprised.

"Because I've seen them. I've been taken back there by students I've met at the Cyprus."

Mark shook his head.

"You're not jealous are you, Mark?" asked Dave.

"Of course not."

I saw Dave and Millie smile. They knew very well that Mark was desperate to go out with Dawn but there was little chance that she ever would.

"The bedrooms all have central heating and are nice and cosy in the winter," continued Dawn, intent on ribbing Mark further. "It's proper central heating too. Radiators; not like the underfloor heating we've got in these houses."

"Yes," added Millie, "Jeanette hardly ever turns it on. It uses so much electric and it's far too expensive to keep putting 50p's in the meter. Anyway, it only heats downstairs."

"It doesn't need to be expensive," said Dave. "Let me have a look in your electric cupboard. I bet your meter is the same as ours and the glass on the front is loose. If you're careful you can shove a wire in it without breaking the glass and stop the wheel from going round. You'll still get electric but the meter won't register the units."

"But won't they find out?" I asked. "You won't be using any electric and they're bound to be suspicious."

"No, because you take the wire out a couple of weeks before the meter reader comes so he won't see it. That means the meter will record some units and you'll still get a bill. The electric board will think that you're hard up and having to economise."

"What happens if they turn up unexpectedly and you haven't removed the wire?"

"That's easy. Before you start fiddling the meter, you put a lock on your cupboard. If the electric man turns up unexpected, you tell him that someone else always keeps the key and they're not in."

"Won't he get suspicious?"

"Why should he? The lock helps stop anyone, including family, from getting in the cupboard to rob the meter."

"Oh," I said, surprised.

"Your parents have never had a slot meter, have they Michael?" asked Millie.

"No," I replied. "Dad gets a bill through the post and then pays it."

"Well, most people round here pay for their electric as they use it. That way they don't have to worry about finding the money for the bill and getting cut off if they can't pay it."

I could have felt gormless for being so naïve but I didn't. What I did realise was how lucky I was that I never had to worry about keeping warm. It was a mark of privilege if you were able to take the necessities of life for granted. I had been given a practical lesson that taught me far more about the nature of inequality than any theoretical out pourings from Marx or Lenin.

"Shall I have a look at your meter then?" asked Dave.

"There's no point," said Millie. "Terry would never agree to it and I can't say I blame him."

"Anyway," said Dawn, "Michael didn't get to tell us about what he was planning to study when he goes to university."

Normally I would have been pleased to answer but given Mark's earlier hostility, I felt that it was better to let the subject pass. Dave however, felt differently.

"Yeah, Michael, what will Bamber Gascoine tell us you're reading when we see you on University Challenge."

"We're all glued to the telly in our house when that's on," said Dawn. "It's brilliant when you know one of the answers."

"So, what's your starter for ten, Michael?" asked Dave with a chuckle.

"It doesn't matter. University's a waste of time," ventured Mark. "All that matters is this."

Putting his hand into his pocket he pulled out his wallet, opened it and took out a couple of fivers.

"Money's all you need and you're wasting time staying on at school and studying. I've learnt far more by working than I ever did at Nicholls."

"The university of life I suppose," remarked Millie, somewhat dismissively.

"Yes. That's right. It's exactly what I mean," said Mark.

"And that's not because you didn't do great at school, then?"

Just like at the Cyprus Millie was quick to jump to my defence but I hoped that she would not fall out with Mark because of it. I could understand his feelings. He had not done well at Nicholls and the stagnation of the engineering and manufacturing sector in Manchester, had meant that twice already he had faced redundancy. It must have irritated him that through staying in education, my passage through life seemed far more comfortable than his.

"I didn't do well either," said Dave, turning towards me, "but I've got a lot of respect for you Michael. You're clever and you've got to work hard to get to university. I was in the top band when I first went to Nicholls but I couldn't be bothered to do the homework. They threatened to drop me into the middle band but I didn't care and took no notice. I started wagging school, so it's what they did. That meant no 'O' levels for me but in the fourth year I saw the careers officer and he told me that if I wanted to get an apprenticeship, I needed good grades at CSE in Science, Maths and English. It was the first time in my life that I listened to some advice. I started working and got them."

"Did you get any others?" I asked.

"What do you think?"

Dave paused, then started to laugh.

"Of course I didn't. Waste my time on geography and history? No chance. They still entered me for the other exams though but I never bothered turning up for any of them."

Dave had spoken. He had given me his seal of approval. It meant that there would be no falling out between Mark and Millie. The former knew better than to continue to criticise my prospective life as a student and a loud knock to the front door directed Millie's attention elsewhere.

"Who's that?" she ventured aloud.

"Well, you won't know, unless you answer it," suggested Dawn.

Getting out of her chair, Millie walked into the hallway. Looking past her, I could see the silhouettes of two figures through the reinforced frosted glass in the front door. As Millie opened it, two young women appeared, heavily laden with large, bulging holdalls. I recognised them as Karen and Linda, sisters in their late teens who lived with their parents in one of the houses in the row in front of Dougie's.

"We wondered if you might be interested Millie," said Linda.

"We've got some nice tops, skirts and a couple of lovely dresses that would be perfect for you or your Jeanette."

"No thanks," said Millie.

"We've not shown you them yet."

"I know, but we don't need anything."

"I might. Hang on."

It was Dawn. She had been listening intently to the conversation and now quickly made her way to the front door.

"You'd best come in," said Millie.

The sisters came into the hallway and the front door was closed behind them. Walking into the front room they placed their holdalls on the floor and proceeded to take out some articles of clothing. Pride of place were two beautiful knee-length dresses. One was white, the other red. Millie couldn't help but admire them.

"They are lovely. Very glamorous. Especially the white one."

Karen handed it to Millie who examined it closely.

"Marks and Spencers," remarked Millie. "I'm not surprised that it's good quality material."

"It's from Marks?" asked Dawn, surprised.

"Yes," said Linda.

"But wasn't it there that you got caught and sent to prison."

"That's right but Karen took it this time and the store detectives don't know her. I took the red one from Debenhams."

Suddenly I realised that the sisters were selling 'knocked-off stuff.' It was why Millie had tried to get rid of them at the door, only for Dawn to thwart her plan. The latter was soon rummaging through the rest of the ill-gotten gains, before returning to look at the dress from Debenhams.

"I do like the design of this red one," she said, "but it isn't really my colour."

"We only want eight pounds for it. It's twenty-five in the shop."

"No, I'm not sure," said Dawn.

"What colour would you prefer?" asked Linda, sensing a potential sale. "They've got others in the same design."

"Well, a pale blue or yellow."

"Oh, we can do that. What size?"

"I've got to have an eighteen, for the top half," said Dawn.

"Are you sure that's enough?" asked Dave. "It can't be denied. You're a big girl."

Dawn and Mark burst into laughter. Millie shook her head but, like the others, could clearly see the humour in Dave's comment. Looking at me she noticed my embarrassment, for even though Dawn was clearly comfortable at her attributes being discussed so openly, I still felt that it was inappropriate. Smiling at me, I sensed that she understood my response.

"Well, eighteen it is," said Linda. "We should be able to bring it at the end of next week."

"Make sure you take it to Dawn's," said Millie. "Don't bring it here. You're lucky that Terry's out tonight. He'll go spare if you turn up with it at the door."

Having put the clothes back in the holdalls, the sisters said goodbye and Millie let them out of the front door. Returning to her chair, she sat down, clearly relieved that they had finally gone.

"I'm sorry," said Dawn. "You've told me before what Terry feels about shoplifting. I didn't think."

"It's alright. We didn't buy anything, so there's no chance of being done for receiving."

"You wouldn't get done for that, even if you had," said Mark.

"That's where you're wrong," replied Millie. "One of Terry's aunties, who lives in Alexandra Park, was always buying at the door and the police had a crackdown on gangs of shoplifters. They had them under surveillance and recorded all the houses that bought off them. Terry's auntie did it several times and so the police charged her with receiving. She was lucky to get a suspended sentence and that was only because the court took into account the fact that she was old."

"But that's stupid," said Mark, "she didn't steal anything."

"Ah, but the cops say that by buying knocked-off goods, you're encouraging crime," said Dave. "If no one buys it, they'd have no reason to steal it. That makes people who do, more guilty than the thief."

"That's right," agreed Millie. "It's why Terry insists that Jeanette turns anyone with stolen goods away."

"It's a big risk that Karen and Linda are taking," I observed, "especially as they aren't asking anything near what the clothes are really worth."

"They can't ask any more," said Mark, shaking his head. "People here haven't got the money your friends in Sale have."

"And they just want enough to be able to go to the Cyprus on a Friday and Saturday night," added Dawn.

"Might be better for them if they got a job," suggested Dave. "Perhaps then, they might have the money."

"Not much chance of that," said Dawn, laughing. "They can make more from Social and shoplifting and just like Mark's students, they don't have to rush to get out of bed in the morning."

"I must admit," I said, "I see the logic. I can understand why Karen may feel that way but Linda has a toddler; she has a responsibility. Surely, she wants a better life for her daughter and to set a good example for her."

"You'd think so," said Millie. "Little Laura was just a baby when her mam was sent to prison and it was lucky that her gran was prepared to look after her. It hasn't made any difference to Linda though and to be honest, most of her friends don't think any the worse of her for doing it."

"That's a fact," confirmed Mark. "There aren't many here that think like Terry."

"Yes," said Dave. "Shoplifters have got loads of customers on the estate and that's without all the knocked off-stuff from Great Universal. It really is stealing to order."

"Great Universal?" I asked.

"Yes," said Dawn. "GUS. Great Universal Stores, the catalogue company on Devonshire Street. They sell absolutely everything on weekly terms. Because people on the estate work in the warehouse, they can steal most things and sell them cheap to friends and neighbours. Mam got a bike for our Sean last Christmas. It was a belter. She couldn't have afforded it from the normal shops."

I looked confused.

"Of course," said Dawn, "you don't have a catalogue at your house, do you? Your mam doesn't have to buy things on tick, does she?"

"Er, no. I suppose not."

"It's alright Michael," said Dave. "We won't hold it against you that you're rich and posh."

"Well, only a little," added Dawn, laughing.

"You're getting quite the education, aren't you Michael? You had no idea about the thriving market in illicit goods in Chorlton-on-Medlock, did you?" asked Millie.

"You're right. All the time I've been staying at Dougie's no one's ever knocked on the door trying to sell him anything."

"That isn't surprising," said Millie. "They know he's old and unlikely to be interested in anything they've got to sell."

"Oh."

"Anyway," said Dave, changing the subject. "I'll have to nip over to the Sherwood for some cigs. Shall I get us a few bottles whilst I'm there?"

Dawn and Mark were enthusiastic but from Millie came a note of caution.

"Yes, okay Dave, but not too many. Remember, we can't get too rowdy. I've got the kids upstairs."

"Don't worry, I'll only get a couple for each of us. It's Friday night and I just fancied a drink. Like I said, I don't want to have too much in case I end up missing the train in the morning."

Millie nodded and Dave got up from the settee.

"Are you coming with us Michael to help carry them back?"

"Yes, of course."

I was surprised. I had expected that he would ask Mark to go with him. I have to say that it pleased me. Dave had been generous in his praise of my academic ability and his words had softened Mark's attitude towards me. It seemed that the most feared lad on the estate liked me and other than the fact that I supported City, I couldn't understand why.

Chapter Eight

"We'd best get them from the Sherwood," said Dave, as we stepped outside. "I'm not paying Giovanni's prices."

For a moment I felt uncomfortable. On the previous occasion that I had been in the establishment, I found the atmosphere more than a little intimidating. It was one of those pubs in which it was wise to sit close to the door, so that you could make a quick exit before it all kicked off. Then I remembered that I would be with Dave and realised that it was as good as having my own personal minder. Being with him, it was unlikely that anyone would target me after we entered the Vault. Nevertheless, there were still several pairs of eyes weighing me up and down as we walked towards the bar. Was it so obvious that I didn't fit in?

Ordering bottles of Carlsberg Special and twenty Bensons, Dave turned to speak to Walt and Cyril, a pair of old men sat at a table to the side. A couple of Albert Steptoe's but scrupulously clean; washed and shaved, wearing collars and ties under neatly pressed pullovers, their best cloth caps laid down on the table. They were looking forward to watching tomorrow's game on television and confident about City's chances, regaling us with their memories of attending the finals in 'fifty-six and 'sixty-nine. It was quite some time since they had seen the team play away. As pensioners it was too expensive for them to attend the game, even if they had been able to get a ticket. As we picked up our bottles and prepared to leave, it was clear that Dave's reputation had reached their ears too.

"Don't take any nonsense from those cockney beggars," advised Cyril.

"If they try it on lad, give 'em a good 'iding from us too," added Walt.

"Now why would I do that?" asked Dave, shaking his head.

"We know lad. The young uns in here talk about you all the time. Don't take any nonsense, do you?" observed Cyril.

"No, that's not me. You've got me mixed up with someone else."

"Get off with you," said Walt, "you're not shy of getting stuck in. The cock of the estate. Aren't you Dave?"

Dave smiled, but said no more. He was a bit like John Wayne in 'The Quiet Man.' Everyone aware of the latent rage and aggression that existed underneath his calm persona.

Back outside the shadows were lengthening. Although I'd been safe with Dave, I was still pleased to be on our way back to Millie's. The Sherwood was such a bizarre place. I could never feel comfortable there, whether it was in the vault or the lounge. Millie had taken me in the latter one Saturday night, before we were going out together, to see the 'turns.' It didn't help when she pointed out a young man sat at a table on the far side of the room.

"Michael, if he comes over, make sure you don't look at him. Turn away and talk to me."

"Why?"

"Well, when he's had one too many, he thinks people are staring at him and starts getting aggressive."

"With anyone?"

"No, only men."

"Oh, I suppose that's all right then."

Millie laughed.

"The landlord's just let him back after barring him," continued Millie. "Don't worry. If he does start, I won't let him touch you."

To avoid my concern, it may have been better for her to remain silent on the matter. Furthermore, I seemed to be the only outsider in the room and began to feel uncomfortable with the fact that I stuck out like a sore thumb, observed warily by those who came over to talk to Millie. When the star turn, a covers band, finally made their appearance, I was struck by the appearance of the female lead singer. Tall and gangly with a long, blonde wig, she appeared like a man in a dress. But this was the Brunswick Estate, Chorlton-on-Medlock. A landscape populated by working-class hard men. Surely, I had it wrong, for every number was greeted by cheers and rousing applause. The singer must surely be a woman.

"The singer," I said to Millie. "Don't you think that she looks a lot like .."

"A man," suggested Millie, finishing my sentence.

"Well, yes."

"That's because 'she' is."

"Oh."

"Are you surprised?"

"Well, you never mentioned it was a drag act."

"It's not. That's how he always dresses. He considers himself female."

"And does everyone in the pub know that?"

"Yes. And that the drummer's his boyfriend."

I stared at Millie. I was shocked, for I had assumed that this was the last place where two men would have openly admitted to being gay. Society in general was intolerant of homosexuality and ironically it exposed my own prejudice in assuming that working-class folk would be at the forefront of hostility towards the gay community. Here in the Sherwood, that was clearly not the case. It was more likely the middle class 'rugger buggers' back in Sale who would be inclined towards 'queer bashing.' Yet at the same time tolerance on the estate had clearly prescribed limits. Whilst black families tended to be accepted by their white counterparts, many with a South Asian heritage were not. Furthermore, even though I was friends with both Millie and Dave, relatively few others on the estate were welcoming to the posh, clever sod from the suburbs, even before they had been given a chance to get to know me.

Entering the back garden at Millie's, I closed the gate behind us. Approaching the back door, Dave stopped and sat down on one of the plastic garden seats placed on the flags to the side.

"I fancy a cig before we go back in. Let's sit here a minute," suggested Dave.

Sitting beside him I placed my bottles on the floor next to his whilst he lit up. Inevitably, talk turned towards the game.

"Do you know Dave, if we're successful tomorrow, it will be the first time I've actually been there when we've won something."

"Really?" asked Dave, surprised.

"Yes. Dougie wanted to take me to the League Cup win against Newcastle but my mother wouldn't let him."

"I've been lucky. Dad took me to St James Park when we won the league at Newcastle in 'sixty-eight. It seemed like the whole of the Kippax were there for that one and to Wembley for the Cup final in 'sixty-nine. I've seen both League Cup wins and the defeat to Wolves in 'seventy-four. That wasn't much fun. It's no good getting to Wembley if you don't win. The only final I've missed is the Cup Winners Cup and only because it was in Vienna. I went to all the home ties in the other rounds though."

I was filled with envy. I could only imagine what it would have been like to savour victory in one of the great matches that had defined our history. I almost felt like a fraud. Here was Dave, just a year older than I. No one could doubt that he was a diehard fan whose credentials were so much greater than mine.

"Never mind," he continued. "You're getting your chance tomorrow."

"Hopefully," I replied, "but it's going to be tough."

"Of course. It's the Cup Final. What do you expect? It's a showpiece; the most important game in the World. Every player wants a chance to appear in it and if they do are desperate to win and create a legacy for themselves. Spurs want it just as much as our lads. But there's no reason to fear them, especially when you remember that it was against them that this season's revival got underway."

Dave was right. Back in late October in John Bond's second game in charge, City had triumphed three-one against Spurs at Maine Road. It was the first league win of the season and ended a run of just four draws and eight defeats. Although Bond had considered his men lucky to win the game, the victory had finally given the team belief and inspired a spectacular run of results that moved them well away from the bottom of the table.

"So, you see," continued Dave, "there's no reason why we shouldn't win."

I nodded, although I wasn't totally convinced, especially given the lingering sense of pessimism that seemed such a natural part of my constitution. Spurs were a decent outfit and favoured by the media, especially the BBC with their traditional bias towards London and the Home Counties. The pundits felt that they had the superior players: the silky skills of the Argentinians, Ardiles and Villa; the dynamic strike partnership of Crooks and Archibald and the creative midfield genius of golden boy Glenn Hoddle. City, on the other hand, were regarded as a committed and hard-working collective, with a lack of exceptional flair. It was a view that we Blues regarded as unfair but most agreed that if we were to win, on the day it would be down to our superior team ethic.

"I'm pleased Hutch is over that pelvic injury," I said, "he came through the Palace game fine, didn't he?"

"Yeah. You know what, when we signed him, I thought Bond was desperate. Hutch seemed to have been around forever. I couldn't see him getting into the team, never mind making an impact. I was wrong. We certainly look far more of a threat when he plays and I'm sure those elastic legs mesmerise opposition defenders."

"Yes, I think they do," I replied with a chuckle. "And he's got the experience to handle the big stage and help the youngsters, just like Gerry Gow."

"That was smart management, keeping him out of the team so he didn't get another booking and banned for the final," acknowledged Dave. "Gerry's going to be crucial to stopping them tomorrow. If he, Mackenzie and Power get after the Spurs midfield like they did Muhren and Thijssen in the semi, they'll hardly create a chance."

"I feel sorry for Tommy Booth not making the line-up but Bond's right, Reid and Caton have been excellent since they were put together."

"Yeah, I agree. You should always select on merit and Tommy's had a great career and already has a winner's medal from 'sixty-nine."

"He reacted to the decision with class," I added, "not like Tueart, demanding 'clear the air' talks because Tony Henry got the sub's shirt."

"Yeah, I was disappointed," said Dave. "Denis is a hero of mine. I'll always remember that overhead kick flying in at Wembley. He should have kept quiet and just accepted it."

"Well, he claims he doesn't want to 'rock the boat' but what must the other players think? No one's got a divine right to be in the side. I think Bond was right to say that if he's unhappy, he can go."

"Anyway," continued Dave, "players and supporters alike, we should be thankful that we're at Wembley at all. If we'd kept Big Mal, we'd be in the second division now."

"Yes, I suppose we would. Dougie doesn't see it that way though. He won't have a word said against him."

"Loyal, the old uns, aren't they?"

"Yes, but I understand why. Dougie had to wait ages for us to win anything; just two cups and one title in over fifty years until Mercer and Malcolm delivered those trophies one after another. When I was moaning at the start of the season, Dougie said I was typical of the younger element who think that everything should be easy. We can't take the rough with the smooth, unlike his generation who'd suffered the club's failures for so many years. We've been spoiled by success and so it's made us impatient and forget that the most important quality for any supporter, is loyalty; to stand by those who have done so much for the club in the past. Dougie was furious when Swales sacked Mal and Skip. He hates Swales; he'll never forgive him. He's still convinced that if we'd stood by Malcolm, the results would have turned."

"Do you think they would?" asked Dave.

"No. Definitely not."

The pair of us laughed. We respected Dougie but were convinced that his assessment of the situation was nothing more than misguided sentimentality standing in the way of good sense.

Given that we were getting on so well, I decided that Dave probably wouldn't object if I asked him what lay behind his fearsome reputation.

"Walt and Cyril seemed to be expecting trouble tomorrow. Do you think it likely, Dave?"

"Maybe, but it won't be like a league game down there."

"Oh?"

"Yes, Upton Park, Stamford Bridge, Highbury or White Hart Lane, it's their territory. They have the advantage of knowing all the little side streets and alleys and where best to ambush you. Wembley's neutral ground and there's so many more cops about."

"Why's that?"

"It's the national showpiece; the cup final. It doesn't look good for the cops if there's bother and it seems like they've lost control."

"But what about the trouble at other matches?"

"It's not the same. There's less coppers and they don't really care if it kicks off. Most cops hate fans, especially the away supporters. As far as they're concerned, if we weren't on their patch, then there wouldn't be any trouble."

"That's daft. You've every right to follow your team."

"It's not what they think. A couple of mates drove down to see us at Wolves. After the game, gangs of their fans were searching the streets for our lot and they couldn't get back to their car. They asked some coppers if they would help. What do you think happened?"

"I don't know."

"They told them no chance. That it served them right for not travelling on the coaches."

"Did they get back all right?"

"Eventually, after they'd hidden down an alley for an hour."

Dave started laughing and I soon joined in. We could both see the lighter side of the situation. Taking advantage of Dave's good humour, I decided to address the burning question.

"I hope you don't mind me asking Dave but why is everyone so scared of you?"

"Are they? You don't seem to be."

Dave fixed me with a hard stare. For a moment I thought the question had annoyed him and then, to my relief, he smiled.

"Had you going then, didn't I?"

"Yes, I suppose you did."

"Getting a reputation is a funny thing," continued Dave. "Are you sure you want to know? You may end up disappointed."

"Well, yes."

"All right, but what I tell you goes no further. You understand, don't you?"

"Yes, of course."

"All right then, I don't suppose there's any harm in you knowing. It goes back a couple of years to when we were at home to Everton. I don't have to tell you how much we hate scousers and they're the same with us. City and United against either Everton or Liverpool, it always kicks off."

"Yes, goes back to the ship canal," I ventured.

Dave looked puzzled.

"Manchester manufacturers taking trade away from the port of Liverpool," I explained.

Unimpressed, Dave shook his head.

"I don't know, you can't forget your history for a minute, can you professor?"

He laughed. Fortunately, he was willing to continue.

"We're always ready to welcome them as soon as they get here. They do the same, throwing bricks down on the football specials in the cutting near Lime Street. This time we'd been drinking in town, rushed to Piccadilly Station and couldn't see any of 'em. We thought we were too late but when we walked out, we saw about twenty Evertonians at the bottom of Station Approach. Well, I'd had a few, hadn't I? I didn't think twice. 'Come on lads, let's get 'em.' I went flying down the slope shouting at the top of my voice and as I got nearer, they just stood there looking at me. I glanced round to gee on my mates and there was no one there. They'd all stayed at the top; I was on my own."

Dave paused for dramatic effect.

"What did you do?" I asked.

"Well, I soon sobered up. I understood why none of 'em had made a move towards me. It was one against twenty and too late to pull out. My only chance was to keep going, let them see I wasn't scared and pray for a miracle. So, I ended up in the middle of 'em, flailing my arms around, shouting and swearing and expecting to get given the biggest hiding of my life. But not one of them wanted to fight. They just laughed. They must have thought I was doolally. And then they walked off. Just left me standing there. After that I looked back to my mates and saw them walking down towards me."

"They must have felt embarrassed, not backing you up."

"I suppose they did, but I think I just took them all by surprise. Anyway, they were well impressed; couldn't believe what I'd done. Charging twenty of them on my own. They thought I was a mad man. And after that the story spread and so did my reputation. 'Don't mess with Dave. He's a real hard case.' And that's why no one round here does."

"Yes, but you can handle yourself Dave."

"Well, that's true. But people's impressions of me would never have been the same if my mates had followed me down. Normally they would have but they didn't and through pure luck I gained my reputation. It was all a mistake really. If I'd known that no one was going to follow me, I'd never have charged them on my own."

"I see."

It was an amazing story and I respected Dave's honesty. Yet I also thought that he was selling himself short. From others I had heard that he was always in the thick of the action, fighting to protect his fellow supporters when they were set on by the opposition. Dave never instigated trouble but neither would he shy away from it. Many had reason to be thankful to him for being prepared to stand his ground and protect them when it would have been easier and safer to run. Nevertheless, it was the incident at Piccadilly that had made his reputation; a young man, the fear of whom, ultimately denied him heroic stature.

Chapter Nine

Having finished his cig Dave stood up. He opened the back door and I followed him into the kitchen. We put the bottles down on the top near the sink and Dave shouted through to the front room.

"We've got the beers in Millie. Have you some glasses and a bottle opener."

Walking into the kitchen, Millie looked at the bottles of Carlsberg Special lined up in front of her.

"I thought you were taking it easy tonight, Dave."

"I am. There's only a couple each."

"More like four or five if you compare it to ordinary lager. It's a madman's drink, like cider."

"No, it's not. Try it. You'll like it," said Dave.

"That's what worries me," replied Millie, laughing.

Getting out some glasses Millie handed a bottle opener to Dave who poured out the drinks. We then carried them through to the front room where Millie joined Dawn on the settee and Dave sat at the latter's feet. I took the vacant chair next to Mark and sat quietly as the others talked about recent events on the estate. The focus of my attention was, of course, Millie. She looked so perfect, her delicate fingers playing gently with her necklace as she listened. Eventually the conversation moved on to the subject of films, Dave mentioning that he had heard good reports about The Long Good Friday, a movie that had recently been released.

"It's a gangster film and pretty violent, isn't it?" asked Dawn.

"Yes, that's right," replied Dave.

"Well in that case you'll definitely be going to see it."

"You can come with me if you like."

"No thanks. It's bad enough when my dad makes us watch those old Cagney and Bogart movies when they're on telly."

"No, this one's different," insisted Dave. "It's set in present-day London and has a much better storyline."

"Well, I still don't fancy it," continued Dawn. "Anyway," she said, looking at me, "what kind of films do you like, Michael?"

"My favourite has got to be Thoroughly Modern Millie," I answered.

It was a feeble attempt at humour and it was unsurprising that it elicited little reaction from the others. Feeling slightly embarrassed I tried to explain what the film was about, only to be cut short by Dawn.

"Professor here thinks that we don't know about the film."

"What, that Julie Andrews starred in it and that it was a musical comedy?" asked Dave.

"No. I didn't think that," I said, concerned.

Dawn observed me closely and then her face broke out into a smile.

"We had him again," she said.

"Yes," said Dave. "He thinks he's upset us."

It was tough knowing just when they were having me on and my look of confusion brought an outburst of laughter with which Millie joined in.

"The look on your face," she said.

"Yes, priceless," added Dawn.

"But I wasn't sure that the film was that well known," I tried to explain. "It was a long time ago."

"Yes, all of a few years and it got nominated for lots of awards," said Dave, chuckling.

"Don't try to justify yourself," said Millie, "you'll only make it worse."

Once again, the laughter rang out. Even in the artificial glare of the electric light it was obvious that my face was beetroot. Desperate, I tried to draw attention away from myself.

"What types of films do you like, Dawn?"

"Horror, just like Millie."

"Why? Do you both like being scared?"

"Yes, but then we know that it's only a film and that stops us getting too frightened."

"Except for the time we went to see Carrie," said Millie.

"Yes," confirmed Dawn. "It was the scene at the end that did it. When her hand came out of the grave."

"Do you remember coming home down Oxford Road?" asked Millie. "None of us would go along the pavement because we were scared that something would jump out of the shadows. We ended up walking all along the carriageway and getting beeped at by the taxis."

"I was never so pleased to get home," said Dawn, "but I was terrified of turning the light out when I got into bed."

"Me too."

"No. That's not true. The two of you are having us on," said Dave, laughing.

"We're not," insisted Dawn.

"And after that you still go to watch horror films?" asked Mark.

"Yes."

Suddenly, the door to the hallway swung open before resting against the arm of the settee.

"Come in Fred," said Millie.

Our chairs being in line with the doorway, both Mark and I could see that there was no one there.

Getting up, Dave closed the door and sat back down on the floor.

"Fred?" I asked.

"Yes, Fred. The resident ghost," said Dave.

"Malevolent spirit, more like," said Millie.

"Really?" asked Mark.

"Yes. It's best you just accept it," replied Dave.

Like Mark I was confused, for Millie had never mentioned Fred before.

"Who's Fred?" I asked.

"Yes, Millie," said Mark. "You've got to tell us about him."

"I'm not sure you should," said Dave, looking at Millie. "You know how nasty he can get if you start talking about him."

"Well, they're both intent on finding out. I'll just have to take a chance, won't I?"

"I suppose so, but don't say I didn't warn you," insisted Dave.

If he and Millie were having us on then there was no sign of it; no knowing nods or winks to give them away.

"It all started," explained Millie, "when me and Jeanette found that some of our underwear was missing. We'd both bought similar packs of knickers from 'Marks' and put them away in the chest of drawers in our bedrooms. They were all different colours and after a few days I noticed that the blue ones were missing. When I told Jeanette, she said it was strange because she couldn't find her red ones. We were confused but assumed that it was just one of those things. Then my red ones went missing and her blue ones."

"Sounds a bit kinky, this Fred, doesn't he?" said Mark.

"Or someone you had visiting the house stole them," I suggested.

"No. There'd been no one in the house and the kids knew better than to play tricks on us. Anyway, when Jeanette asked them, they had no idea what she was on about."

"Fair enough," I said, "but is that all there is to it. Just a few pairs of missing underwear?"

"I wish it was," replied Millie, "but then odd items started disappearing from the kitchen drawers. I couldn't find my hairdressing scissors and that's when Jeanette said, 'Oh, it must be Fred who's taken them.' She'd given 'him' a name. A few days later, the scissors turned up again. After that, every time something was moved or taken, we'd simply say that it was Fred. Even the kids did."

"What did Terry think?" asked Mark.

"He said we were barmy; that we'd misplaced things because we were careless or forgetful. Then again, men don't like to face up to things they don't understand, especially if it seems sinister and supernatural."

"That's right," agreed Dawn. "They don't want to admit that they're frightened."

"Well, a few missing items isn't very frightening, is it?" scoffed Mark.

"Well, that's true," said Millie, "but then other things started to happen and it became very sinister."

"I suppose it was our fault," said Dawn. "We shouldn't have held that séance."

"Perhaps," replied Millie, "but we didn't know what would happen."

"You held a séance?" I asked, surprised.

"Yes, a group of us. Dawn got hold of an ouija board and we thought it would be a bit of a laugh to hold one. Jeanette and Terry had gone out, just like tonight, so we held it around the table in the middle room."

"An ouija board," said Mark, "a friend's sister had one. I wanted to know if I would pass my driving test. It said yes but then I failed. It's all nonsense."

Mark seemed determined to treat the subject of Fred as dismissively as possible, even though he hadn't heard the rest of the evidence. Perhaps Dawn's belief that men were afraid to acknowledge the validity of the supernatural, had more than a little merit.

"That's because you didn't create the right atmosphere," said Dawn. "We did. We drew the curtains, burnt some incense and lighted the room with candles."

"At first we asked simple questions and everything was fine," continued Millie, "but we had Annette with us and someone suggested that we should try to contact Kieran and she agreed."

"Who's Kieran?" I asked.

"Annette's friend. He was killed in a car crash after going home to Ireland to visit his parents. His car just left the road. It was a mystery as to why it happened. She was heartbroken."

"They were more than friends though," said Dawn. "She met him working in Liverpool. He was in the Church and they fell in love. He was giving up the priesthood for her. He never told anyone, so Annette didn't feel able to go to the funeral."

"When we asked if he was all right, the room went cold," continued Millie.

"The candles flickered," added Dawn. "We could sense an evil presence."

"And then, that piercing scream and we all jumped to our feet. It was Annette. She was holding her arm. I turned on the light and opened the curtains. Just above her wrist there were three long scratches with trickles of blood coming from them."

Millie paused. There was silence. Sceptical as he was, even Mark was waiting eagerly for her to continue.

"We thought that Fred had done it; that he was angry because we were interfering with the mysteries of the dead. It seemed the only explanation."

"Perhaps he'd been sent by the Devil," suggested Mark. "He'd taken Kieran's soul and wanted his girlfriend's; the sinner who'd turned him from the Church towards the dark side."

"You're not funny, clever arse," said Dawn, angrily. "What you said could well be true."

"Of course, it's not," scoffed Mark. "You're having us on with all this about the scratches."

"No, it's definitely true," said Dave, "I saw her arm a few days later."

"Huh. She could have got those scratches off anything, Dave. You didn't see it happen. How can you know? They think we're completely gormless."

"Well, I believe them. I don't see why they'd make it up," argued Dave.

I had to admit that Mark had a point and as a historian I would always be suspicious of the evidence, but I had been watching Dawn and Millie carefully and it was clear that there were no signs of collusion between them.

"Anyway, after that," continued Millie, "Fred's presence just continued to get stronger, until finally he made an appearance to Jeanette."

"What happened?" I asked.

"Jeanette went to the bathroom in the night and heard a noise at the bottom of the stairs, looked and saw a shadowy figure. She thought someone had broken in and she rushed to wake Terry. He grabbed the hammer from under the bed and went out on the landing. He came straight back, closed the door and jumped into bed. Terry insisted that there was no one there but Jeanette asked him how he knew, as he hadn't the time to go downstairs. Terry told her to be quiet and go to sleep. It was so unlike him and when she touched him, he felt cold and clammy. Jeanette thought he was scared and had been confronted by something on the landing. Whatever it may have been, it wasn't of this world."

"Come off it," said Mark. "It was the middle of the night and they were both half-asleep. Your Jeanette's too highly strung."

"That doesn't sound like Jeanette to me," I observed. "She always strikes me as being very self-assured. And Terry's not frightened of anyone. If it had been an intruder, he would have got stuck in, no bother. No, it does seem strange."

"I thought so too," added Dave.

Mark rolled his eyes. He clearly thought the two of us were far too gullible.

"Anyway," said Millie. "It got to the point where Jeanette asked me if I'd go to the Holy Name with her. She thought that they may be able to help."

"Oh no," said Mark. "They must have thought you'd been watching The Exorcist."

"Well, that's where you're wrong, clever clogs, because it wasn't the first case they've dealt with on the estate. The park and some of the houses are on top of the old Rusholme Road Cemetery. When the Corporation took over the land, they never removed the bodies. There are over 60,000 remains and at the Holy Name they believe that there are other restless souls like Fred who are still searching for peace. They said that a priest would come to perform a simple exorcism which would protect the house against evil."

"So, what happened?" I asked.

"A young priest turned up. He had a cross in one hand and shook holy water from a bottle in the other. He did the downstairs saying his prayers and everything was fine until he climbed the stairs and reached the landing. Then suddenly, his hand started to shake and his voice began to break. He rushed through mine and the kids' bedrooms but stopped dead in the doorway of Jeanette's. He shook a few drops of water into the room and turned back. He was white; he wouldn't go in. Downstairs he said everything was fine but something had frightened him. We offered him a brew, but he refused. He couldn't get away quick enough."

"It could only have been Fred," said Dawn.

"Anyway," said Millie. "Jeanette and I thought about it and it seemed to us that Fred only got nasty when men were involved. He was angry at the attempt to contact Kieran, then at being confronted by Terry and the priest. We decided not to make any fuss when things went missing and touch wood, Fred has been all right."

"Of course he has," said Mark, laughing. "That's because he doesn't exist."

"And is that what you think?" asked Millie, studying me closely.

Soon after meeting Millie I had learned just how much she valued honesty. I therefore knew that she would not appreciate my support against Mark if I were simply trying to please her. I therefore attempted to give an honest opinion about the existence of Fred based on the evidence I had heard.

"Well," I said, "I suppose there is a danger that it's easy to imagine these things, but …"

There was an almighty bang as once again the door flew open and hit the arm of the settee. It was with a force greater than before and as I looked sideways and into the open hallway, there was no one in sight. Shocked, Mark and I both let out a shout, jumped out of our chairs and dived across the room. My heart was in my mouth and unashamedly I rushed to Millie, my refuge in a storm, squeezing in beside her on the settee, whilst Mark backed up against the wall. Yet our friends had not reacted, unsurprised by what had happened. Getting up, Dawn shut the door and invited Mark to sit back in his chair, but there was no response. Mark didn't believe in the presence called Fred, but the hallway door had both he and I seriously doubting the laws of physics and the nature of the universe.

And then, once more, the door began to open, but slowly this time. Unable to see into the hall, I took a sharp intake of breath. I held Millie's hand tightly in mine, for if it was Fred, I wanted to face him together. The seconds ticked agonisingly by, my heart pounding deep within my breast. Then finally, I let out a sigh as slowly, Craig and Gary peeped around the door. Relieved even more than I, Mark sounded triumphant.

"It's the kids. They've been doing it. I should have known."

"Doing what? asked Craig.

"You know what," said Mark. "Pushing the door open and running up the stairs before we could see you."

"We haven't."

"Of course you have."

"No. We've only just come down. There was a bang and all the shouting woke us up and we came down to see what was going on."

"Yeah, I'm sure," said Mark

"Auntie Millie, we're not telling lies. It's true," said Gary.

With his angelic little face, he looked as if butter wouldn't melt in his mouth.

"I know," said Millie. "Anyway, there's nothing for you to worry about. It's only Fred. Go back to bed and get to sleep. I'll be up to check on you in a few minutes.

"All right," said Craig, nodding his head. "Can we have a drink?"

"Yes, Corporation Pop. Use the beaker in the bathroom."

The kids were disappointed. They were hoping for something fizzy and sweet and thought that with all the commotion, they would be able to stay up a bit longer. Yet Auntie Millie was anything but soft and they knew better than to protest.

"Good night," said Gary.

As he and Craig made their way back upstairs, Mark shook his head and smiled.

"Kids, hey? Had us going though, didn't they?

"No," said Millie. "They wouldn't lie to me and if they had been playing a joke on us, they'd never have been able to keep a straight face. Especially Gary."

"Anyway," said Dawn, "for all you don't believe in the supernatural, you were scared stiff when that door banged open. Weren't you Mark?"

"No, I wasn't. I was just playing along for your sake," insisted Mark, trying to summon up as much bravado as he could.

"Oh, really?" said Dave, laughing.

"Yeah. Really."

Stretching his neck and shoulders, like a boxer waiting for the bell, Mark hoped to convince us that he wasn't scared of anything. But we had all seen his fear and he wasn't fooling anyone.

"Come on, Mark," said Dave. "You've got to admit it. Things have happened tonight that you simply can't explain."

Yet Mark was having none of it. Craig and Gary's appearance had saved him. Once again, his belief systems were intact and he wasn't having them questioned.

"What's to explain? We've been had by a couple of kids. They should go on the stage when they get older. They deserve a pair of Oscars."

Yet for me, the events were shrouded in uncertainty and Dave, who had kept a straight face throughout, was adamant that he had experienced Fred's wrath before. Best to keep an open mind I thought and hope that by doing so, I would avoid any unpleasant encounters with Fred in the future.

Chapter Ten

The alarm set off at six. Immediately, I leapt out of bed. I had left Millie's at eleven after arranging to call round again at nine on Sunday morning. She was surprised that I would be up so early, expecting that I would either be celebrating or drowning my sorrows well into the night, depending on the game's result. When I insisted that I would, she smiled at my eagerness to see her, fully aware of the important place she had now assumed in my life.

Six o'clock was too early for Dougie. He had stayed at the King Billy till 'chucking out' time and our train didn't leave Piccadilly until just after nine. Given that we were just a short walk from the station, he was determined to have another hour's sleep. Dougie had been to many finals and it had always gone without a hitch. Yet I was desperate to see my heroes at Wembley and eager to set off as soon as possible, just in case. Having a wash, I quickly got dressed. Downstairs, I put on my shoes and jacket and draped my scarf around my neck. There was a job I had to do. Walking through to the kitchen I saw Shep waiting at the back door, his tail wagging furiously. It was time for walkies but as usual he was being barmy. Needing to go out he also wanted to play, jumping up and licking my face; not allowing me to fasten his lead.

"Shep! Stop it! Don't you want to go out?"

It was a legitimate question. Sure, it was. The only trouble being that Shep couldn't reply. My growing frustration only increased Shep's playfulness and his satisfaction at messing me about went on for some time before finally, the lead was attached and we were on our way. Taking him over to the park, I let him have a run and nodded to a couple of others who had brought out their own little pals too. The latter, like Dougie, were unusual in that they didn't allow their dogs to join the pack of others that roamed the estate throughout the day.

Having returned, Shep took a long drink from his bowl and got into his basket, ready for a snooze. I breathed a sigh of relief. He could be hard work at times but it was impossible not to love him and I knew how much of a companion he was for Dougie. It was now twenty to seven and time to get on with breakfast but as I began to fill the kettle, the kitchen door opened and in walked Muriel carrying a large shopping bag.

"Morning, Michael. Is that good for nothing grandad of yours up yet?"

"Er, no. Not yet."

"There's no surprise," she replied, with just a hint of satisfaction. "No doubt he had a skinful last night."

"I'm not sure he did. He probably took it easy with going to Wembley today."

"You're a good un, aren't you cock? Wouldn't let anyone say anything bad about him, would you?"

I was silent. I didn't know what to say. Muriel looked at me, shook her head slowly, smiled and put her bag down on the top. Opening it, she brought out a pack of bacon, eggs and some tins of tomatoes as well as a fresh, sliced loaf.

"I don't expect he's bothered getting anything proper in for breakfast, has he? And what with taking his grandson all the way to Wembley. Can't expect a growing lad like you to go all that time without a proper breakfast inside you, can we?"

They were rhetorical questions; statements of fact and I wasn't expected to reply. Dougie, of course, would never concern himself with any such arrangements. In his eyes, domestic matters lay very much within the woman's domain.

"Football, beer, racing and that dog," sighed Muriel, as she looked towards Shep. "That's all he's bothered about."

Glancing up at her, Shep faintly wagged his tail, then lowered his eyes. There wasn't a chance that he would leave his basket. He was always on his best behaviour when Muriel was around, for she was the voice of authority.

"Get the frying pan down."

Wondering why Muriel was back so soon after yesterday's departure, I failed to register her request.

"I don't know, you're as bad as your grandad. Head in the clouds, I don't doubt."

"Uh?"

"You, having me stood here like piffy."

"What?"

"Stop gawping and get me the frying pan down. I can't very well cook bacon and eggs without it. Now, can I?"

"Oh, yes. Of course. I'm sorry Muriel."

I fetched a chair from the middle room and put it by the cupboards. Standing on it, I was able to take the frying pan from off the top where it was kept along with the saucepans. Getting back down, I handed it to Muriel.

"Thanks cock," she said, smiling.

"I suppose it's only natural, you being in a daze," she continued. "You're worrying about the match. It's a big day for you, isn't it? Your grandad's not stopped going on about taking you to Wembley. He's real pleased that you're going. Said that all the times he'd been before, he'd wondered what it would be like to have a son to take with him. Now he's got you."

"Did he?"

"Oh yes, he's not shut up about it. He's dead proud of you, you know. Tells everybody that you're doing well at school and that you'll be going to university. First in the Fraser family he says."

I was surprised. Dougie rarely expressed any kind of emotion towards me. In fact, he treated me just like he would any of his friends and I'm sure that he wouldn't be pleased if he knew what Muriel had told me. Feeling slightly self-conscious, I laughed.

"It's true," Muriel confirmed.

"But he's always telling me that I'm a daft bugger"

Realising what I had said I felt my face going red. I had used bad language in front of a woman and for the older generation in Chorlton-on-Medlock, that was unforgivable.

"I'm sorry Muriel. I didn't mean to swear."

"Don't worry cock. I've heard far worse. But don't let me hear you do it again."

Muriel fixed me with a firm stare, reinforcing the point.

"Anyway, go and knock your grandad up and tell him that I'm doing some breakfast for the pair of you."

As I got to the top of the stairs Dougie was coming out of the bathroom. Washed and shaved, he was about to get dressed.

"Muriel's here."

"Muriel?"

"Yes."

"Why's she turned up?"

Typical Dougie. Not a sign that he was pleased that she had returned after their disagreement. Then again, it was matchday and there was no allowance to be made for female sensibilities.

Back downstairs, there was no place for idle hands as Muriel directed me to set the table in the middle room.

"Should I put out a place for you, Muriel?"

"No, I'll get something later."

It was probably a wise decision. I knew from experience that Dougie would be expecting someone to be available to do his fetching and carrying should the need arise.

Having completed my task I watched Muriel take the bacon from the frying pan and place it on two plates that were put back in the oven to keep them warm. Returning the frying pan to the gas, it hissed and spat as the first eggshell was cracked and its contents slipped into the bubbling fat.

"Stay back, cock. I don't want you getting burnt."

Retreating towards the window, I watched proceedings from a suitably safe distance as Muriel prepared double eggs and fried bread for Dougie and I and placed them on the plates in the oven. Opening two tins of tomatoes, Muriel emptied them into a saucepan before adding some of the bacon fat from the frying pan into the mix. It was an authentic treat and when I got stuck in, I could almost feel like a bona fide member of the working-class. Back home in Sale, breakfast wasn't anything like this. Mother insisted we must follow the middle-class trends of muesli, croissants, freshly squeezed orange juice and coffee. Here, everything was washed down with a strong, sugary mug of Co-Op 99 tea. It smacked of building sites and the factory floor; men with dirty, grimy hands. There was no jasmine, darjeeling or lapsang souchong here. This was a real, not an imaginary world.

As the tomatoes came to the boil, Dougie appeared in the doorway.

"Have you done me any fried bread?" he asked. "You know how I like it."

I found it hard to believe, even by Dougie's standards. No hello, or nice to see you; his concern being only for his stomach.

"When have I never made you any fried bread for your breakfast?"

"Well, I'm just saying."

"You're a cheeky beggar. You're lucky I'm giving you any at all."

"Well, I didn't ask you to," replied Dougie, appearing to be hurt by the suggestion that he could possibly be taking advantage of her.

"I'll have you know that I was only thinking about the lad. You're lucky that there's a bit over, or you wouldn't be getting any at all."

I had the sense that she was really doing it for Dougie but she wasn't going to admit that.

"Anyway, why are you here?" asked Dougie, straight to the point as usual.

"Why am I here? That's just typical of you, isn't it? Men. I don't know."

Muriel shook her head and sighed. Dougie, none the wiser, stared at her hoping for enlightenment.

"You can't just go off like that without a concern for the dog. Leave him all that time and just think that he'll be all right."

I looked at Muriel. She appeared deadly serious. If she was, it certainly was a surprise, given that Shep was an unwanted rival in her quest for Dougie's affection.

"Shep's all right," insisted Dougie. "I've asked Cyril to come and let him out."

"Cyril! He's neither use nor ornament. He'll be blind drunk in the pub at dinner and sleeping it off for the rest of the day. No. I might think you spoil that dog rotten, but I won't see the poor little mite left all alone while you swan off to football."

I suspected that concern for the 'poor little mite' was Muriel's way of retaining her self-respect. It threw a veil over the real reason that she was here; a desire to make it up with Dougie. She was throwing him an olive branch but if he failed to grasp it, then there would be no loss of face. I found it hard to resist the urge to smile, for they struck me as being just like a pair of teenagers who were forever falling in and out of love.

"Well, yes. Fair enough," said Dougie, looking thoughtful. "I suppose you might have a point there."

"I know I have."

"But he'll need a walk, you know."

"Of course, he will. Do you think I can't take him?"

"Well, no love."

"He behaves better on the lead with me than he ever does with you."

"Oh, I know that."

Sitting down at the table we waited quietly whilst Muriel brought our breakfasts to us and then returned to the kitchen to finish making us a brew. As expected, the food was superb, Dougie and I eating it with real gusto. As we finished off our drinks I looked up and could see Muriel looking at her watch.

"Go on then. Get your coat and shoes on. It's time you were off or you'll miss your train."

Muttering, Dougie made his way to the cupboard in the hallway. Putting on his coat and shoes, Muriel was far from finished.

"You've got the match tickets, haven't you?"

"Yes, they're in my wallet."

"Show me."

Tutting, he took them out so that she could see them.

"And the train tickets?"

"Course I've got them."

"No, I want to see them. You can't get to Piccadilly without them and let the lad down. Can you now?"

Although irritated, Dougie did as he was asked.

"And you'll not forget to make sure Michael gets something solid inside him, will you?"

"No, I won't."

"That breakfast won't last him all day, you know."

"I said, I won't!"

"And you make sure he does," she said, turning to me.

Quickly nodding my agreement, I could see why Dougie often became irritable with her. Muriel really did treat him as a child but then he acted like one. In fact, it was hard to deny that Muriel was good for him. When she was around, he had the reassurance of knowing that the day would run with regularity. Dougie was getting a good deal and so, I suppose, was Muriel, who found satisfaction and a purpose in being able to look after him.

Satisfied that Dougie was ready, Muriel kissed him on the lips, stepped past him and opened the front door.

"Come on then. Are you going to stand there all day? You've a train to catch."

Dougie stepped outside and I began to follow.

"Oh, hang on a minute," said Muriel.

Thinking that he had finally escaped, Dougie stopped in frustration.

"What is it now?"

"Your hearing aid. Where is it?"

"What, love?"

Dougie's voice had suddenly become soft and gentle. There was a vacant expression on his face. I had to admire his genius; pretending to be deaf whenever his hearing aid was mentioned. And Muriel. Why did she always fall for it? He had been hearing her all morning without it. How had she not realised that? Or was Muriel playing games too? Did it suit her to believe that his disability made him even more dependent on her and perhaps, that is what she really wanted after the unhappiness of her marriage.

"YOUR HEARING AID," repeated Muriel loudly, mouthing the words slowly so that Dougie could lip read.

"Oh, yes love," he replied. "I think I left it on the table."

Muriel nipped back into the house and handed it to him.

"Thanks," said Dougie, slipping it into his coat pocket.

"No, put it in your ear."

Dougie stared back blankly.

"PUT IT IN YOUR EAR," continued Muriel, again speaking slowly and loudly whilst pointing to her own ear to underline the point.

"Oh, aye," replied Dougie, with an enlightened nod.

Taking the hearing aid out of his pocket, Dougie put on a sterling performance of carefully fitting it into his ear and then twiddling with the volume so that it let out a screech. He always did it. Aiming to reassure us that he really did need it.

"I don't know, it's just the same getting him off to work," said Muriel, turning to me and shaking her head. "Every morning, I breathe a sigh of relief when he's finally out of the door."

Outside, we quickened our pace. It wasn't long before Dougie took the hearing aid out of his ear and returned it to his pocket. It would not come out again until after we had returned. Yet that was of little concern as finally, we were on our way to Wembley.

Chapter Eleven

When we arrived at Piccadilly, Dougie's pals were waiting on the concourse. They were gathered beneath the destination boards by the gate to platform five, from where the train to Euston would be departing. We weren't the only ones heading for Wembley of course. The station was awash with sky blue and white; scarves, hats, sweaters, tee shirts and the recently released special match shirt to be worn for the final. Fans were everywhere and it was impossible not to feel the collective positive energy that hung in the air, generated by the excited nervousness of Blues desperate to get to Wembley and see their lads lift the Cup. Many were waiting by the departure boards for their train to be announced, whilst a steady flow of fans made their way through the barriers ready to board the trains that kept on arriving at their platforms. Circling the concourse were photographers from the Manchester Evening News hovering around the close-knit groups of family and friends, most of whom were eager to pose together behind their home-made banners with their beaming smiles and defiant, positive gestures. All were hopeful that one of today's editions would carry a photo that would forever provide them with a memento of the day.

A total of four thousand fans were departing from Piccadilly Station that morning and the demand for seats had been satisfied by the laying on of thirteen football specials. The Evening News had informed us that: "British Rail will be taking no chance with hooligans. There will be a heavy police guard and a total alcohol ban on ten of the trains." At the other end of the spectrum the Manchester City Executive Club had hired the use of a luxury Pulman train to be wined and dined as they travelled to the game in style. Unsurprisingly the cost was considerably more than the £10 needed to buy a ticket to ride on one of the specials. A cheaper option was to buy a seat on one of the thirteen official Supporters Club coaches for £7.50 and these had already departed from Maine Road at seven-thirty.

It was the regular 'intercity' service for us however, as there was no chance of my travelling companions taking one of the cheap football specials. They were for the younger element and the tales of wanton destruction on several such trains, was highlighted by the media to demonise football fans in general. Such incidents did ensure that older supporters rarely considered the 'specials' as an alternative way of getting to the match. Not that Dougie and his mates were at all apprehensive about rubbing shoulders with a potentially hooligan element. Older, they still retained the mental toughness that had been gained through their testing wartime experiences. Even now, in a tight corner, these men knew that they could depend on one another. There was no chance that they would back down to anyone. After all, they had been friends since childhood. Born and brought up on Cresswell Street, just up from the 'George and Dragon,' they had attended Mansfield School and watched City together since the final days at Hyde Road.

Albert Smith, Bert, lived in Beswick on Wellington Street Flats. He appeared the most traditional of them all, the one who, for want of a better word, appeared old. It was an impression reinforced by the appearance of the grey tufts of hair that peeped out from beneath his cloth cap and nestled around his ears and his well-tended sideburns. Wearing a pair of large, brown-framed glasses, his face was kind and gentle. It was clear that Bert's heart lay firmly in the past and his recollections of early married life in the old terraced streets of Beswick were made more poignant by his enforced relocation to the flats.

Like Dougie, Vic Hayes still lived in Chorlton-on-Medlock. He and his wife Elsie had been given a property on the Brunswick Estate; a maisonette on Hursthead Walk. For that reason, Dougie and Vic drank regularly together at the King Billy. Vic was an encyclopaedia of knowledge when it came to the Blues and his word was final when there was a dispute on any aspect of the club's history. As such he had a kind of quiet authority, mild of nature and features too.

Ken Thomas, 'Red Ken,' lived off Plymouth Grove in Longsight. Lean and wiry, he had fierce eyes that seared into the depths of your soul, searching out if you were friend or foe. His was an ominous presence that belied his smallness of stature and when Dougie introduced me, I couldn't help but feel intimidated. Ken's opening question sounded like one continuous growl.

"So, you're going to university to study history. Is that right lad?"

"Er, yes. Yes, it is."

"Well, then. You'll do for me."

Ken offered me a brief smile which relieved, I gratefully accepted.

He was wearing a City bobble hat to cover his baldness, the sky blue providing a bizarre contrast to the ruddy stubble that covered his chin. As I got to know him, a red cap of liberty would have seemed more apt, for it was soon apparent that his nickname was not due to the colour of his hair, but for his passionate championing of the left-wing revolutionary cause. I soon began to appreciate that spending time with him brought my study of the French Revolution to life. A self-employed plasterer, Ken resembled the skilled artisans who were the heart and soul of the sans-culottes. The more he railed against the shortcomings of government and society, the more he reminded me of those members of the Enragés, so desperate to drive the revolution onwards for the benefit of the most vulnerable of their fellow citizens. There was one thing for certain, Ken was a living, breathing enemy of the capitalist classes and he would never bend the knee to anyone.

Being the youngster in the group I was naturally designated to do the running about; any fetching and carrying that may be necessary over the course of the day. It began almost immediately as Dougie and his pals decided that they could do with some reading matter for the journey down.

"Here you are," said Dougie, handing me a pound note. "Nip over to 'John Menzies' and get some papers for the train."

"Sun, Mirror, Express," I suggested.

"Yes, fine," replied Dougie.

"Not for me," growled Ken.

"Even the Mirror?" I asked, thinking it to be a good, solid Labour paper.

"Especially not that," replied Ken, dismissively. "Nothing more than a tool for Foot, Healey and their cronies, the lickspittles of the establishment, to control the minds of the feeble-minded."

"Oh," I said, surprised.

"Oh?" asked Ken, disappointment etched into his face. "Your education suggests you've got promise lad, but don't let your middle-class prejudice have you believe that us working men can't think for ourselves."

"I'm sorry. I didn't mean that."

"He knows you didn't," said Dougie, laughing. "He's having you on."

I nodded weakly. Ken may indeed be having me on but it was almost impossible to tell. His was a grim demeanour; a face like granite that gave nothing away.

"You'll need a thick skin lad if you're going to spend the day with us," added Vic.

"Come on, leave the lad alone," said Bert. "He doesn't know whether he's coming or going."

I felt embarrassed. I didn't want Bert, however well-meaning he may have been, to step in on my behalf. I wanted them to see that I could take it; that I could roll with the punches and surprise them with some shots of my own. I too could be one of the lads. It was then that I suddenly realised that despite the vast difference in our ages, I wanted to be accepted as one of their own.

"Well Ken," I said, changing the subject, "what paper should I get you?"

"A Grauniad. Pathetically liberal it might be but it's the original Manchester daily and at least there's some content I can get stuck into."

"Fair enough."

I began to walk towards Menzies, when Vic shouted after me.

"And bring back the change, young man. Don't be buying any of those dirty books."

"Why?" I shot back. "Have you brought one with you?"

Vic went red and the others, including Ken, burst out laughing.

"The lad got you there," observed Bert.

"Well, the little bugger!" said Ken.

He pretended to show his displeasure by shaking his fist at me, but I knew that my quick rejoinder had impressed him. For all my middle-class imperfections, it seemed that they had accepted me. Today at least, I would be one of them.

Once I had returned with the papers, we made our way on to the platform. I was surprised to see that Dave and a couple of mates were waiting to board the train too. The latter were wearing lumber jackets, jeans and trainers with a scarf knotted around their necks. To the uninitiated, they looked pretty hard.

"Hi Dave, I thought you were going on one of the specials."

"No, you get met by the cops when you come in and they're always looking for someone to collar."

"And it'd probably be you, I suppose," suggested Dougie.

Who, me?" asked Dave, feigning surprise.

"Yes, you."

"Of course not."

"You and your pals aren't bloody hooligans, are you?" asked Ken.

"No. We never start any trouble," said the taller of Dave's mates.

"But we don't avoid it if it comes our way," said the other.

"And I've no doubt that it does," said Dougie.

Dave's mates started laughing but I noticed that he didn't join in. It struck me that he had no wish for Dougie and the others to think badly of him.

"You should save that aggression for the real enemy," said Ken.

"And who's that?" asked the tall one.

"The class enemy. The bosses that are trying to keep you down."

The lad's mouth was wide open. Confused, it was obvious that he didn't have a clue what Ken was on about. Turning towards me, Dave smiled.

"Well, I can see you'll be in your element today professor. You've got someone to plan the revolution with on your way down to Wembley."

Before I could reply there was a sound of jeering coming from the top of the bridge located further up the platform.

"You've no chance! Come on Spurs!"

We looked up and could see a couple of youths gesturing towards us. Having seen our scarves, they were letting us know what they thought of our club and its chances. They were hoping for a reaction and as their taunts continued, Dave's mates didn't disappoint.

"Effing Reds," said the tall one. "If we didn't have to get on the train I'd have 'em."

"Why can't we?" asked his mate. "If we're quick enough we can still catch 'em."

"Come on then."

The two of them set off running whilst their targets retreated across the bridge towards the far platforms and the safety of Fairfield Street. Yet the pursuit was quickly brought to a halt as Dave bellowed after his mates.

"Get back here. We're ready to go."

The two of them stopped immediately, turned around and walked back towards us.

"They were only kids," said Dave. "Too stupid to know any better."

"Doesn't matter," said the tall one. "They need a good hiding."

"Yeah. Teaching some respect," said his mate.

"I say, they don't," said Dave.

His words were quietly spoken, whispered even, but there was no mistaking that they had a chilling quality. I couldn't help but feel affected by it myself, even though I wasn't the intended recipient. I watched as Dave's mates glanced down at the floor, a sign that they had deferred to his judgement.

"I'm sorry about that," said Dave to Dougie and his friends.

"I don't know," said Bert, "When we were younger it was never like that. I can't say that any of us four ever did, but there were lots that used to go to Maine Road one week and Old Trafford the next."

"I find that hard to believe," said Dave.

"Well, it's true kid," replied Bert. "Back then we weren't all full of hate. We could see that it didn't really matter if we were Blue or Red, the main thing was that we were all Mancunians."

"Aye, that's true," said Vic. "Could you imagine, just for a moment, Manchester coming together today if, God forbid, there was another Munich?"

"Well, no," said Dave "and I still find it hard to believe the stories I've heard of our fans crying in the street when they heard the news. I don't understand why they did that."

"That's because you didn't live through the War son," explained Bert. "We thought that we'd seen an end to the loss of youth and innocence, but Munich took so many young men. It was such a waste. Talented boys with great careers ahead of them, just taken in an instant. It was a tragedy and I think, a reminder to so many families of those they had lost to the conflict just a short time before."

Dave nodded. He understood and so I think, did his mates who remained respectfully silent.

"And of course," noted Vic, "Blues fans naturally had close connections to the tragedy through Swifty and Busby."

"Swifty and Busby?" asked the tall lad.

"Yes, Swifty and Busby."

Vic stared back at him, shaking his head in disappointment. It was clear to him that the lad didn't have any idea what he was talking about.

"That's the trouble with you young uns," said Vic, "you don't have a clue about your club's history. Do you?"

Dave's mates looked embarrassed. They loved the Blues and followed them all over the country, but they sensed that this old man was suggesting that they were mere charlatans; that they weren't committed enough.

"Swifty. Frank Swift. City and England keeper," said Dave, helping them out. "He and Matt Busby were league and cup winners with us in the Thirties. You should know that lads."

"Swifty was on the plane working as a journalist. He was killed and Matt was at death's door for weeks after," added Vic. "Yes, Blues and Reds both have reason to remember Munich."

"My Dad reckons that Frank Swift's our best ever keeper and England's too," said Dave.

"A close call between him and Trautmann, I'd say."

"What, as good as Big Joe?" asked the tall lad.

"There you go again," said Vic, with a smile, "thinking the club didn't exist before the days of Mercer and Allison."

"Well, I'm just saying."

"We've had a lot of great keepers," explained Vic. "Big Swifty, Bert, Charlie Williams and Jack Hillman. Joe's good lad, I'll give you that, but certainly not the best. You need to read up on the old uns and get a sense of the club and its history. We're all part of something magnificent; it's bigger than us all. Only when you can truly feel that will you be able to say that you're a Blue."

Vic's passion was undeniable and although the meaning of his words had soared high above their heads, Dave's mates stared in wonder at the unassuming figure stood before them. I looked at Dave and I could see that he got it too. For Vic, following the Blues wasn't just a pleasurable distraction; a chance to ditch his responsibilities and have a drink and a laugh with his pals on a Saturday afternoon. It was far more than that. City was in his soul; a part of that very essence that distinguished him as a man. I had felt the emotion of his words, the peculiar tenderness with which he spoke about his lifelong passion for the club. There was a connection there that couldn't be denied; a love that more ordinary folk could never understand. But I could sense it and I felt that Dave could too.

"Vic's right," said Ken. "Loyalty and solidarity. It's what the working classes are all about and it's why this great game will always be ours."

I nodded and looked towards the train. The doors had been opened and the guards were calling us aboard. Glancing to the side, another party of travellers were eager to take their seats. Three elderly women, kitted out in their best coats and frocks, overnight bags by their side, ready no doubt for a short break at some swanky hotel in the big city. I smiled at them and politely stood to the side, only to be greeted by a ghastly collection of withering looks. Disapproving of football supporters, they were rather put out that we would be travelling on the same train. Herding them together in a somewhat apologetic manner was a distinguished looking elderly gent. Immaculately dressed, his brilliant white collar and regimental tie were displayed through the lapels of his dark, double-breasted, Crombie overcoat. Well-groomed and oiled, his brogues were black and shiny, his voice calm and reassuring. His thick, grey hair swept back from his forehead, he appeared the very image of John Le Mesurier and as he continued to fuss politely around the women, helping them gently on to the train, the more he reminded me of Sergeant Wilson.

"Might see you at the other end," said Dave. "If I don't, behave yourself."

Dave grinned and patted me on the shoulder, then he and his companions moved further along the platform, their intention to take seats on a different carriage. I suspected that the latter found our presence to be somewhat inhibiting. Dave's friends could respect the lifelong commitment that Dougie and his pals had given to the Blues but they regarded their constant references to the past as irrelevant to the here and now. I suppose they were young men who just wanted to be themselves; louder and more raucous. But if they had only known these venerable old men in their youth, the antics that they had got up to, their prejudices would have been shattered into a thousand pieces. But like Vic had said, these lads lacked the capacity to imagine a time before Mercer and Allison and as such, the ability to contemplate the notion that those who today were old, could ever have once been young, was an impossibility. It made me realise that I was different to most of my generation, willing to engage with my elders, recognise their humanity and not regard them as unwanted relics of a bygone age. And always, when I looked at Dougie, I could never escape the realisation that for all his greying hair and furrowed brow, he was still essentially the fiery and idealistic young man whose lifetime of memories could, if only they would listen, be gifted to those who came after.

Chapter Twelve

As there were five of us and only four seats to a table, it was clear that we would have to divide our party across both sides of the carriage. Taking an aisle seat, I indicated to Dougie that he and his pals should take the seats opposite.

"It's all right Grandad, I'm fine here. You can sit with your pals."

"No, lad. I'll sit with you. We're right next to them anyway."

"One of you could always sit on Vic's knee," suggested Ken.

"Get off with you," replied Vic.

Ken and the others laughed. The banter was well under way.

Sergeant Wilson's party had already boarded before us and the old ladies were now nervously settling into their seats whilst their chaperone struggled manfully to squeeze their luggage into the tight, narrow gap that gave access to the rack above their heads.

"Do you need a hand?" asked Grandad, standing up.

Wilson continued to struggle. It wasn't clear if he had heard the offer of assistance or hoped that by ignoring it, Dougie would sit back down.

"Hey pal, "insisted Dougie, "you're doing it all wrong, let me."

Moving forward he reached up and took hold of the case and tipping it back, eased it into position.

Wilson, left standing like a spare part, appeared ill at ease. It seemed that Dougie had exposed his inadequacies and worst of all, had done so in front of his admirers. Yet it was clear that these elderly damsels in distress hadn't lost any faith in their charming Sir Galahad. After all, it was natural for these ladies to regard matters of fetching and carrying as God given tasks for the working man. It was what they were good for. Seeing their adoring eyes looking up at him with admiration and affection, Wilson pulled himself together. Had he forgotten that it behoves a gentleman to show his manners and sense of appreciation?

"Thanks, old chap. Don't make these fit for purpose, do they?"

He laughed somewhat nervously. During the War, men such as Dougie were under his command and although he was never regarded as a disciplinarian, back then he had the reassurance of knowing that they must obey his orders without question. Now times were different; everything was mixed up. 'Jack' no longer doffed his cap or tugged his forelock but thought that he was as good as his master. One of the old school, Wilson had never quite got around to accepting the existence of the new social reality, where class differences still existed but had become blurred around the edges. He had always considered himself a rather benevolent figure when it came to his dealings with members of the working-class, yet he could never shake off his disregard for their importance. To Wilson they would never rise above their station and although the factories, back alleys and cobbled streets were increasingly becoming a thing of the past, he was convinced that their unsavoury odour would attach themselves to Dougie and his pals forever.

"Do you want me to help you with the others?" asked Grandad, motioning towards the rest of the party's luggage.

"No, I'll be fine, thank you. I'm sure I've got the hang of it now."

"All right," said Dougie, returning to his seat. Sitting down he pulled a packet of Bensons out of his pocket and offered one to Vic and Ken.

"Now you know I prefer roll-ups," said the latter.

"Yeah, but you don't often turn anything down when it's going for free," replied Dougie.

"He's bothered about his image," remarked Bert. "It's what these political arty types smoke."

"Oh, I just thought he was a tight get," said Vic.

Bert and Dougie burst out laughing.

"Oi, less of the tight. I'll have you know that it's a better quality of tobacco I'm smoking. You're getting the sweepings up off the factory floor with that pre-packaged muck."

"Aye, I suppose it's another capitalist plot," said Dougie.

"That's right," replied Ken.

"Well, I'll have one," said Vic, taking one from the proffered packet.

"You don't smoke, do you Rick?" asked Bert.

"No."

"I thought all you youngsters did," said Ken.

"Well, I tried them when I was younger but I didn't like them."

"Neither did I," said Vic, "then all my mates said that I'd get to like them if I persevered and now, I can't give 'em up."

"Yeah, just like me," remarked Dougie, "but at least my Bensons aren't as strong as your Woodbines. I don't know how you can smoke 'em."

"Well, I suppose I've got used to 'em."

As my companions drew on their cigarettes, bluey-grey clouds floated into the air before dispersing across the carriage. Wilson's ladies were sniffing the air uncomfortably but this was a smoking compartment and there was nothing that they could do about it. When Dougie had returned to his seat after helping Wilson, I had observed a wave of relief wash over the faces of these ladies. The last thing on their minds when they boarded the train to London, was that they would be sharing the journey with a band of ageing football hooligans. For hooligans was all they could be. The Daily Mail and the Telegraph insisted that it was what football supporters were. The spectre of Dougie inserted into their midst had raised the alarm that they would be pulled into that dark and dangerous world. It was no place for women of gentility. Only when Wilson had pushed the last stubborn suitcase into the luggage rack had they finally been able to settle into their seats. Yet Dougie had been close, uncomfortably close and at least one of their number couldn't help but express the fear that their ride down to the capital could turn into a nightmare.

"I told you that we should have gone first-class."

She had a face like a shrivelled prune, a pair of thin lips curled up into a sneer made prominent by the all too liberal application of shocking, scarlet lipstick.

"Yes, I know, Phyllis. You've no idea what you'll come across these days, do you?"

She spoke quietly. Unlike her friend she feared that her words, if overheard, may antagonise us. She looked very prim and proper wearing her smart blue two-piece suit and elegant rolled brim wool fedora.

"But we decided Vera. First-class is so expensive and the money saved has gone towards a much nicer hotel."

Finally, a voice of reason and conciliation; an acknowledgement that the world and the people in it were not as bad as her friends were suggesting. The owner of the voice had a kind, gentle face with ruddy cheeks and welcoming eyes. Features that had softened gracefully over the course of time.

"That may well be, yet it was before you got to see the types of people that we've to contend with. Wasn't it, Constance? I do recall telling you that we could expect this type of thing. But as usual my advice was ignored."

Phyllis looked accusingly at Constance, who was unable to regard her words as being anything other than a stinging rebuke. Lowering her eyes, Constance fell silent. It wasn't the first time that I had seen her friend intimidate her. When Dougie had helped place the case in the luggage rack, Constance had flashed a grateful smile. It had quickly vanished however when Phyllis had given her a withering look; one that silently screamed 'don't you dare give any encouragement to that awful man!' It was hard to escape the conclusion that Phyllis was nothing but a bully and difficult to understand why Constance would offer her the hand of friendship.

Yet it would be wrong to say that Wilson and his party were the only ones among the passengers who seemed to lack an appreciation of the football supporters in their midst. Once seated I had watched as other passengers had come into the carriage, spied the couple of window seats that were available next to Dougie and I and then glancing at our scarves, had moved hurriedly along. I suspected that unless there were any other Blues boarding the train, we would be left alone until Euston.

As the train pulled away from the platform, we slowly began to pick up speed and had soon covered the short distance to Ardwick Station. It was now that I looked out of the window. It was what I always did when travelling on this line for we were now approaching holy ground; about to cross the bridge over Bennett Street and Hyde Road, where on wasteland next to the railway arches, Ardwick FC had obtained a lease in 1887 to develop the club's first enclosed ground.

Staring out of the window I was lost in thought, wondering about how exciting it must have been to live through those early years, when a great club had been forged from such unremarkable beginnings. Dougie looked at me and smiled.

"A proper Blue. That's my grandson lads," he remarked proudly to his pals.

"Oh aye?" asked Bert

"Yes, he's well up on the history. Just like Vic."

Vic looked over and saw me turning back from the window.

"Good lad. You were looking over to where the old Hyde Road ground was, weren't you?

I smiled and nodded, pleased that he had recognised my awareness of our history. After all, that history was at the heart of our culture and community. It drove the club forward and gave us the identity that connected us all.

"We saw the last years there before the move to Maine Road," continued Vic. "Dougie, all of us. I miss those days but Maine Road gave the club the opportunity to increase attendances and push the club on to be the best in Manchester and then the country. Hyde Road was fit to bursting and hemmed in by the railway and houses. It was impossible to redevelop the ground and increase the attendances. When the main stand burned down, it was the last straw."

"You must have witnessed some great occasions there."

"Aye, that's true lad. The game I remember most was against Burnley when we won three-nil. March 1921 that was. They'd gone thirty games without losing and looked odds on to run away with the league, but we were playing well too and thought that if we won, we could catch them and take the title. It was packed to the rafters. Everyone wanted to be there. Loads of fans climbed on top of the roof over the Popular Side and they stood all along the edge watching the game. Others were clinging to the girders underneath. I'd have been scared to death if it were me. Some of us kids were lifted out and put on the side of the pitch so that we wouldn't get crushed. Fans who'd been locked out made it worse by forcing some of the gates. We were brilliant that day. Horace Barnes scored two, one a forty yards free kick and Tommy Johnson the other."

"But we didn't manage to win the league, did we?"

"No, lad. We had to wait another sixteen years. They went and beat us at their place and for the rest of the season they never let up. Never mind. They were a good side. Sometimes you have to hold up your hands and accept it. We were pleased to be runners-up but I don't think a lot of you youngsters would see it that way today."

"Probably not."

"But you've not told him about the greatest occasion at Hyde Road," said Bert.

"Oh aye. What's that then?" asked Vic.

"You know," replied Bert, with a wink.

Vic looked slightly confused, that is until Bert nodded his head towards Ken, who was quietly reading his Grauniad.

"Yes, of course. How could I forget. It was probably the most important day in the club's history."

"Oh, it's got to be," replied Bert, raising his voice to disturb Ken's concentration. "Other than turning up for the odd cup final, when does the monarch honour a football club by attending one of their games?"

"Yes, I remember it well," said Vic. "Ours was the first provincial ground that a reigning monarch had ever visited. It was certainly a special day when George V came to watch us play Liverpool in March, 1920. We won as well, which made it even better."

"The players were made up, weren't they? Being introduced to him on the pitch," observed Bert.

Dougie was listening with interest. Like me, he was aware that his pals were baiting the hook, confident of reeling Ken in. As the latter was a staunch republican, it was only a matter of time before their conversation would take his attention away from the newspaper. Yet Dougie had no intention of joining in. Although amused and eagerly awaiting Ken's inevitable reaction, he too had no love for the monarchy and so wouldn't pretend that he did in order to participate in the wind-up.

"Yes, it must have inspired them. It was said at the time that when the King was sat in the grandstand, he was clapping away when City were attacking."

"He must have been a Blue then," said Bert.

"Yes. He must," agreed Vic.

"A Blue!"

The Grauniad was flung down on the table. Ken was about to explode. The mention of royalty had taken his attention away from his paper and what he had heard had not pleased him at all.

"You pair of gormless old fools. Do you honestly think that he, or any of these royal scroungers, give a damn about the working man's game? Hunting and shooting, with lackeys like you running after them, bowing and scraping. That's all they're interested in."

"Now come on Ken. That's hardly fair, is it?" asked Bert, his voice excessively calm and reasonable.

"And," added Vic, "you can't say that the royals don't like their horse racing. That's where they're really in tune with the People. Now you tell me. What working man doesn't like to have a bet now and again? They wouldn't be able to if there weren't those like the Queen who run their own racing stables."

"Racing," fumed Ken. "Gambling's yet another way by which the Establishment keeps the working classes down; keeps them poor by telling them that they can risk money they can ill afford on the forlorn hope that they might make a pathetic few quid in return."

"Come on Ken, gambling's just a bit of fun."

"It might be to those that can afford it, like your royal pals. That's why they call horse racing the sport of kings. It just brings misery to the working classes."

It was fascinating to watch Ken once he got on his soap box. He was often overbearing but I had to admit that I admired his passion and had already been forced to recognise that although he lacked formal education, Ken had a depth of knowledge and understanding equal to, if not greater, than anyone I had met.

"No, Ken," said Vic with a shake of his head. "That's not fair. Other than that Edward and he was gone soon enough, the monarchs who've reigned over us, have been pretty decent."

"Yes, you can't say fairer than that," agreed Bert. "They've all shown a real interest in their subjects. That's why George V was at Hyde Road. He wanted to show us that he was one of us; an ordinary Mancunian."

"Yes. it must be really hard for them," added Vic, smiling. "It's a tough life. All those royal visits and having to be so formal all the time. I can see why George V enjoyed it so much when he had a chance to relax and be himself at Hyde Road."

"He enjoyed it all right," spluttered Ken, raging like a volcano that was about to erupt. "He enjoyed it because he was having a laugh at silly beggars like you and your ilk who think the sun shines out of the royal backside. Can't you see them laughing at you every time you bow and scrape and sing the national anthem? They've got you just where they want, snivelling and slobbering on the floor!"

"You say that now," said Bert, with a twinkle in his eye. "I bet you cheered him like everyone else at the time though, didn't you? After all, you would have only been six or seven."

"I was old enough to know," said Ken proudly. "I've always known what that lot were about. My dad made sure of it. When he came back from the trenches he told me what it had been like. He said that he'd had enough of 'King and Country' after he got buried alive on the Somme in 1916. You're deluded you two. Do you think a royal would ever give a toss about City, or Mancunians for that matter? His advisers knew how popular football had become, so they got him to show his face to encourage mugs like you that he was one with the People. After all, Manchester's got a proud, radical past and they wanted to keep everyone in line, didn't they?"

"What are you going to do today, just before kick-off, Ken?" asked Dougie.

"What do you mean?"

"Well, the Queen Mother. She'll be on the pitch meeting the lads, won't she?"

A slight, mischievous smile flitted across Dougie's lips and I could see that Vic and Bert were straining hard to keep a straight face.

"There's no way I'd shake her hand if I was playing," said Ken

"But they might sub you before the kick off if you did that," said Bert.

"I wouldn't care. I'm choosy over whose hand I shake."

"But she's lovely, the Queen Mum," insisted Bert.

"And all the wonderful things she did in the War," added Vic. "Her and the King. They held the country together through the Blitz, didn't they?"

By now Vic was hardly attempting to hide the fact that he was pulling his leg but Ken was so intensely committed to his politics, that he failed to recognise it.

"Held the country together!" he fumed. "The East Enders hated the pair of them. Censorship. That's what stopped anyone knowing about it. When they toured the bomb sites they got pelted with stones and told to 'so and so off' and do you know what she said when a bomb landed in the grounds of the Palace when they were safe in their bunker?"

"No," replied Bert, pretending to be interested.

"That she was pleased they'd been bombed so that the East Enders wouldn't be able to have a go at them anymore. Huh, the royals getting bombed! Secure in their shelters. They weren't in any danger. Not like the tens of thousands of casualties in the East End."

"Never mind that," said Dougie, "you've not said what you're going to do about her being at Wembley."

"He could wait outside the stadium until after they've kicked off," suggested Vic.

"What and give her the satisfaction of ruining my day."

"She wouldn't know that she had," said Bert.

"That's not the point. It's the principle of the matter."

"So, what will you do?" asked Dougie.

"It's simple. I'll nip down to the concourse until they're just about to kick-off and then I'll come back. She'll be off the pitch by then and I won't miss a kick."

"Well," said Vic, trying hard not to laugh. "You've got it all worked out, haven't you?"

"Yes. You'll never see the day when the Establishment puts one over on me."

Ken appeared proud and defiant, a look of satisfaction on his face. Yet almost immediately it was gone as his friends, unable to contain themselves any longer, burst into laughter. Finally, he understood that his passion for the cause had blinded him to the fact that all this time, Vic and Bert had been having him on. Their conversation about George V was all about angling for a response; casting out the line and hoping that Ken would bite. Their friend had duly obliged and was now left with the realisation that he'd fallen for their wit and raillery hook, line and sinker.

"Well, you …"

"Ah, ah, ah," said Bert, admonishing him with his finger. "There's ladies present."

Ken breathed in hard and shook his head. He should have known better than to fall into their trap but then again, they were his lifelong pals and knew exactly how to get a reaction. A brief smile acknowledged their skill but Ken was still eager to end the matter with his dignity intact.

"Yes, fair enough. Laugh all you like boys but remember, one day you'll wake up and realise just how right I am."

Ken's words drew a temporary line under proceedings as the band of brothers turned to their newspapers for some alternative entertainment, yet it wasn't long before the banter was flowing once more.

"Crikey, look at that," said Bert, putting the Sun down on the table in front of him and nodding towards the Page Three girl.

"You shouldn't be looking," said Vic.

"Why not?" asked Bert.

"Because you'll be having a heart attack, that's why," explained Vic.

"Rubbish, these photos keep me young. It's the first page I go to after I've picked up the paper from the newsagents."

"What, you don't start at the back page?" asked Vic.

"No. That comes second. I like to start the day on a positive note."

"Yes, I can see that," said Ken, looking admiringly at the topless young lady. "She's very nice."

At first his comment surprised me. Surely, I thought, a radical like Ken would be sympathetic to the feminist condemnation of the peddling of such images in the popular press. Then I recognised my naivety. I had failed to appreciate that the movement was dominated by men. Whether workers, unionists or academics, most wouldn't think of assessing the value of such photos in any other terms than the pleasure they would derive from looking at them. The notion that Page Three and the Sun were reinforcing negative female stereotypes and the sexualisation of women, wasn't under consideration. And who was I to assume the moral high ground for if I did, I would be nothing more than a hypocrite. I had to admit that the young lady had grabbed my attention too. I found it impossible not to be drawn towards the photo, her attributes more than pleasing to the eye. And therein lay the real issue; just how could feminist logic and reason overcome the power of the male libido.

"I don't know Bert," said Vic, a feigned hint of disappointment in his voice. "You should be ashamed of yourself, gawping at young women like that."

"Why should I?"

"You're old enough to know better."

I don't see why. I'm not past it," insisted Bert.

"Linda Lusardi's my favourite," said Ken. "Now she'd brighten up any man's day."

"You never know," said Bert, "maybe she likes an older man. You might be all right there, Ken."

"She might want a sugar daddy," suggested Dougie, "but I don't think she'd be interested in someone older than her grandad."

"Hey. Less of the old man," said Ken. "Always say you don't know."

His friends started laughing but Ken didn't join in. He was loathe to give up the idea that a Page Three model could find him attractive.

"Well, perhaps he's got a point," suggested Bert.

"I don't think so," said Dougie.

"How do you know," replied Bert. "Women aren't only interested in looks. They're after other qualities too. Ones such as trust, understanding and security."

"And do you think that they're likely to get that from Ken?" asked Dougie, with a chuckle.

"I'll have you know that I'm very understanding," insisted Ken.

It was a response that drew forth howls of laughter from his friends.

"I'll tell you what Ken," said Vic, as the general hilarity began to subside. "The only chance that any Page Three girl would look at you would be if you had a nice, fat bank balance."

"Well, there's an end to it," said Dougie.

The others, including Ken, nodded in agreement. It seemed as if he had now accepted that his desire to go out with Linda Lusardi was merely wishful thinking.

It seemed such an amazing conversation. How on earth could Ken's friends give serious consideration to the possibility of him becoming romantically entwined with Linda Lusardi? But I understood that I was an outsider looking in and so unable to fully appreciate the dynamics of the tight relationships that existed between these long-standing pals. Bizarre conversations regarding unlikely and impossible scenarios were all part of the quick-fire repartee that took place between them. No subject seemed off limits if it offered up the opportunity for ridicule. In fact, the longer I spent with them the more I recognised the presence of an adolescent mindset that would not have been out of place among my contemporaries. Perhaps it was a fact too, one to which many wives would attest, that men never truly grow up.

For a few minutes we all turned back to our newspapers until Vic asked Dougie about Muriel.

"Has she been round?"

"Who?"

"You know who. Muriel."

Dougie did know, but he would never admit that he did. It was the image he wished his pals to observe. One of unstudied indifference.

"Yes, she came round this morning before I got up."

"See. I told you she would," said Vic.

"Made us a nice breakfast before we set off, didn't she Rick?"

"Yes, that's right. She's staying to look after Shep too," I added.

"Well, I don't know," said Bert with a sigh. "You always fall on your feet where women are concerned, don't you Dougie?"

"Well, I never asked her to. She offered. I wasn't going to turn her down now, was I? Not where Shep's concerned. He's important to me."

"Muriel isn't then?" asked Ken, with a chuckle.

Dougie shrugged his shoulders. He always played his cards close to his chest where his feelings about women were concerned and when he did refer to Muriel it was with such an air of practiced nonchalance, that it was impossible to know if he really did care so little about her.

"I told you she'd understand," said Vic. "Once you point out to them that there's more important things in life than birthdays…"

"Yes, like football," interrupted Ken.

"Then they'll see reason," finished Vic.

"Is that right Vic," said Bert, laughing. "So, you didn't have to soft-soap your Elsie, like you did before the semi, so that she'd let you come along today?"

"That was different. I told you. She'd arranged for us to go to her sisters long before we got on the cup run. I could understand why she was a little upset but I was firm with her; football comes first. She understood."

"Did she really?" asked Bert, his words laced with irony.

"Of course."

The others burst out laughing.

"It's true. I can do what I like."

"Yes, of course you can. Just so long as Elsie agrees," said Bert.

A red flush slowly crept across Vic's face. We all knew that Elsie wore the trousers in their house. Remaining silent, Vic knew that it was pointless to reply.

"And you Dougie," continued Bert. "You don't know how lucky you are. You should feel honoured that Muriel seems to think so much about you."

"Yes, you're right there," said Vic, grateful that he was no longer the centre of attention. "Remember before the War, when we all started courting? Muriel was the one we all wanted to go out with. She was the prettiest girl in Ardwick, Chorlton-on-Medlock and probably, the whole of Manchester. There were lots of disappointed young men when Muriel got married."

"That's right," said Bert. "She could have had anyone. It's just unfortunate that she chose a wrong un."

"I never liked that Tommy Smith," said Ken. "He'd rob you blind as soon as look at you."

"He didn't treat her well either," added Vic. "He was always carrying-on and knocking her about. I don't know why she put up with it."

"Didn't have much alternative back then though, did she?" replied Ken. "At least she's rid of him now."

"And a very eligible widow," said Bert. "Still looks good for her age and she's a decent lass. Generous to a fault. In fact, far too good for you Dougie. You don't know how well off you are. A woman like that interested in a miserable old beggar like you."

Dougie shrugged his shoulders, refusing to be drawn.

"You're not getting any younger," continued Bert. "How many more women are likely to want to be around to look after you in your old age?"

"That's all well and good," replied Dougie, "but you seem to be doing all right on your own."

"You might think that but I'm lost without our Annie. They say that time's a great healer but if you really love someone, then life can never be the same once you're parted."

"You've never thought that you might find someone else?" asked Vic.

"No, because there isn't a woman out there who could ever replace her. Annie looked after me. Yes, I could kid myself on about being the man of the house, like most of us do, but I always knew that she was the boss. All I had to do was go out to work, whilst she looked after the house and dealt with everything else. She made me feel safe, provided me with security and I loved it."

"Yes, I know what you mean," said Vic. "A good wife. We do depend on them. Us men would be finished without the love of a good woman. I don't know what I'd do without Elsie."

"Well, that might be the case for you lads but I've done well enough without," insisted Ken. "I've tried marriage once and six months of that was enough for me."

"I don't know," said Bert, "She must have been terrible. How could any woman not get on with a kind, considerate and good-natured chap like you."

As his friends began to chuckle, Ken shook his head in disappointment. How quickly the mood had changed. Through the emotions of Bert's heartfelt sadness, Vic's homespun philosophising and Ken's bitterness, the conversation had ended, almost inevitably, in humour. It was indicative of the fact that these men had lived such full and varied lives.

Chapter Thirteen

"Well, I don't know about you lads but I fancy a beer," said Dougie. "Rick can go and get us some cans. Who else wants one?"

It was a daft question. They all did. As his pals fumbled in their pockets for change, Dougie handed me a ten pounds note.

"It's alright lads, I'll take care of it. You've plenty of time to get 'em in later."

"What should I get?" I asked.

"Bert and Ken like Newcastle Brown. Me and Vic prefer McEwan's Export or Youngers if they don't have it."

I nodded and set off down the aisle only to be recalled by Ken.

"Hang on a minute lad. I'd best come with you in case they won't serve you."

"It's alright. I'm sure they will. I've bought beers on the train before."

"Ah," said Ken, "but I bet you didn't have a scarf on then, did you? They'll think if they sell you booze that you'll turn into one of those drunken hooligans."

"What, our Rick?" asked Dougie, with a chuckle. "He's as soft as they come."

"Yes, but they don't know that," said Ken. "Don't want the kid to waste time queuing up, not getting served and having to come all the way back to fetch one of us."

"That's right," agreed Vic. "We'd be losing valuable drinking time."

"It's what I was thinking," said Ken. "We can't afford that now, can we?"

"You'd best have this then," I suggested, offering the money to Ken.

"Give it me when we get to the buffet. You'll still need to come. I'm not carrying the cans back. Like they say, you don't have a dog and bark yourself."

It was Ken's way of making it clear that he wasn't concerned about saving me the embarrassment of being refused service, or the inconvenience of a wasted journey. No, his sole purpose in calling me back had simply been to optimise his pals' drinking time. Or perhaps that was what he wanted them to think, for I suspected that he was exhibiting a more generous spirit. Yet to admit that would never do, for these men had lived through hard times and as youngsters they had rarely been given and did not expect, a helping hand. They had learned to toughen up almost as soon as they had toddled out into the cobbled streets. Collectively, they were convinced that today's youngsters were spoiled rotten; cossetted by a feeble-minded society that had low expectations of juvenile behaviour and responsibility. Of course, they were prepared to make exceptions to the rule, but I knew that although I had made a good start on creating a favourable impression among Dougie's pals, there were more tests to pass before I would receive their full seal of approval.

The cans secured, Ken and I made our way back to our seats. As we approached them, there was a sudden jolt as the train traversed a bumpy section of track, forcing the carriage to sway. Instinctively throwing out my arm to grab the top of a nearby seat, the cans escaped from my grasp and fell with a thud on the table beneath. Looking down I could see my hand resting just a few inches away from Constance's head. There was a look of terror on her face. I could have been forgiven for thinking that she believed that I had attempted to hit her. Quickly, I apologised.

"I'm ever so sorry, I couldn't help it. I lost my balance and was trying to stay on my feet. Are you alright?"

"All right? Of course she's not all right," barked Phyllis. "You've frightened the life out of her and us too."

The sharpness of her response and the fierce look in her eyes produced an impression that was far removed from fear. If anything, I was the one faced with hostility and aggression. It seemed as if my unfortunate stumble had provided Phyllis with an opportunity. Now she could take out her frustrations at having to travel second class, on the louts that she had the misfortune to share her journey with.

"I'm sure the young man didn't mean it," suggested Constance. "It was just an unfortunate accident, wasn't it?"

Constance offered me a weak smile. Her words were hesitant; her voice tremulous. Yet I wasn't the one that she was afraid of upsetting. Glancing nervously towards Phyllis and Vera, her main concern was how her companions would respond to her conciliatory gesture.

"Yes, it was. I can only apologise," I politely replied. "I only hope that you ladies can forgive me for being so clumsy."

It was the clipped and precise tone that I used when talking to the wives of the committee members at the local tennis club. There it was something that I needed to do for the purpose of 'fitting in' and to ensure that I retained my place in the team, but in these circumstances I suddenly felt ashamed. Knowing that Ken could hear my every word, I was concerned that he would regard my attitude as unduly deferential. In my defence, I had always hated confrontation and would often attempt to mollify those who threatened it. This time however, my actions had left me feeling disappointed and inadequate. For all my pride in the rich working-class heritage that I had inherited from Dougie, all my radical notions had been betrayed. I was unable to escape my polite middle-class upbringing, see clearly without uncertainty or ambiguity and tell Vera what I really thought of her. I looked at Ken apologetically, embarrassment writ large on my face. In return, he merely grinned back at me. I could only think that he had misread my words and demeanour as a contemptuous form of ridicule.

"Well, everything's fine then," said Ken, smiling at Constance. "Get the cans Rick and we'll get sat down. Me and the lads are desperate for a drink."

As I picked up the cans from the table, it seemed that the incident was over. Phyllis however, had other ideas.

"I don't think it's fine!" she snorted. "It's not fine at all. Throwing your drinks around and all but striking poor Constance, you think that you can do whatever you like. Don't you?"

"Yes, that's right," agreed Vera. "Don't you think it's about time that you showed some consideration for people other than yourselves?"

"Look, love," said Ken, speaking calmly to Vera. "There's no harm done and Rick here's apologised. I don't think there's any reason for you to be getting a cob on now, is there?"

Ken seemed unusually affable, almost amused. He was certainly responding to some rather provocative comments with admirable restraint. Hoping to defuse the situation, he looked at

Constance for some support but after her friends' outbursts, it was unlikely to be forthcoming. Averting her eyes, Constance pressed herself firmly back into her seat, almost as if she wished that it would swallow her up. And although it had not been his intention, Ken's words had simply added fuel to the fire. Vera's face had turned a deep shade of red. She was furious at the suggestion that she had a 'cob on.' A phrase that struck hard at her genteel susceptibilities.

"How dare you speak to me like that!"

"Like what?" asked Ken, bemused.

"Like I'm one of the floosies you've picked up on your travels."

"Floosies?"

It was a rare sight. Ken lost for words, his obvious confusion leaving him unable to respond.

"You should be thoroughly ashamed of yourself," added Phyllis for good measure. "You're old enough to know better, yet you and your friends have been acting like hooligans from the moment you were waiting to board the train. Your sort aren't fit to be around decent people."

Now, there was no confusion. Ken fully understood. It was the language of social superiority and snobbery. This was the class war and it no longer mattered that his protagonist was a woman. Now she would receive no special dispensation for her gender. Ken's response would be unrelenting.

"Oh, excuse my ignorance love. I didn't know that wearing fancy clothes and owning a few bits of smart luggage gave you the right to tell the rest of us what to do."

"Well, I never!" said Phyllis, bristling with indignation.

"Is that right?" asked Ken. "You're in England love and me and my mates fought a war so that we wouldn't be told what to do by the likes of you. We saw off the Nazis and come the revolution, 'your sort' won't last too much longer."

Phyllis and Vera stared at him open-mouthed, unable to respond. Ken had adopted the former's own phrase, eager to use it against them.

"Do you know what love," Ken continued, "it's 'your sort' that are the worst of all. The lower middle-classes. You aspire to live in the suburbs, have your holidays abroad and drive your fancy cars, speak with an affected accent and pretend that you're part of the establishment. They'll never accept the likes of you. In their eyes you're no different than me living in a council flat in Longsight. Wake up. You're one of us and the sooner you realise it, the better it'll be for you."

It was almost possible to hear his victims squirming in their seats. Although they would never accept the truth of what he had said, his words had certainly cut them to the quick. Finally, Phyllis responded.

"Well, I've never been so insulted in all my life!"

"Really love? You mean to tell me that no one else has ever taken exception to your warm and welcoming personality?"

I wanted to laugh but I held back. After all, I was starting to get concerned that matters may get out of hand. Ken was clearly blameless but if the guard was made aware of the incident, there was every likelihood that we'd be stopping at the next station and the police would be coming on board. And there was only one way that would end; the football hooligan would never get a fair hearing against the hysterical claims of two irate old women. Yet for Ken there was a principle involved and he would continue to argue his corner. I could envisage a situation where he would be prepared to be handcuffed, taken off the train and away to the cells, where he would miss his beloved team's appearance at Wembley.

Fortunately, a resolution to the disagreement was about to be found. The catalyst for it would be Sergeant Wilson. He was sat next to Constance and I'd been observing him as the exchange between Ken and the old ladies had unfolded. His face was drawn; his breathing shallow. It seemed to me that he was reluctant to get involved and that he had initially hoped that Vera and Phyllis would follow Constance in being prepared to accept my original apology. In one sense he and I were kindred spirits, for he too disliked confrontation. Yet that ceased to be an option once Phyllis and Vera had made it clear that they were spoiling for a fight and the former had shown her determination to insult Ken. Nevertheless, Wilson had waited. He had ignored Ken's barbed comments in the hope that it would bring the argument to an end only for Phyllis to issue her final cry of despair; one that no self-respecting English gentleman could possibly ignore. A lady had been insulted and as her travelling companion and protector, his own reputation was now firmly on the line. Wilson knew that if he continued to sit there in silence, he could never expect his companions to look at him in the same way again. Getting to his feet, the carriage rattled across an uneven section of track. Stumbling, Wilson threw out an arm towards me. Holding him firm, I ensured that he stayed on his feet. His sense of relief was all too brief for quickly he felt that his physical frailties had been exposed and furthermore, realised that he was in my debt. Whatever he was about to say, Wilson suspected that it was unlikely to have much effect, particularly as he felt it was incumbent upon him to thank me for my help.

"Thank you, young man," he said, with the faintest trace of a smile. "That was very kind of you."

"That's alright," I replied.

Wilson bowed his head in acknowledgement and turned towards Ken.

"Now look old chap, I think you owe the ladies here an apology."

"And what gave you that idea?" asked Ken.

"Because one doesn't speak to a lady in that fashion," insisted Wilson.

His comment only served to illustrate the gulf that existed between himself and Ken. Wilson was a prisoner of circumstances; trapped in the outmoded ideals of a now distant past. A strict world of etiquette that had governed the upper-middle classes in the last, fading days of empire. But now it had lost its relevance and men like Ken were determined to challenge the old social conventions, break down the barriers between classes and establish new, egalitarian relationships based on mutual respect. Unsurprisingly, he had little sympathy for Wilson's suggestion.

"Ladies? I don't see any ladies here," asserted Ken.

Pausing, he looked down towards Constance who, still looking timidly towards the floor, had pressed herself even further back into her seat.

"Except for this kind lady here," continued Ken, nodding towards Constance. "After all, she showed understanding towards Rick here. A generous spirit and sense of decency that these others would do well to take note of."

His words were sharply delivered and a clear rejection of Wilson's request, but the latter had to admit that they somewhat reflected his own ideas on the matter. Perhaps then, there was still an opportunity to secure some limited form of apology from Ken that would satisfy his companions' susceptibilities.

"Look old chap, it's easy for these things to get a little heated; a bit out of hand. Just apologise to the ladies and we can forget about it. What do you say?"

Wilson sincerely believed that he was holding out the generous hand of friendship; officer to enlisted man. Yet if he thought that Ken's ire could be so easily extinguished, then he was a poor judge of character. For Ken, the disagreement had become nothing less than a matter of principle and any apology, even one that was half-hearted, would be tantamount to an acknowledgement that Phyllis and Vera were his social superiors.

"Now look here, pal. Rick apologised for dropping the cans and Constance here, accepted. These other old crones," continued Ken, with a flourish of his arm towards Phyllis and Vera, "had no reason to get involved. I don't know, perhaps it's because they're old that they've become so bitter."

Pausing, Ken fixed Wilson with the fiercest of stares.

"There's nothing more to be said," he continued. "Come on Rick."

Wilson knew that he should let it go but to take the sensible option and do nothing offered up the prospect of losing face. Old he may be but just like with Ken, age had brought no diminution of his masculine pride. And of course, there were ladies present. A proud peacock like Wilson simply could not allow his feathers to be ruffled by some jumped-up, self-opinionated scoundrel.

"No, I'm afraid that just won't do. I must insist on an apology."

"You can insist all you like pal. You're not getting one."

The two of them looked closely at one another. It was like a stand-off in the school playground; which one of them would blink first. I thought of suggesting to Ken that we should go and sit down, but I knew that he was unlikely to thank me for it. Wilson had issued a challenge and there was no way that he was going to back down. I waited, wondering how the situation would be resolved. Surely these two old men weren't about to exchange blows. And that I believe, was the thought that crossed Vera's mind too. It was something that had to be avoided at all costs. An altercation on the train to London and her party at the centre of it. The details would no doubt be reported in The Manchester Evening News and possibly, Lord forbid, in the 'nationals' too. How could she and her friends ever live the shame of it down? Their protector had defended their honour and that was satisfaction enough. Now it was time for him to stand down.

"It's all right Brandon. You've made your point. There's no need to get involved any further."

"Come on, Brandon. Sit back down," agreed Phyllis. "Don't give him the satisfaction of lowering yourself to his level."

"Yes, there's a good lad, Brandon. Do as you're told."

Ken chuckled as Brandon sat down. Relieved that a potential punch-up had been avoided, Vera and Phyllis didn't rise to the bait. In Ken they had met their match and he was the one who could claim the moral victory.

"Have you got those cans lad?"

"Yes, Ken," I replied, holding them up in front of me.

"Come on then, let's get down to some serious drinking."

Chapter Fourteen

Having returned to our seats, I put the cans down on the table and then handed them over to Dougie and his pals.

"It's about time," said Dougie. "I thought we were all going to die of thirst."

"Did you get us some glasses?" asked Vic.

"Here you are lads," said Ken, handing them out.

"Plastic. Wouldn't you know it," complained Bert. "Ale never tastes the same when it's not in a glass."

"Well, they knew that hooligans like you were on the train. Didn't want you smashing them to use as weapons."

"Typical. Haven't they got any common sense?" asked Bert. "As if old beggars like us are going to start any trouble."

There was a general murmuring of discontent as Ken's pals turned the plastic vessels over in their hands.

"What took so long?" asked Vic.

"There was a bit of a queue," said Ken. "They needed more staff on."

"And you were talking to those old women," replied Dougie. "I saw you."

"Oh, was he now?" remarked Bert, grinning widely.

"Trying to catch yourself a rich old widow, eh?" asked Vic.

"You must be joking," said Ken, with ill-concealed disgust. "Having to put up with one of those old bats would be a fate worse than death."

"Oh dear. Something happen, did it?" asked Vic.

"We had a little disagreement on the way back," I added.

"About what?" asked Bert.

"Nothing really," replied Ken. "Come on, lads. Get your cans opened. We didn't traipse all that way just for you to be sat staring at them."

There was a pronounced hiss as four ring tops were pulled almost simultaneously, followed by a gurgling sound as the liquid cascaded out.

"Have you been shaking them lad?" asked Vic, as he watched a mountain of froth creeping up his plastic pint pot.

"No," I hastily replied, hoping Ken wouldn't tell him that I'd dropped them.

"It'll be all right. You just need to give it time to settle," said Dougie, coming to my rescue. "Cans of McEwans are always like that. Look, mine's already settling down."

Vic looked over to confirm the fact and looking back at his own drink could see that the froth was almost magically turning to liquid.

"Fair enough," said Vic.

Ken's earlier reply to Bert, had made it clear that he had no interest in discussing our disagreement with Wilson. The incident had certainly caused me some anxiety, especially as I was concerned that matters would get out of hand and that it would ruin our day. Yet in Ken's world disputation was a way of life and consequently he took disagreements in his stride. Be it at work, in the pub, over politics or football, a man as opinionated as Ken could hardly avoid an argument and most were quickly dismissed as soon as they were over. Settled back into his seat, Ken now turned his attention to the most pressing matter of the day, our prospects of victory at Wembley.

"I know we're putting a decent side out," said Ken "and we've won some tough games to get here but I can't help feeling nervous."

"And it's the nerves that kill you," said Vic, "especially at Wembley. Sam Cowan and Roy Paul both realised that when we ended up as losing finalists. They were determined to learn from the experience, remember the disappointment of defeat and make sure that the players were ready for it when we got back there."

"Those two were proper leaders," said Bert. "We haven't got anyone like that now."

Dougie and Ken nodded, murmuring their agreement.

I wanted to interrupt and disagree. How could they ignore our current captain's contribution to the cause? Paul Power had been a revelation this season. He had scored in every round of the Cup, except at Peterborough and his brilliant free-kick in extra-time had got us past Ipswich in the semi-final, a tie few experts expected us to win. Power was full of energy and drove the team forward, whether playing in defence or midfield. He was a Manchester lad, brought up a Blue and unusually had insisted on completing a law degree at Leeds Poly, before signing professional forms for the club. His academic background clearly resonated with my own but it would never carry much weight with Dougie and his pals. They were never likely to put Power on the pedestal that they had erected for Paul and Cowan. Like most senior supporters they looked with favour on the halcyon days of the past when the game was played by real hard men; tough and uncompromising, no quarter asked or given. And it was an age where skill abounded too. When heavy, exacting pitches and sodden leather footballs, as hard as a rock, were no impediment to the artistry of Maine Road legends like Fred Tilson, Eric Brook, Tommy Johnson and the greatest of them all, Peter Doherty. Yes, the older generation had marvelled at the achievements of the Mercer-Allison era, acknowledging the prowess of Bell, Lee and Summerbee, yet they would never regard these younger men as anything other than mere pretenders who could never achieve the status of their idols. And perhaps that also reflected the belief that City's 'Holy Trinity' were embodiments of the swinging sixties, a decade where social and economic change had undermined so many of the old values and certainties of the past. It was therefore unsurprising that feeling increasingly marginalised in an ever-changing world, Dougie and his friends took comfort in the conviction that the best of the older generation of players would always be held up as superior to those that followed.

Or so I thought, for it soon became apparent that Vic, with his encyclopaedic knowledge of the club, was able to put any notions of generational bias to one side and had retained the historian's sense of objectivity.

"I think young Rick here, might disagree with you," said Vic.

"Oh aye?" asked Bert.

"Yes. I think he'd have every right to make out a case for Paul Power being a sound captain."

"Yes, but where was he before Gow, McDonald and Hutchison arrived?" asked Dougie. "Bond had to bring them in to restore confidence in the team and steady the ship. It was only then that we started to perform."

"But Sam Cowan and Roy Paul relied even more on experienced team mates when they were captains," noted Ken.

"You're not talking into account what a young side Power was leading at the start of the season, thanks to Malcolm getting rid of so many senior players. I can't say that I ever saw the lad's head go down. Can you?"

"Well, no," replied Dougie.

"But Cowan and Paul didn't just drive the players on, they directed the play too," said Bert.

"Yes, they did," replied Vic, "but the captain's role has changed since Sam Cowan's day. Now it's the manager's job to set the tactics on the field. For the captain, it's all about geeing up their team mates and leading by example. I agree, he's not the most gifted player to pull on the shirt but right now, I wouldn't want anyone else leading us out on the pitch."

"Well, he's alright I suppose," said Bert, somewhat reluctantly, "but you can't deny that Cowan and Paul were far better players."

"That's right and Skip was too," added Dougie. "And he led us to four trophies and Power's not done it once yet."

I felt like reminding them of how I'd seen them leaping in the air, howling like a pair of Banshees with thousands of others on the Holte End, when Power's free kick hit the back of the net in the semi at Villa Park. Perhaps wisely, I thought better of it.

"I won't disagree with either of you on Paul Power the player but as captain, I still rate him."

Vic paused before continuing.

"What you have to remember as well lads, is that as good as it is for us to celebrate the past and all the great players, you can't stop the clock. The club will always move on. We can tell Rick here that Pete Doherty is our greatest ever player but he's never seen him in action. The young uns need their own heroes; players of the here and now that are part of their own experience and we shouldn't begrudge them that. And it's important that we don't ignore the merits of the players of the present because we're too sentimental about the past."

The others were silent for a moment, seemingly prepared to accept Vic's point of view until Dougie, with a grin, responded with characteristic and forthright conviction.

"Yes, all right Vic, but Power still wouldn't have got into any of the winning teams in 'thirty-four, 'fifty-six or 'sixty-nine. And he's soft. Roy Paul was as hard as nails and didn't take any nonsense from anyone. In the tunnel at Wembley in 'fifty-six, he threatened to give the other players a good hiding if he didn't get to lift the Cup."

Bert and Ken burst out laughing, whilst Vic shook his head and smiled.

"You know what lads," said Ken, "I wish we were sat here having lost the final last year and then I'd feel far more confident about today."

His words took me by surprise and noticing my look of confusion, Vic seemed disappointed.

"You haven't forgotten your history, have you lad?"

The penny suddenly dropped.

"Of course not," I said. "We lost the final in nineteen thirty-three to Everton and then won it the following year against Portsmouth. Then in nineteen fifty-five we lost to Newcastle and beat Birmingham a year later. Both Cowan and Paul, after the first defeat, insisted that we'd be back at Wembley to win the following year."

Vic smiled, further impressed by my awareness of the club's history. I sensed that my statistical knowledge reminded him of a younger version of himself.

"Come on Ken," said Bert. "Don't be talking like that. You'll have us getting all superstitious."

"Well, I can't help it," said Ken. "It's what I'm thinking."

"But if I remember right," said Dougie, "You were all doom and gloom on the way down to Wembley in 'fifty-six. You weren't thinking about what Paul and Cowan had said then. Were you, Ken?"

"No, that's true," replied Ken, "but let's be honest, Birmingham were fancied more than we were and then there was that injury to Jimmy Meadows in the Newcastle final that ended his career and lost us the match."

"But why were you still bothered about that? It was a year later," asked Dougie.

"Because we went down not knowing what the team would be. Johnstone, Leivers and Spurdle were all injured and Les McDowall couldn't name a side ..."

"Yes, I remember," interrupted Dougie.

"… and all I could think, was that he'd have to pick them and they'd probably end up like Meadows and it would end up worse than against Newcastle."

"Were you nervous in 'sixty-nine against Leicester, Ken?" I asked.

"No. Nobody was. They were already relegated."

"But we only just got past 'em," said Bert. "Cup finals can be real levellers. Just ask Leeds. No one saw that one coming against Sunderland."

"Damn funny though," replied Ken, before he and his mates burst into laughter.

The mention of Leeds prompted me to ask Vic about the fabled 'Revie Plan' that was so unique to City's style of play at the time of their fifties' finals.

"It depends on who you believe," said Vic. "It was generally accepted that Les McDowall came up with the idea of using a deep lying centre-forward, after watching the Hungarians hammer England at Wembley in nineteen fifty-three. They'd used Hidegkuti in that role and we tried it out in the Reserves for a season before Revie, or sometimes Bobby Johnstone, were asked to do it in the first team from the start of the 'fifty-four, five season. Yet I've spoken to Ken Barnes and he says it had nothing to do with McDowell or the Hungarians. He said the Reserves were already playing that way before Hidegkuti came to Wembley and it was down to Johnny Williamson being moved to centre-forward. Being an inside-forward, Johnny continued to drop deep to pick up the ball from his inside-halves and that confused the opposition's centre-back."

"But why was it such a success?"

"Because it gave the centre-half a choice. Did he track Revie as he dropped back, or simply ignore him? If he ignored him, Revie could wander all over the pitch and create mayhem and if he followed him, Ken advanced into the space and opened up the game with defence-splitting passes. In fact, Roy Paul said that by dropping deep and dictating the play, Revie was only following what Alex James had done as a creative half-back in the successful Arsenal side of the 'thirties."

"So, the Revie Plan wasn't anything new at all then?"

"Well, not really," said Vic, "but it was different to how everyone else was playing and the newspapers were keen to latch on to it as we seemed to be doing so well."

"Nevertheless," I continued, "it's obvious that you older Blues admire Revie, don't you?"

"At the time the whole country did," said Bert. "He got the player of the year award in nineteen fifty-five."

"He's one of the best players we've seen in over sixty years," added Ken.

"You see," said Vic, "older fans aren't like you youngsters. We don't hold it against Don for being at Leeds, or the disaster he made of the England job. We remember him as a brilliant centre-forward who helped us win the Cup. It was an honour for all of us when he was named footballer of the year. He was the first Blue to get it and only Bert and Skip have won the award since."

Vic was right. His generation had known Revie the player, whereas mine had only experienced him as a manager. Most importantly, the brilliant Leeds side he had put together in the 'sixties and early 'seventies, was thoroughly detested by the fans of other clubs and nowhere was that hatred felt more than in Manchester, whether it was on the blue or red side of the city.

"Your grandad's favourite player from 'fifty-six wasn't Don Revie though," said Vic, "it was Bobby Johnstone. Wasn't he, Dougie?"

"That's right," said Grandad.

"And do you know why?" asked Vic.

"Well, I know he was a brilliant winger, won league titles in Scotland with Hibs and then scored in the final in 'fifty-six to help win us the Cup. I'd say it was the Scottish connection, but then my grandad never makes much of his Scottish heritage and always wants England to beat them in the Home Internationals."

"That's right," said Dougie.

"It's none of that," said Vic. "Your grandad sees Bobby as a kindred spirit."

"Why's that then?"

"Because he was a painter and decorator like me," said Dougie, smiling proudly.

"Yes," said Vic. "He served an apprenticeship as one before he turned professional."

"That may be so," said Bert, "but there's little else to say you're much like him."

"What do you mean?" asked Dougie.

"Well, for a start," replied Bert, with a cheeky grin. "You could never have raced after Bert's clearance and smashed it into the net like Bobby did for that third goal and he also paid his tax and insurance."

Dougie looked on silently as his chums burst into laughter, his deadpan expression indicating that he was unimpressed by his friend's attempt at humour.

"He is right though. Isn't he Dougie?" asked Vic, "The tax man's never likely to get anything out of you, is he?"

"And why should he?"

"Because us silly beggars all have to pay."

"Yes, but you're different. You see, I look at it this way. When the bad weather comes and I'm losing all my outdoor work, you don't see me going to the unemployment and claiming benefits. I've never asked the government for anything, so what gives them the right to expect something in return? I don't bother them, so they shouldn't bother me."

"But it can't be easy, struggling through the winter when people aren't looking for decorators. You'd probably end up getting back in benefits, if you claimed them, anything you laid out in tax and national insurance."

"No, I value my independence," said Dougie, proudly. "I can get by. I always have. I don't need to rely on the government for anything."

"But you go to the doctor's, don't you?" asked Bert.

"So?"

"Well, what do you think tax and insurance pays for?"

"What, you'd begrudge a man who fought for his country a visit to the doctor's now and again?" asked Dougie, a pained expression etched on his face.

"So did we," said Vic, with a sigh of resignation, "but we've always had to pay tax and insurance."

"That's not my fault. I never asked you to."

The conversation was proving a revelation. I had known for a long time that Dougie got up to some dodgy practices when he was putting one over on his customers. When I was younger, I had regularly gone with him into town early on Sunday mornings and searched through the builders' skips for empty tins of Crown and Dulux white emulsion. We would then take them home and I would help Dougie clean them, inside and out, so that later he could fill them up with cheaper Johnstone's paint. These cans would then be taken to the homes of his wealthier customers, where Dougie would pass them off as the genuine article and charge accordingly.

"But Grandad," I once asked, "won't they ask you for a receipt for the materials? If you don't have one, then won't they suspect that it isn't the real thing and you'll be in trouble?"

"No, don't worry lad, they won't." He smiled at me, touched by my naivete and concern. "The tins look just like new and Johnstone's paint is every bit as good as Crown or Dulux. They're not getting an inferior product and no one's ever contacted me to complain that the paint has started yellowing. And they won't ask for receipts because I ask them whether they want me to get the paint or buy it themselves. I offer it cheaper; tell them I get a tradesman's discount. They think they're getting a bargain."

Dougie was no mug. He had it all worked out. I could see the logic of what he was saying and I suppose no real harm was done and although it still seemed dishonest, Dougie was such a likeable rogue that I could never do other than smile about it. Yet now I'd found out that he was defrauding the State. It was amazing that he'd got away with it for so long but after being demobbed at the end of the war, he'd always worked for himself and never offered his services as a sub-contractor. All his jobs were cash-in-hand and with no receipts given, there was no paper trail left in his wake. As far as the Inland Revenue were concerned, he simply didn't exist. Dougie had found that rare, sweet spot where he remained invisible to the system.

"Well, I've nothing but admiration for you Dougie," said Ken. "Don't give 'em anything that you don't have to. There's enough of them rich beggars hiding their money from the tax man in their off-shore accounts and the Royals don't pay a brass farthing. What's good enough for them, is good enough for you."

"Well, you would say that, wouldn't you, Ken?" said Bert, with a chuckle. "You do enough fiddling yourself, don't you? Pay your own tax and insurance and never declare any of the cash jobs, hey?"

"His middle-name should be 'cheaper for cash'," suggested Vic.

Everyone started laughing even Ken, who although he tried found it impossible to keep a straight face. As employees, Bert and Vic came under the provisions of PAYE and so couldn't avoid making their full contributions towards the nation's finances. Nevertheless, neither felt any resentment towards their pals. After all, they weren't hypocrites and knew that if they too had the opportunity to avoid paying, they would gladly have taken it.

"Hey lads," said Dougie. "I think we're nearly there."

He was right. It was some time since I had seen the outskirts of London make their appearance outside the carriage windows and now the train had started to slow down. It wasn't long before the announcement came over the carriage tannoy that we would shortly be arriving at Euston. Looking to my left, the three huge tower blocks of the Ampthill Estate came into view, whilst on the right, long rows of flats and maisonettes stretched into the distance. The post-war urban renewal of the capital was changing the once familiar landscape. The dramatic height and uniformity of buildings that seemed to enclose the station, had the effect of providing anything other than a warm welcome to its visitors. Not that it concerned Dougie and his pals, for their arrival in London was nothing more than a means to an end. They had come to get to Wembley and see their boys raise the Cup. Getting to their feet with the train still in motion, they crammed their newspapers into their coat pockets and made their way down the aisle to the carriage door. As we passed Sergeant Wilson's party, still sat firmly in their seats, I saw Phyllis give us all a withering look, whilst Vera tutted quietly to herself. I couldn't help but smile, pleased to know that the pair of self-appointed moral guardians were still irked by Ken's delivery of some choice home truths.

Chapter Fifteen

Dougie and his pals had last been down to Euston in 'seventy-six and were familiar with the station and its layout. Consequently, once we had shown our tickets at the barrier, we were quickly on our way. I noticed immediately that there was an unusually large number of policemen present on the station concourse and outside the entrance too, as we emerged on to the large piazza beyond where lots of Blues were congregated.

As we paused to get our bearings before making our way to catch the tube at Euston Square, I wasn't the only one who noticed that we were being observed by a small group of the guardians of law and order.

"Yes lad," said Bert. "It's you they're watching."

"That's right," said Vic. "They're wondering if you're a young hooligan."

"That's daft," I replied. "I wouldn't be travelling with you if I was, would I?"

"Now then," said Ken. "You're assuming that they've got some common sense. Police and intelligence aren't words that normally go together."

"I see that there's quite a few specials about," observed Bert.

"They're the beggars you've got to look out for," said Ken.

"Why's that?" I asked,

"Volunteers. Keen as mustard and desperate to make an arrest so they can feel all important. It'll make their weekend if they do. Normal coppers can't stand 'em. Specials turning up unpaid does the regulars out of their overtime."

"Well," said Ken, "it doesn't look like there'll be any shortage of overtime today. If they've got this many coppers here they must have loads out and about all the way to Wembley."

"I noticed it changing when we came down in 'sixty-nine," remarked Vic. "When we were here in 'fifty-five and 'fifty-six the London coppers were quite friendly. Now they seem to hate all Northern fans."

"Not as much as they hate Dougie's lot when they come down for the home internationals," said Bert, winking at Vic.

"My lot? They're not my lot lads," insisted Dougie.

"Come off it, Dougie. Of course they are. You can't deny your heritage that easy," said Vic.

"I'd love to see those tv pictures again," said Bert. "Of their fans on the pitch when they beat England at Wembley. If we looked closely, I bet Dougie was one of them that swung on the crossbar and bust it."

"Get off with you," said Dougie. "You're being daft."

"Better watch out lads," warned Ken. "He'll be coming after us with his claymore."

As his pals burst out laughing Grandad shook his head, a look of resignation on his face. Although he had known that they were having him on, Dougie just couldn't avoid being drawn in by their good-natured banter.

"It didn't help encourage sensible policing though, did it?" observed Vic. "Stories in the papers claiming that the 'Tartan Army' had taken over London, made it look like the coppers had lost control. Now they over-react at all the big games."

"Scotland had a decent side back then," said Bert, changing the subject. "They should have done far better in Argentina. The way they played against Holland I reckon they could have won it if they hadn't been poor in the first couple of games."

"It was only goal difference that did 'em," said Ken.

"Yeah, it looked like they'd get through and then Johnny Rep smashed that one in from thirty yards. The Scots deflated like someone had popped their balloon. What a shame," observed Dougie, with a chuckle that left no one in doubt where his national loyalties lay.

"There were a couple of Blues in their line-up," noted Bert. "Willie Donachie and Asa Hartford."

"Denis Tueart, Dave Watson, Mick Channon and Peter Barnes were in the England squad at that time too," added Ken.

"Makes you sick," said Dougie. "All those good players. Only an idiot like Swales could have thrown it all away so quickly."

"Don't forget it was Malcolm who wanted those players out," replied Vic "and Skip went along with it too."

"No. It was Swales's job to look after the club," insisted Dougie, not prepared to hear a word against Big Mal. "He shouldn't have agreed to the sales."

"Well, whoever's to blame, none of it will ever make any sense to me," insisted Ken.

"Come on lads, let's be positive," said Bert. "If we win today, then we can draw a line under the whole sorry episode."

"And before that we need to get to Euston Square," said Ken.

"Can't we catch the tube here?" I asked.

"No, we need the Metropolitan Line," replied Ken "and that doesn't run through Euston."

"You know what," said Bert, turning to look at Euston's long colonnaded frontage. "You can't help being reminded of just what an eyesore this station is."

It was unsurprising that the steel, concrete and glass anonymity of the modernist design did not sit well with a man who felt more comfortable with the familiar styles and traditions of the past. Bert soon made clear his preference for more classical styles.

"Remember when we first came down here in 'thirty-three against Everton? The style of the place. It was grand. The entrance hall with the big double staircase, the reliefs along the tops of the walls and the mouldings on the ceiling."

"Yeah," said Dougie. "And that amazing giant arch outside the entrance too."

"And it was all still here when we came in 'fifty-six," replied Bert.

"It was all looking a bit grimy by then though, wasn't it? observed Vic.

"Yeah, it was," agreed Ken. "And to be honest it wasn't designed to make those such as you and I feel comfortable with it. All too grand for my liking. It was from a bygone age when all they cared about was pandering to the tastes of a wealthy elite. No, it's a new world now and so the station needed to have a different design and I'm pleased we've got it. There'll be those who claim that Euston looks too bleak and severe. Condemn the steel and concrete with its uniform lines and absence of ostentation or striking gestures. But that's perfect," insisted the committed socialist, "just as it should be. It's British Railways; the people's railway. The station should reflect that; egalitarian and functional."

"Get off with you and your fancy words," said Bert. "Egalitarian and functional? The only thing that anyone can say for certain is that it looks damn ugly!"

"Anyway," added Dougie, "if Thatcher and her cronies get their feet under the table, we might well find ourselves going back to the old days and the railways being privatised."

"It won't be 'the age of the train' then, will it?" observed Vic.

The re-development of Euston was virtually completed just after I was born. Unlike Dougie and his pals, I had never seen the original station. Nevertheless, I didn't find it difficult to sympathise with Bert's sentiments. When looking back at the station's exterior I felt completely underwhelmed. The frontage was characterless indeed and it was almost as if I was seeing a reflection of the architecture of Piccadilly Plaza, Forts Beswick and Ardwick and worst of all, the Hulme Crescents.

"Right, come on," said Bert, "shake a leg. We need to cross over Euston Road here and make our way to the station."

Bert pointed over to the busy road a short distance in front of us and slowly we started to set off. Discussing the architectural merits of Euston Station, there had been nothing to disturb us other than the ever-present sound of traffic; a monotonous hum that dulls the senses of all those unfamiliar with the streets of central London. But suddenly, everything changed. A barrage of chants and shouts rending the air like a series of explosions. Startled, I looked around. Chaos. A blur of movement as bodies raced across the piazza tumbling together, back and forth like the onrushing tide. And we were at the centre of the maelstrom. Struck from behind I stumbled before being knocked to the ground, wincing in pain as a boot crashed into my leg. Shaking my head, I realised that we were under attack. One of those ambushes that Dave had told me about. Clearly, they didn't care that our group was elderly, for these morons were after anyone who had the temerity to wear sky blue. And as I looked up there were two of them ready to move in for the kill. No older than me, Spurs scarves tied around their wrists; denim jackets, jeans and the ubiquitous Dr Martens boots. Evil glints in their eyes and relishing the thought of what they were about to do.

"You Mancy barstard," said one, "you should of stayed at 'ome."

"You'll fackin' wish you 'ad," said his shorter, pimply mate.

But their chance had gone; their words redundant. A sickening crunch and the first one doubled over, blood gushing from his nose and then his mate was on the floor, his arm forced up his back, his legs pinned tight as Vic hooked his free arm around the lad's throat and started to tighten his grip. Unable to resist he was struggling for air. For all his advancing years, Vic was tough, wiry and surprisingly agile. Dougie had told me that his pal had served in the Royal Marines and it was obvious that all these years later, he had forgotten none of his training. He had taken my attackers out in almost a blink of an eye and now he seemed so cold and efficient that I started to believe that he actually intended to suffocate the young hooligan for the temerity of his attack. Vic was ruthless and his prey didn't have a chance. Rising slowly from the ground I wanted to ask Vic to let him go, but unable to speak, I was grateful to see Dougie laying a hand on his shoulder.

"Come on, pal. Best let him go. There's coppers coming."

Vic relaxed his grasp and got to his feet. The lad, still lying on the floor, took in a large gulp of air before coughing uncontrollably.

"I don't think he'll be comfortable swallowing for a while," observed Bert.

"Probably be sucking soup through a straw," added Ken, with a chuckle.

"Well, it serves the beggar right," said Dougie. "Attacking our Rick."

"Well, he should be thankful. He's got off lightly. Have you seen the other kid?" asked Bert.

Trying to put distance between us, the other lad was staggering slowly away. Still bent over, the front of him was covered in blood.

"Hellfire, Vic. It's a wonder you didn't kill him."

"No, Bert. I only tapped him," replied Vic, unconcerned.

The others laughed. The altercation had been over relatively quickly but the violence was sickening and it had shaken me to the core. Yet Dougie and his friends had taken it all in their stride, almost laughing it off as if nothing had happened. Suddenly, I felt ashamed. I was younger and supposedly fitter and I had let them down.

"I'm sorry, I wasn't much use, was I?"

"That's alright lad. It's not your place to get involved in this kind of thing."

Vic's generosity, only deepened my sense of guilt and inadequacy.

"But I was useless. Pathetic. I should have got off the floor and fought back."

"They caught you by surprise," said Bert. "There wasn't much you could do."

"And do you want to turn out like them?" asked Vic. "Thick beggars. No, lad. It's your place to use that mind of yours, or what's the point of all that education? It's the responsibility of those like us to protect decent people like you."

"A man who uses his brain is far more dangerous than one who use his fists," added Ken. "Just think about Vladimir Illyich."

"Yes," I replied, "but Trotsky could do both."

"But we don't want you ending up like him," said Ken.

It was a lesson I'd heard before. Like Dave and Millie, Vic and his pals had now accepted me as one of their own, whilst still insisting that I was different. They were firmly of the opinion that the studious lad from Sale had no business getting involved in anything unsavoury. They were insistent that I should avoid, where possible, the tough, physical challenges that they regularly had to deal with as residents of some of Manchester's roughest estates.

Across the piazza, the pandemonium had almost subsided. Looking across to the station entrance, I recognised Dave. It seemed that for the moment he'd escaped the clutches of the law but there was no sign of his mates. The police were now mopping up, having finally regained control of the situation. They were marching an assortment of young men towards a number of black Marias that had been brought in to whisk away the miscreants. I noticed that some young Blues were among the number; hardly fair I thought as quite clearly the trouble had been initiated by the locals and like us, they had been forced to defend themselves. Although they had been around the station in large numbers, the police had been slow to respond. Losing control, it seemed that many of their officers now felt that they had a point to prove and were looking for opportunities to make it. Just how vindictive they could be, I was soon to find out.

"Oi! You!"

The bark came from nearby but I chose not to look round.

"I said you!"

The voice was louder; getting nearer. I looked at Vic. He was confused too. Suddenly two of them were up close in my face. A rotund sergeant, all bristling 'tash and firm-set jaw and a loyal PC wearing a supercilious smile and eager to add another name to the list of arrests.

"Right sonny, let's be off with you."

Placing his hand on my shoulder, the sergeant was about to lead me away. Yet he had underestimated my elderly companions, who moved quickly to confront him.

"Hold on, Sergeant. What do you think you're doing?" asked Dougie

"What does it look like? Arresting this troublemaker. Now clear out of the way, sir."

The sergeant's tone was condescending, but whilst he was clearly used to having his instructions obeyed, his younger colleague gave off an air of uncertainty.

"I'll have you know that this is my grandson and he's no hooligan."

"So why is there blood all over his scarf?" asked the sergeant.

I looked down. He was right. I could only assume that it had sprayed over me when Vic had punched the Spurs lad on the nose.

"That's nothing to do with Rick here. It's off the hooligan that attacked him. And I should know," said Vic, jabbing his finger into the sergeant's chest. "I was the one who smacked him in the face, to get him off the lad."

"It's a bloody disgrace," said Bert. "We're here minding our own business and some of your cockneys come over and lay into a defenceless lad who's never been in any trouble in his life. And now you're trying to frog-march him off, so you can chuck him in the back of the black maria and beat the living daylights out of him."

"And no witnesses," said Ken. "Out of sight and it never happened. You're all the same you coppers, aren't you? The law applies to everyone except you lot, doesn't it?"

It seemed to me that my protectors were merely being assertive and standing up for my rights, but they had made their points forcefully and Vic, having laid a finger on the sergeant, could be accused of having carried out an assault. I had no wish for any of them to get into trouble, but I knew that if they gave up on me, I was destined for the back of a black maria and an appointment with a beating. Battered and bruised, I would have 'fallen over' whilst resisting arrest and up in court, I would face conviction and possess a criminal record that could ruin my chances of getting into university.

"Don't make matters any worse," said the sergeant, responding to Ken. "In fact, if you persist in taking this attitude, then you're all in danger of being arrested for obstructing an officer in the course of his duty."

His words were formal and intended as a serious threat. Yet a tone of conciliation could be detected in his voice, a tacit acceptance that the arrest wasn't proceeding as smoothly as anticipated. His colleague meanwhile, had taken the opportunity to step back from the situation and was now moving quickly to summon reinforcements. He soon returned, accompanied by an inspector and a couple of constables. My companions could see them approaching and knew that they no longer had the numerical advantage. It was the moment of truth. Would they now quietly abandon me to my fate?

Once again, I felt ashamed. How could I have possibly doubted the support of my grandad and his pals. To them, loyalty was everything and it was clear that no matter what the guardians of law and order intended to throw at them, they were not going to yield an inch. There was no chance that they would stand idly by and allow me to be taken away.

"What's all this Sergeant?" asked the inspector.

"We've apprehended this young hooligan, sir. We were just about to escort him away when these gentlemen here took exception to us doing so."

The inspector looked carefully at Vic who was standing closest to his colleague. Assessing the situation, he could see that

Vic and his friends were remaining relatively calm. There seemed no immediate cause for a robust support of his sergeant's proposed arrest. Seeing that four elderly men had united in my defence led him to believe that perhaps his colleague had been mistaken. The inspector thus decided to question his sergeant further.

"I see. And why are they objecting then?"

Having his actions questioned by his young superior, the sergeant felt uncomfortable. These were changing times and now, he believed, there was far too much concern for public opinion. Not long ago, his superiors would have backed his judgement to the hilt. They understood that firm discipline and a 'clip round the ear' was necessary to keep troublesome youngsters in line. And if occasional excessive force was used, then there was protection and understanding for those working on the frontline. Now the 'do-gooders,' a coalition of bleeding-heart liberals and leftist teachers and social workers, were intent on molly-coddling young hooligans and too many senior officers were pandering to their wishes. Although unhappy with the conciliatory attitude of his inspector, the sergeant knew that he could not afford to appear disrespectful.

"Well sir, they claim that this young man here was a victim of an attack by opposition supporters and that he wasn't the instigator of any trouble himself."

"That's right," said Vic. "The lad hasn't laid a finger on anyone."

"My grandson, Rick here, isn't guilty of anything," added Dougie. "He's a quiet, studious lad. He's certainly no troublemaker. I'd never allow it. He'll be going to university in September."

"Yes, I see," said the inspector. "My name's Baines. I'm in charge of operations here at Euston today. I can appreciate what you're saying, but you're going to have to let me finish talking to my sergeant. I can't make a decision without hearing what he's got to say."

Baines paused to make sure that Vic and Dougie had understood. He was as smooth as they come, friendly but eager to project his authority. Satisfied, he turned back to his colleague.

"Well, sergeant?"

"I suspect otherwise. I don't believe the lad's an innocent bystander at all."

"But have you actually seen him start any trouble?"

"Well, no, but ..."

"And have you?" asked the inspector, turning to the PC who had fetched him.

"Erm. Well, no. Not really."

The hesitant replies, added to the lack of any hard evidence, made up the inspector's mind.

"It's all right sergeant. You can leave the young man here and go back into the station with the other officers. We've got a couple of 'specials' coming in soon."

"Yes. Of course, sir."

Dutifully, the sergeant and constables walked away towards the station entrance.

A calm voice of reason, Inspector Baines cut a rather surprising figure. Slight of build, bespectacled and just about reaching the minimum height for entry into the Metropolitan Police, he appeared exceptionally young for his position; no older than his late twenties. I could see that my companions were rather surprised by this. Having been present at a talk delivered by an inspector from the Greater Manchester Police, I was not. He had informed us about a new graduate training programme that could provide accelerated promotion to promising candidates. It was now possible for graduates to achieve the rank of inspector in just a couple of years, unlike ordinary and ambitious recruits who would have the much longer and traditional route of working their way up through the ranks. This proved unpopular with many current officers, who had given years of service without any real chance of advancement. Yet nationally, the police had an image problem. The organisation was seen as lacking dynamic and innovative leadership and it was believed this was partly because the profession was unattractive to graduates. The perception of 'PC Plod' was still strong in the media and it continued to hold sway over the minds of the public. Britain's supposedly 'best and brightest,' had no wish to be tarnished by its unwanted image. If rapid promotion and large salaries could change this, it would provide the perfect solution to challenging popular misconceptions and improve the Force's image.

As far as Vic and his pals were concerned, Baines' conciliatory tone had made little immediate impression. After all, why should they be grateful when they knew that I had done nothing wrong? Furthermore, rather than appreciating the fact that he was trying to be reasonable, having spent a lifetime dealing with coppers who were tough, uncompromising, often arrogant and hostile, Baines simply struck them as being inexperienced and unsure of himself. The inspector had thus opened himself up to criticism and unsurprisingly, Ken was quickly on the attack.

"It seems to me that despite all this manpower, you've still been caught out. In fact, you haven't got a clue what's going on, have you?"

"Well, to be fair sir, our intelligence didn't alert us to the fact that anything was likely to happen and we did respond quickly and effectively once the disturbance broke out."

Baines seemed very satisfied with his response. It was couched in words that resembled an official statement that had just been released to the press. The fact that he remained calm and assured showed exactly why he had been selected to be part of the new breed of senior officers. Yet if his intention was to draw a line under the matter and retreat quietly back to his men, he was to be sadly disappointed. As far as my companions were concerned, the conversation was far from over.

"I don't see how you can say that," said Dougie, angrily. "My grandson got attacked and just look," he continued, pointing to a couple of ambulances further along the piazza. "Innocent fans have got badly injured and if you lot had known what you were doing, that wouldn't have happened."

"The truth is," added Vic, "for all your fine words, you lot don't care. You think that football fans are the scum of the earth and you don't give a damn what happens to us."

"That's not true," pleaded the inspector. "We do care. Why would we bring so many officers here to Euston, if not to keep supporters from Manchester safe?"

"Oh, don't come that," said Ken, laughing. "It's all politics. You're only here to make a show of force for the benefit of the so-called general public. Reassure them that you won't let any nasty football fans spoil their day."

"We're here to protect everyone," insisted Baines, "Whoever they are."

"So, you claim," replied Vic, "but that doesn't make sense. You told us that you weren't expecting any trouble, so the only reason you've got so many officers here is to reassure the public."

"And to intimidate the Blues fans when they arrived," added Bert.

Baines was stunned. He winced with embarrassment, his confident demeanour suddenly deserting him. The inspector had been caught out. He had not counted on the perceptive intelligence of his working-class protagonists and by underestimating them, realised that he was guilty of being smug and complacent. It was not surprising that he had made such a mistake. Having gained a first in economics from the LSE, he was highly commended by his tutors who were disappointed that he did not go on to complete a PhD. He had quickly impressed his superiors at the Met too and was predicted to have a bright future. Given the corruption scandals that had rocked the organisation and Sir Robert Mark's tireless work in trying to get rid of the 'bad apples,' he was identified as someone who could be relied upon to provide upright leadership and uphold high moral standards among the rank and file. The upward trajectory of his career had instilled Baines with enormous self-confidence and a belief that all things were possible. It was natural for him to assume that it would be easy to disarm the criticisms of my companions. Yet now, he was struggling for an answer and without his officers to extricate him from this embarrassing situation, he had no alternative other than to see it out.

"And you talk about using intelligence," added Bert. "You can't even distinguish a small number of hooligans from the decent, law-abiding fans. Innocent youngsters, pensioners, hard-working husbands and fathers. Then again, it's a lot easier to lump us all together and treat us as the enemy. Isn't it?"

"And you forget that we're all tax payers too," added Vic. "We and fans like us pay your wages and on a day like today, it doesn't seem like we're getting anything in return."

The inspector looked overwhelmed and for a moment I felt sorry for him. After all, he had treated me fairly and overruled his sergeant's desire to arrest me. I was thankful that he had dismissed his officers, for I wondered how they would have reacted to seeing him at the centre of a storm of protest. Perhaps, they would have been pleased at Baines' discomfiture and regarded it as a salutary lesson to him, given his insistence on pursuing a softer approach to matters of public order.

"I'm sorry, you're still unhappy," replied Baines, eventually. "You are, of course, at liberty to complain to the Assistant Commissioner for Operations and Administration who will look into my handling of matters here today and take any action he sees necessary."

Having had his confidence shaken, the inspector had returned to the official tone and language that enabled him to believe that he had regained control of the conversation. Baines was also astute enough to know that his working-class protagonists would be highly unlikely to invest any time or effort into registering a grievance with his superior. His instincts soon proved to be correct.

"Huh. As if he's likely to agree with us," said Ken, shaking his head.

"We'd just be wasting our time," agreed Vic.

"Well, the opportunity exists if you want to use it," replied Baines. "And now, if you'll excuse me, I need to return to the station."

Relieved, the inspector moved quickly away from the withering glances of Dougie and his mates. The latter were visibly unimpressed by the softer face of modern policing. It would take far more than good manners and clever PR to convince them that it was ever possible to trust a copper.

"What a tosspot," said Vic, shaking his head.

The others laughed.

"Well, I don't know about you lads, but I'm feeling a bit hungry," said Bert. "We've still got plenty of time, so how about us finding a café and getting something to eat before we get on the underground?"

"Aye," agreed Dougie. "The lad'll need something to eat. Muriel was nagging about it before we set off."

"Well, we've no option then, have we," said Vic. "We almost lost him once to the cops so we don't want Rick wasting away now, do we?"

The others laughed. They all wanted to take a breather after their exertions against the hooligans and the dispute with the police, but conscious of their age and that they weren't as fit and healthy as they once had been, they were reluctant to admit it. And that's where I came in useful, duly designated as the somewhat delicate young man who couldn't quite stand the pace.

"That's right," said Ken. "Come on then, let's head over to the main road, there's bound to be a café there."

Chapter Sixteen

We soon found a café and looking inside could see that there were already quite a few customers sat at the tables.

"This looks alright," said Ken. "Should get a decent brew in a proper mug in here."

"And it smells like they do a fry-up," added Bert.

"Look, there's some Blues in there," said Vic, pointing through the window. "They look happy enough."

"Come on then lads. Let's go in," said Ken.

For my companions, the café seemed acceptable. The older generation were not impressed by the accelerating advance of the fast-food outlet, with its bland, tasteless products, served with plastic and cardboard. What they desired was the familiar. The traditional meals that they had grown up with presented on proper plates and eaten with stainless steel cutlery.

Stood at the counter, the proprietor acknowledged us as we entered and sent over a waitress to seat us at a couple of tables near the window. Having settled us down the waitress pulled a small notebook out of a pocket in the starched white apron that covered her black knee-length dress and smiled.

"We're not too late to order a fried breakfast, are we?" asked Bert.

"No, darling. We do them all day."

"What do you get?"

"It tells you on the menu, gormless," said Vic. "Three rashers of bacon, two sausages, a fried egg, beans or tomatoes, fried bread and a mug of tea"

"That's right," said the waitress, smiling.

"No black pudding?" asked Bert, sounding disappointed.

Our waitress looked confused.

"Never mind him love. He should know that you don't eat it down here," said Ken.

We could tell that she had made an impression on him for Ken was smiling at her, something he rarely did to anyone. She must have been in her early forties but carried her age well. The apron pulled tightly around her displayed a shapely figure and I too could not help but find her attractive. Her light-brown hair curled around her ears and she had a very pretty face. A small, cute nose, soft, hazel eyes and long eyelashes that fluttered attractively when she smiled. Her lips were full, rosy and looked ever so inviting when she rested her pencil softly against them.

"So, what would you like?" she asked, pencil at the ready.

"That's easy for me," replied Ken, "I'll have the breakfast love but knowing these lads, they'll probably want to look at the menu."

Ken looked across at his pals and raised his eyebrows. It was his way of telling them that he wanted a bit of time to chat with the waitress. Whilst I could see a trace of a smile on the faces of Vic and Dougie, the slightest shake of the head from Bert told me he thought that Ken was being ridiculous. Nevertheless he, like his friends, picked up the menu to grant Ken's request.

"What's your name love?" asked Ken.

"Val. What's yours?"

"Ken."

"You don't look like a Ken to me."

"What's a Ken supposed to look like?"

"Well, I always think of Ken Barlow but he's a teacher and you don't look like one of them, do you?"

"You're right there, love. I do a proper job."

"What's that."

"Self-employed plasterer."

Val seemed far from impressed.

"It's good money. Better than teachers' earn," said Ken, trying to justify himself. "Anyway, how long have you been doing this?"

"Waitressing?"

"Yeah."

"Ten years. Since my other half bought this café."

"Oh. Are you running it then?"

"No, he is. My Stan. There at the counter. He's a trained chef and does all the cooking too."

Ken looked over. He could see that Stan was watching them closely, perhaps unhappy that he was giving his wife a little too much attention. This was confirmed when Stan called out to her.

"Val. I think the other gentlemen are ready to order now."

"Yes, Stan. I'm on it."

Val quickly began to take our orders. Unsurprisingly, all of us had decided to have the fried breakfast so confirming what our waitress had already suspected, that we had delayed ordering so that Ken would have a chance to chat her up. It was clear that she approved of our actions, taking the order back to Stan with a beaming smile on her face. In no time at all she had returned with our food and once she had departed, Ken's pals were eager to rib him about his pursuit of her.

"You can't really believe that she'd be interested in someone like you, Ken?" asked Bert.

"Why not? I reckon if her husband hadn't been here, I'd have been well in. We definitely clicked."

The others started laughing.

"You're dreaming," said Vic. "She was only being friendly. It's part of her job to keep the customers happy. Anyway, you're far too old for her. You'd never keep up," said Vic.

"She's a good-looking lass though," said Dougie. "I even noticed our Rick eyeing her up. Isn't that right lad?"

As he looked towards me, I could feel my face slowly turning red. It was the cue for his pals to explode into laughter.

"Hey, Rick. You never know, she might like someone young and energetic," suggested Bert.

"I'll bet she could teach you a thing or two," said Vic. "She'd complete your education all right!"

"She'd eat him alive," added Bert, with a chuckle.

"No, the lad might appreciate the chance to look, but he wouldn't touch," said Dougie. "He's already spoken for and nothing like me when I was his age. Rick's old faithful."

"That's because unlike you, the lad's got his head screwed on," remarked Vic. "Millie's a lovely girl."

"Yes, she is. You're a very lucky lad, Rick. Just make sure you don't forget it."

"I know I am Bert. I won't."

The discussion of my love life was becoming embarrassing and I was grateful when Ken noticed Dave staring through the window from outside.

"That's Dave, isn't it? asked Ken.

"Yes," I replied. "He doesn't seem to have seen us though, does he?"

"I suppose he got mixed up in the shenanigans at the station. His mind'll be elsewhere if the cops are looking out for him," suggested Vic.

"Aye, it could be," said Dougie.

"Rick, go and tell him to come inside. I wouldn't like the lad to get arrested and miss the game."

Despite his reputation for trouble, Dave had made a favourable impression on Dougie and his pals, especially Vic. The latter was impressed by the respect that Dave showed for his elders and in addition, he had warmed to the young man's impressive knowledge of his club's history. Having nipped out, it wasn't difficult to persuade Dave to come and sit with us.

"We're over here," I said, pointing towards the tables by the window as I closed the door behind us.

"Right you are Rick. I'll go and get myself a brew and come over."

As Dave headed for the counter, I returned to my breakfast. In my absence, the conversation had got round to considering the disadvantages of living in the South. I could only assume that it had evolved out of Bert's grumbling about the absence of black pudding from what otherwise, he acknowledged, was quite an acceptable fry-up.

"There's loads of things they don't have down here," said Vic. "Not just black pudding."

"Yeah, that's right," agreed Dougie. "At the chippies you can't get steak and kidney puddings, mushy peas or gravy."

"And have you ever been in a decent chippy down here?" asked Ken. "These Southerners eat anything. A London chippy wouldn't last five minutes in Manchester. They'd have no customers."

"The beer's normally flat an' all," added Bert. "I noticed it right away when I got stationed down 'ere in the War and it hasn't improved much since then."

"Get off with you," said Vic, laughing. "It's not stopped you supping it when we come down though, has it?"

"Well, I do my best," replied Bert, "but it's not great and it doesn't help when they don't sell Boddies."

"Most of the landlords are miserable beggars as well," added Dougie. "They're quick to sell you a pint at last orders, then they're chasing after you to drink up as soon as you've bought it!"

"Yeah, but that's Southerners all over, isn't it?" remarked Ken. "None of 'em are very friendly. I mean, just try stopping someone and asking for directions. Most'll walk on without looking at you."

"Probably think you're going to lamp them," suggested Vic. "It's that fierce look on your face."

"Who, me?"

Ken's mouth opened wide in disbelief, causing his friends to roar with laughter.

"You know what," said Bert, "for all we've called 'em, when I was down 'ere in the Blitz, I'd only got admiration for how they were able to put up with it."

"Aye, you're right there," said Dougie. "The Manchester Blitz was terrible but the East End got it night after night."

Bert's comment seemed to restore balance to the ongoing appraisal of the Southern character yet once Dave had come over to join us, it did not last very long.

"What happened to your pals then?" asked Ken.

"Huh, them," replied Dave, dismissively. "The pair of 'em were away as soon as they realised how many of 'em there were. It took me by surprise though. You don't normally get trouble at Euston."

"You didn't run off though lad, did you? I saw you getting stuck in," observed Ken.

"Well, I had no choice. It was a matter of honour."

"But there were coppers all over. You were taking a chance hanging about, weren't you?" asked Bert.

"It didn't matter. Most weren't Spurs fans, they were Cockney Reds. I wasn't going to run away from them."

"Cockney Reds?" asked Ken.

"Yeah. United fans from London. Or, when they feel like it. A couple of lads at work are Reds and they said that when they come down and there's trouble, if they're outnumbered the Cockney Reds throw their scarves away and join in against them. Open their mouths and they've got the twang and so they get away with it. The lads tell me the same ones 'll be at Old Trafford the following Saturday supporting United."

"I can believe that," said Bert. "Our kid did his national service in Malaya and when his unit went on patrol in the jungle, he said that you couldn't trust a cockney not to run and leave you in it if you were attacked."

"You were there during the emergency as well, weren't you Vic?" asked Ken.

"Yeah, but as far as I'm concerned you could always rely on the cockney lads. Then again, we were marines and there from the start of the emergency. That's before the Briggs Plan got underway and the 'new villages' separated the guerillas from the locals. In time, it stopped them getting food and intelligence and made the fighting less difficult."

"The 'strategic hamlets' set up by the Yanks in Vietnam were a similar idea, weren't they?" I asked.

"Yes, but they didn't work," replied Vic.

"Why not?"

"Different times Rick. We were ruthless but it was before tv and journalists started chasing atrocity stories, like they did in Vietnam. Pathe News followed our lads around and produced features for the cinemas, but they were positive and wanted to reassure people at home that the boys were doing a good job. After the War it's what everyone wanted to believe."

"People just accepted government propaganda," said Ken. "The Daily Worker didn't go along with it though, did they? Printing those pictures of the heads."

"Heads?"

"Yes, Rick. They showed photos of the decapitated heads of dead communist guerillas. In one of them, a couple of heads were being held up by a marine," admitted Vic.

"Oh."

"We need to be honest," continued Vic. "I won't lie to you. It was brutal fighting in Malaya. You don't play by the rules if you want to stay alive. It was just the same in the War. You can ask any of us. We all did and saw things that we would never have believed before we went off to fight."

"He's right," said Ken. "War's not just a game."

Dougie and Bert nodded in agreement.

"But you're not likely to find out about it in the history books," continued Vic. "Not the bits that the government don't want you to know about."

"Classified information," added Ken. "You'll never get access to the records in your lifetime."

"But they can't stop us old soldiers talking about it," said Vic.

I looked at Dave. Like me, he was fascinated and listening intently.

"I remember one time when we were attached to a field regiment sent to destroy a guerilla force out in the hills near Kampar. Our unit had to go out, locate them and determine their numbers. If possible, we were to engage them. If not, we were to call in reinforcements. We found them as it was getting dark. They were camped outside a cave. They had more men than us but the captain was confident. We waited till dawn, took out their sentries and moved in. We did lots of 'em before they had a chance to fight back and the rest retreated into the cave. It was a stand-off. We had no heavy weapons and if we'd tried to rush the entrance, we'd have lost too many men. The captain radioed back to camp and explained the position. A couple of hours later this colonel from military intelligence flew in by helicopter and shortly after a couple of twenty-five pounders were brought in. I was with the captain when he explained the position. He said that our interpreter had shouted to the guerillas that they were surrounded and we were waiting for them to lay down their arms.

'And how long will that take?' asked the colonel.

'Well, they'll have to surrender eventually,' replied the captain.

'We're not messing about like that,' said the colonel. 'We've got the twenty-five pounders. We'll bury them in the cave.'

The colonel ordered the two guns to be lined up ready to fire. Our captain asked for another chance to get the guerillas to surrender.

'You've got two minutes,' said the colonel.

He was ruthless. Studying his watch, he refused any extra time for the interpreter to shout out the warning. The guerillas hadn't a chance. They couldn't have laid down their arms and got out in that time, but he didn't care.

'That's it, times up. Fire!'

The shells exploded inside the cave and brought the roof down, sealing the entrance.

'These people need to know just who they're dealing with. Carry on captain.'

And he was off. A huge smile on his face. It was the first time we felt as if we were the ones acting like terrorists, rather than the guerillas. Perhaps it was necessary but it did make me think. After all, it wasn't like the War. Then we were fighting against Hitler and pure evil. In Malaya it was all about protecting the tin mines and rubber plantations and the profits of the big companies. I was proud to be a royal marine but when my time was up, it made me decide not to re-enlist."

"Good for you, Vic," said Ken. "You recognised the real enemy. The class war."

"No, I'm not like you Ken. I don't see things in black and white. I accept that there'll always be rich and poor and that'll never change. There's too much greed; people always wanting more. I'm not for changing the world but neither am I prepared to help the cruel and the avaricious and since leaving the forces I've only ever worked for decent companies and honest bosses."

"Come on," said Bert, "we need to make a move. Wembley awaits."

"Best you come along with us Dave," said Vic. "The cops won't be interested if they see you walking along with a bunch of old men."

"Yes, thanks," replied Dave. "There's quite a few of 'em at the tube. That's why you saw me hanging about outside. I was waiting for it to calm down a bit."

As we got up and put our chairs under the table, I saw Bert with some coins in his hand.

"Have you got something for Val, lads?" he asked.

"Dougie and Vic quickly put their hands in their pockets and handed over some change.

"What about you, Ken?"

The latter sighed before reluctantly handing over ten pence.

"You tight beggar and to think you were trying to chat her up," added Vic.

"I'm not being tight. Tipping someone is demeaning to them. It's saying they're no better than a personal servant."

"Get off with you," said Bert. "You've always been dead mean. You wouldn't give anyone the steam off your tea."

As his pals burst into laughter, Ken made his way quickly outside. Putting the coins under his empty plate, ready for Val when she came to clear away, Bert gave our waitress a cheery wave and followed us to the door. Fed and watered, our journey to Wembley was about to resume.

Chapter Seventeen

By now, the area outside the entrance to the underground at Euston Square was packed with Blues. It meant that although they had a large force of officers present, the police had little chance of identifying and arresting any individual. Ken's concerns for Dave turned out to be unfounded. In fact, impressed by the unusual alacrity of the staff in their desire to move supporters quickly through the station, the officers on duty had made a conscious decision not to interfere in the continuous flow of excited humanity eagerly making its way down to the Metropolitan Line and the journey to Wembley Park.

Having bought our tickets, we joined the heavy press of supporters moving slowly through the barriers. There was still plenty of time to get to the stadium and the general mood of John Bond's sky-blue army was relaxed and good-natured. Singing and chanting and hardly a Spurs fan in sight. Manchester had come to London all right and it felt like we were taking over. Confidence was high; you could sense it in the air. The cynic could point out that spirits were buoyed by the liberal consumption of alcohol, but they would be wrong. This was no booze-fuelled day out to Blackpool, or a coach load of wide-eyed provincials come to experience the sights and sounds of the capital. All of us were here on a mission. Our heroes had come to play a match of historic proportions and thirty thousand of us had travelled with a purpose, backing them to win.

And we were sick and tired of the national media; the tv and press who told us that we hadn't a chance. It was the Chinese year of the cockerel and if that wasn't auspicious enough for the Londoners, Spurs had won trophies in 1901, 21, 51, 61 and 71. It was now another year ending in a one and the omens were stacked against us. We may as well have stayed at home. The orchestration of subliminal messages favouring our opponents went even further, as 'Top of the Pops' and Radio One wore out the grooves of 'Ossie's Dream.' Written and performed by Cockney knees-up artists Chas and Dave, the Tottenham squad croaked along unconvincingly in the background. It may well have been the worst football song ever recorded but that didn't matter to the London based BBC who, by playing it, made clear which side they were favouring in the nation's showpiece final. Not that we cared, for back home we had the refuge of Piccadilly Radio, where 'me old cock sparrers' didn't have a chance of getting on the airwaves. In the period leading up to the final, Radio One FM's audience figures in Manchester plummeted, confined to the red side of the city.

So, despite all the optimism surrounding Tottenham, we Blues continued to believe.

"He can dream all he likes," said Dougie, on hearing the song. "He'll never see a winner's medal."

It was a view shared by his pals and all their elder brethren, who had no time for the Argentinian imports, Villa and Ardiles. After all, Wembley was no place for the unpredictable Latin temperament. It was football's biggest stage and the Spurs men would never handle the pressure.

"But surely grandad," I pointed out, "why should being foreign make a difference? What about Trautmann's heroics in 'fifty-six? Playing on with a broken neck and refusing to leave the pitch."

"Aye, but you forget lad, he was German. Same character as us. Tough and ruthless as required."

"That's right," added Ken. "He was brought over near the end of the War and he learned our ways. In fact, he's just like a proper Englishman," he added, with obvious approval.

"And think on, Rick. All the experts said those Dutch lads, Muhren and Thijssen, would run the show against us in the semi, didn't they? What happened there, eh?" asked Dougie.

I stared back silently. It was obviously a rhetorical question.

"Yeah. That's right," he continued. "They couldn't handle the pressure once our lads set about them. Like I said. It's all about character and most foreigners don't have it."

It wasn't long before we had reached the platform, where a seemingly impossible number of bodies were crammed tightly together.

"Come on," said Ken, "there's some room along the back. Let's get ourselves further down the platform. It'll probably open up a bit."

Following Ken's lead, we squeezed ourselves through the narrow gap between our fellow passengers and the white tiled wall. Difficult at first, Ken's judgement was vindicated as the press of bodies began to relent and the tiled platform floor began to emerge clearly beneath our feet.

"People are daft," commented Ken, as we made our way along to the platform's end, almost reaching the tunnel. "They'd rather be packed uncomfortable, just like sardines, rather than walk a short distance further on."

"Well, most of 'em are young uns," insisted Bert. "They're gormless, aren't they? Too daft to realise that staying at that end blocks everyone else who's trying to get on the platform."

Looking back, I could see that others were now following our example and moving towards us, but there was still a heavy throng pressed up to and in some places over, the yellow line near the edge of the platform. Observing it, I found myself moving further away from the track. After all, I had no desire to prematurely end my visit to Wembley by being inadvertently pushed into the path of an onrushing train.

Euston Square was part of the original Metropolitan Line, which was London's first underground railway. Located along an east-west axis underneath Euston Road, it had been built using the basic cut and cover technique. The evidence of this could be clearly seen above our heads. There could be found the exposed steel beams placed between the large brick arches that supported the weight of the ground above. Although not a deep level station and despite the cheery singing of our supporters, Euston Square still struck me as being quite gloomy. The dull, artificial glare of the overhead lights reflecting off the cold, white tiled walls, did not help. As the headlights of our train peered through the darkness of the tunnel and the rattling of the wheels grew to a crescendo, the air seemed to crackle and hum in anticipation of its arrival. As it rushed in along the platform, the air sweeping in beside it, the atmosphere became electrically charged. The taste and smell of hot metal, ozone and argon assaulted the senses.

Well along the platform, we watched as the train came to a halt, its wheels screeching in protest. Alongside the front carriage, we waited for the doors to open. Stepping on board there were enough seats for all of us. As the doors closed and the train hummed back into life, I looked around our fellow passengers. Most scrutinised the books, papers and magazines that lay in their laps, or stared blankly into space. One bright young thing, her parents more affluent than the rest, listened to a Sony Stowaway, the harsh, jangling headphones extinguished by the thrumming of the carriage as we rushed headlong through the tunnel. And finally, one young couple, so obviously in love, whispered sweet nothings to one another, oblivious to all around them. It was an insular environment full of lonely, isolated people. Here there were no slight nods of the head or smiles of acknowledgement that you would get back home. It was so unlike Manchester, where the traveller on public transport almost inevitably found themselves in conversation with a stranger. After all, it passed the time whilst waiting at the bus stop or when sat on a long journey. Inevitably, conversations started small; the nature of the weather, the unreliability of the timetables, but then could develop into discussions on matters of great import. Here in the capital however, people did not possess the warmth or trust of their Northern counterparts. Already unfriendly and suspicious of strangers, being draped in our club colours was unlikely to alter their attitudes.

In little over a minute, we had reached Great Portland Street. Of similar construction to Euston Square, from the well-lit interior of the carriage it appeared brighter and more welcoming. The circular lights suspended above the platform and the colourful posters placed in the recesses along the brick wall beyond, caught the eye as we waited for the train to depart. 'It's made for you' advertised London's first Wendy Hamburger restaurant, whilst Morphy Richards proclaimed 'The Shape of Toast to Come.' Marlboro cigarettes, National Savings Certificates and London Transport with their 'Best of London for £2' offer, all soliciting our support.

Off again, it was another short, rapid ride to Baker Street.

"Where is he?" asked Dougie.

"Who?" replied Vic.

"Who do you think? Sherlock Holmes, of course."

"Probably getting ready for Wembley with Watson," suggested Bert.

"Bet they're supporting Spurs," said Vic.

"Bound to be," remarked Ken. "Rich Southerners."

"Wouldn't want a strange pair like them supporting us," remarked Bert.

"Elementary," replied Ken, with a chuckle.

"It's not far to Lords from here you know," said Vic. "It's a pleasant stroll up to the ground alongside Regents Park."

"Oh," I said, surprised. "I didn't know you liked cricket."

"Of course, I do and Bert does too. We often go to Old Trafford in the summer. You thought we were like your grandad, didn't you?"

Dougie hated cricket and blamed my sheltered upbringing in the suburbs and attendance at a 'posh' grammar school for my liking of the game. From the beginning of May to the latter part of August, he was lost without his football and refused to countenance the idea that the sound of leather on wood might prove some compensation for its temporary absence.

"Well, yes. I suppose I did."

"You shouldn't just assume," said Bert.

"No. I suppose not. When did you go to Lords then Vic?"

"Me and Bert went in 'seventy-two when we played Warwickshire in the Gillette Cup final. It was when Lancashire got the hat-trick of wins."

"Clive Lloyd's match," said Bert, proudly. "A brilliant century. One hundred and twenty-six."

"They had a damn good side as well, Warwickshire," added Vic. "Full of test players. Mike Smith, Lance Gibbs, Amiss, Kanhai, Kallicharan, Murray and Willis."

"But they'd no chance when they'd to face Lancashire lads like little Harry Pilling, David Lloyd, Hughes, Simmons and Bond," insisted Bert.

"I remember watching the closing stages on tv," I added. "I felt nervous because only Hubert and Harry Pilling seemed to get on top of the bowlers."

"You don't waste your time watching cricket like that daft pair, do you Rick?" asked Ken.

"Yes. I play for the school as well."

Ken gave a wry smile and shook his head.

"You don't like cricket then, Ken?"

"No."

"Why not?"

"Because it's a toff's game."

"Rubbish," said Bert.

"No. I'm right. It's all gentleman and the players," scoffed Ken.

"Not anymore," said Vic. "All that's over now."

"Since when?"

"Since they made Len Hutton captain of England. That's when."

"So you say, but you can't deny that there's still too many public schoolboys playing the game, whether they've turned professional or not. And don't talk about the MCC, that's just another part of the Establishment. The running of the game's not changed since the days of the 'bodyline series.' Miner Harold Larwood, salt of the earth, working-class hero, bowling just as Jardine asked him to and because he did, never got to play for England again. The MCC never criticised Jardine though, did they? They didn't tell him to apologise to the Aussies, only the working-class oik."

I had to hand it to Red Ken. He didn't like cricket but he'd done his research. I knew it because I was fascinated with the bodyline tour of Australia and had read up on it myself.

"There's no point arguing," said Vic. "Everything's a conspiracy to you."

"That's right. You're finally learning," said Ken, with a smile of satisfaction.

As we left our next stop at Finchley Road, the train finally reached the surface and emerged into the light. We were now racing into suburbia with its rows of neat and tidy semis and heading towards our final station. Arriving at Wembley Park, we quickly left the carriage. In front of us, there was a heaving mass of Blues slowly making their way along the platform, heading towards the stairs that led out of the station. The proximity of the stadium instinctively triggered a wave of songs and chants and it was impossible not to get swept along by the general feeling of euphoria. We were close now and the nerves had gone, well at least until the match got under way. Positivity, a sense of destiny and purpose, was the order of the day.

Walking through the barriers, left open to ease congestion, we found ourselves looking down on the crowds moving along Wembley Way towards the famous twin towers. Joining them it was readily apparent that there was now an intermingling of supporters. The opposition's navy blue and white scarves and navy, white and yellow caps becoming as numerous as their sky blue and white counterparts. Here and there friendly exchanges of banter took place between small groups and individuals and the mood was generally good-humoured. It was the self-control and good sense of the vast majority, concerned only about the football, that ensured that there were relatively few altercations. Certainly, there were a lot of police officers on duty, but in the congested conditions it would have proved difficult for them to contain any serious outbreaks of trouble. Having reached the stadium, we stopped in front of the towers. Considered to be iconic, up close they seemed less impressive. Perhaps the weather didn't help. It had been raining in the night and the skies had been grey ever since we had arrived in the capital. It was dull and damp and the large white blocks of which the towers were constructed, didn't radiate any of the gleaming quality that I had expected. In fact, the towers themselves were distinctly box-like in their construction and the domes that topped them gave the impression of being something of a fanciful afterthought; nothing more than an attempt to provide an attractive focal point for what was otherwise a rather standard, utilitarian arena. Perhaps it wasn't surprising that the stadium was no architectural showpiece given that it had been built for the purpose of hosting the British Empire Exhibition of 1924 and it was expected that it would be demolished after the event's completion. Yet despite its dilapidated appearance, almost sixty years later Wembley had become a national institution and that was because it hosted the greatest game in football; the FA Cup Final. And the Empire Stadium was where the players and fans dreamed of ending up when the draw for the third round of the competition took place.

"Still a bit early to go in yet," suggested Vic.

"We can stay out here a bit longer. Let the young uns watch the crowds go by," said Bert.

"Dave's seen it all before," I said. "He's a veteran of Wembley."

"Yeah, but not like us," said Dougie. "He wasn't even a twinkle in his father's eye when we were here in 'thirty-three. The ends were completely open back then and on both sides the roof only covered the fans sat at the back."

"For the national stadium, it's a bit of a dump really, isn't it," agreed Bert. "It's not that great inside either and you're too far away from the pitch when you're stood behind the goal. Maine Road's far better."

"Well, you wouldn't expect the rich beggars at the FA to put their hands in their pockets to improve it," said Ken, "or the government. No. Spend money on a stadium for the working-classes? You must be joking!"

"You know what annoys me?" asked Vic. "It's the fact that all this lot," he continued, nodding towards a large throng of Spurs fans threading their way past us, "only have to come down the road to see the game. They don't have the expense and inconvenience that we have to get here."

"That's right. It's the same for all the London clubs when they get to the final. It's like a home game for them," said Ken.

"Huh. Do you remember how the Chelsea fans complained when they had to travel to Old Trafford, for the replay of the final against Leeds?" asked Bert.

"Wouldn't you complain, if you had to play there," said Dougie, laughing.

"Well, of course, but that's not what I meant."

"I know."

"I agree that it's awkward getting down here and it's not cheap," said Dave, "but I like playing at Wembley. It's the only time that the whole country takes notice of you. When we won the league in 'sixty-eight, we weren't in the spotlight like when we beat Leicester in the Cup. You can't get away from it. If you want to be seen as a great club, then you have to get to Wembley. If they decided to play the final somewhere else, it just wouldn't be the same."

"No, Dave, I can't agree with you lad," said Bert. "It's time things changed. If we're ging to have a national stadium, why isn't it in the middle of the country? That's fair for everyone."

"And historically, all the best clubs are in the North and Midlands," insisted Vic. "It makes sense for us all to have less distance to travel."

"Do you really think that they would build a new stadium in the middle of the country? That's never going to happen," said Ken. "All your toffs and politicians having to leave the big city for the day and the poor old royals having to give up their free tickets because they can't just nip down the road from the palace. 'Darling Harold' was supposed to be a mad, keen Huddersfield fan, but he never suggested building a national stadium further north, did he? No, keeping the cup final at Wembley is just another way that the Establishment keeps its knee pressed down hard on the necks of the workers."

"I don't know," said Vic, "coming down to London doesn't half bring out the revolutionary in you."

"Because Ken's like Lenin," I suggested. "His every waking moment is steeped in revolution."

As soon as I had said it, I sensed that my observation was ill-advised. I had let enthusiasm get the better of me. Vic, Bert and Dougie turned towards me with suspicion. One rabid radical in their midst was enough for them to cope with and they had no wish to see or hear from another. Falling silent, I hoped that they would let the matter drop.

"Perhaps having an education isn't always such a good thing," suggested Bert.

"You can say that again," said Dougie.

Yet whilst he and Vic slowly shook their heads, Ken's reaction was different. Examining me closely and with a barely disguised smile, he nodded his head approvingly.

"Do you know what kid? You're all right. Don't take any notice of this lot."

Thankfully, before I could respond, Dave spotted his mates walking towards us.

"Eric! Pete! Over here!" shouted Dave, waving his arm.

The two of them moved quickly towards us.

"Dave," said Eric, sounding surprised "We didn't expect to see you again."

"Why not?"

"We thought you'd got nicked at the station," explained Pete.

"No chance lads. They'll have to be a lot quicker to catch me."

Dave looked at the pair of them closely. It seemed that something wasn't quite right. Observing them I realised that whilst Pete, the taller lad, had his scarf tied around his wrist, his pal's was nowhere to be seen.

"Where's your scarf, Eric?" asked Dave.

"Er, I lost it."

"Lost it?"

"No, he didn't," said Pete.

"Shut up," snapped Eric. "You don't know what you're talking about."

"Oh, don't I?"

"No."

"I do. You gave it that Tottenham lad so he didn't give you a good hiding. I saw you."

"When did that happen?" asked Dave.

"Just after we split up," said Pete. "When the Spurs lot attacked us outside the station and we had to make a run for it."

"It's not like he said," explained Eric. "I was cornered. Couldn't get away and there was quite a few of 'em. They would have laid into me if I didn't hand it over. I wouldn't have stood a chance."

"Huh," said Pete, unimpressed.

Dave looked at him closely.

"So why didn't you help him, Pete?"

"Yeah, why didn't you?" asked Eric, feeling less embarrassed.

Pete was silent now that his attempt to make fun of his friend had backfired.

"Smart move," declared Dave. "He who fights and runs away, lives to fight another day."

"That's what I was thinking," said Eric.

Dougie and his mates burst out laughing. It was obvious to them that neither Eric nor Pete were hard men, a fact established when they had tried to prove themselves by chasing after the young Reds at Piccadilly. It was clear that both lads were eager to impress Dave but it seemed to me that he was unconcerned; disinterested in judging how far his partners in crime measured up to his own daunting reputation.

"When some of our coaches arrived earlier, their lot were waiting," remarked Pete. "They set on the youngsters, didn't they? The word's gone out for us to go round to their end and see if we can find 'em. That's where we were going when you saw us."

"Yeah. Give 'em some payback," added Eric.

"Well, I suppose we'd better get round there," said Dave.

Dave was back in familiar territory. He'd had a quiet time of it with us but now excitement beckoned and it was time for him to return to his regular matchday routine.

"Hey, lad. Make sure you behave yourself," said Vic. "We don't want to hear that you've ended up missing the match."

"You know me," replied Dave. "I'm just going to have a look. I won't miss seeing us walk out at ten to three."

Dave grinned and Vic shook his head. He and his pals liked Dave. I suspect that they saw something of themselves in him when they were his age. Seeing how they'd handled the trouble outside Euston, I'd no doubt that they hadn't shied away from confrontations in their youth. It was clear too that they were impressed by the respect that Dave had shown towards them; relatively unusual for young men his age.

"You make sure you don't," added Bert.

Dave nodded and then disappeared with Eric and Pete into the streams of supporters mingling together as they made their way around us.

Chapter Eighteen

Vic looked at his watch. It was nearly two o'clock.

"I think it's about time we were making a move," he said.

"Yeah," said Dougie, "our Rick needs to soak up some of the pre-match atmosphere."

"No. I'm all right, grandad. There's no need to rush on my account."

"Oh," said Bert. "You're not bothered about getting in so that you can listen to the brass band then?"

I was unsure how to respond but my silence made it clear that it was something I could do without.

Ken laughed.

"Don't worry, Rick. You don't have to listen to the old fogey's music."

"You can't really hear them anyway," said Vic. "Not with the noise of the crowd and these days it's a struggle to get anyone to sing along to Abide with me."

"Of course it is," said Bert. "Youngsters don't know the words, do they? And there's no point putting them in the programme because they don't read them anyway."

"It's old fashioned now," said Ken. "How many kids are interested in singing hymns? I bet it's not long before they have to give up on it."

"It's tradition though, isn't it?" noted Bert. "The community, both sets of fans coming together. I wouldn't like to see it disappear."

"Huh, I can't say there's much chance of me feeling any sense of community with those cockney beggars," observed Ken.

"You're not wrong there," said Dougie.

"Come on then," said Vic, "let's get going."

Slowly we made our way through the crowds along to the East side of the stadium, the end that we had been allocated. The club had officially been given thirty thousand tickets but there would be Blues present in other parts of the ground too; those who had been fortunate enough to lay their hands on some of the numerous tickets that the FA distributed every year to their local associations. As we arrived at Turnstile D there were still lots of fans content to wait outside, drinking their cans with friends and joining in the waving of scarves and flags, singing and chanting along with the hundreds around them.

Entering the stadium, we headed for Entrance 17 and into our standing section located in the lower half of the stadium, not far from the tunnel from which the players would emerge on our right. For £3.50 we had no reason to complain, especially as the cheapest seats were priced at £13; complete profiteering as far as Dougie and his pals were concerned. Moving up the terracing towards the back, we positioned ourselves behind a crush barrier. At a reasonable height, we had a good view of the whole pitch right down towards the far distant goal.

As we settled down, we could see that both sets of players were slowly making their way towards us as they completed their pre-match inspection of the pitch.

"The players look smart in those suits, don't they?" observed Bert.

"Our Elsie read an article in the Evening News that said City would be the smartest team ever to hit Wembley," said Vic. "Apparently, they got a special sky blue, terylene wool worsted cloth woven at a mill in Bradford and then had it made into suits by a fancy tailor in Leeds."

"What?" said Bert in disgust. "They got the suits from Yorkshire. What's wrong with Lancashire?"

"I doubt they can find a mill round us that can make top quality material anymore," suggested Ken.

"Probably," replied Vic. "Anyway, the club said how proud they were for the players to wear them, as 'British is best'."

"I hope Villa and Ardiles have taken note," said Bert.

"But the thing is," said Ken, "the club's supposed to be hard-up. I'm surprised Swales paid for 'em. He should have got a cheap job-lot from Longsight Market. It would have made more sense."

"Aye, but he likes showing off, doesn't he?" noted Dougie.

"Ken's got a point. I don't think we can afford to," said Vic. "The club's in serious debt. It seems we need to win today to get into Europe and have a chance of clearing it."

Vic was right. The club did have crippling debts and it was all a legacy of Malcolm's profligate spending in the transfer market. Far be it from me to point that out however, knowing that Dougie and his pals still idolised the great man. And of course, the money couldn't have been spent without the agreement of the chairman, so in that sense it seemed fair enough for my companions to direct their criticism at Swales.

As usual, there was a timetabled programme of pre-match events of which traditional brass band music was a part. Vic was right, the Massed Bands of the Royal Marines were on the pitch but too far away for them to make much of an impression. They were not the only entertainment on offer. As this was the hundredth final, the FA had gathered an array of surviving cup winning captains to be presented to the crowd on the hallowed Wembley turf. It proved to be a moving experience for my companions who roundly cheered the appearance of Roy Paul, the tough, uncompromising Welshman who had led City to triumph in 'fifty-six. Although roaring our appreciation for him, Roy's impact had been made long before we younger Blues had made our way to Maine Road, but then the great Joe Mercer was known to us all and present too for his captaining of Arsenal in their defeat of Liverpool in 1950. The loudest cheer from our supporters was probably given to Tony Book, Joe Mercer's captain in 'sixty-nine and such a huge part of the club as player and manager over the following years. Skip's legacy remained very much intact, despite the disappointment at the start of the season that had led to his and Malcolm's replacement.

Finally, it was time for the teams to make their appearance. As they emerged side-by-side from the players' tunnel the whole stadium erupted in an explosion of sound, both sets of fans unleashing a torrent of pent-up up nervous energy, relieved at last that the action was soon about to start. All around thousands of flags, banners and scarves were waving, both sides of the stadium intent on exceeding the other in their enthusiastic commitment to the cause. Leading out our boys was John Bond, followed by captain Paul Power, the pair affording hardly a glance towards Keith Burkinshaw and Steve Perryman of Spurs alongside them. The boss was striding purposely across the turf and he had an aura about him; confident that we would win. He had been bullish all week. Unshakeable in his belief. "I have no doubt that we will win the Cup," he had declared and now I could see that these were no mere words. He was convinced that it was our destiny.

Having reached the halfway line at the edge of the pitch, the two teams lined up at right angles to the Royal Box underneath which the red carpet was ready for the guest of honour, the Queen Mother, to walk to receive the presentation of the teams. I glanced around me. Ken was nowhere in sight as the royal party halted for the playing of the national anthem, the observation of which was not as universal as it would have been when Ken attended his first final back in 'thirty-three. As the final strains of the band disappeared beneath the expectant roar of the crowd, the Queen Mother walked on to the pitch where Paul Power was waiting to introduce her to his teammates. Moving relatively quickly along the line of players, a customary handshake and the briefest of words given to each one, she then joined his opposite number, Steve Perryman, to be conveyed along the line of our opponents.

The presentation over, the players ran back to their supporters for the final warm up as the marching band made their way off the pitch in precise military fashion. Ken was now stood beside me.

"You were as good as your word then," I said.

"Of course I was. You didn't expect any different, did you?"

"No," I replied, smiling. "There were quite a few who didn't sing it."

"Including you, I hope."

"There's no way I'd ever join in. One of my teachers tried to force me when we had to attend speech day and I refused. I was lucky that the headmaster backed me. He said that I had every right to my own political opinions and commended me for having an independent mind."

"Huh. He sounds unusual."

I nodded in agreement, pleased that he had not asked me about his pals. Whilst Dougie had remained silent, Vic and Bert had sung out the words loud and proud. Then again, I assume that he suspected they would.

"It took a bit for the singing to get going around us," I added.

"Yes, but there's always those who'll join in and you can bet that all their lot will have sung it. Typical cockneys. They love the royals, don't they?"

Looking towards the centre circle we could see that referee Keith Hackett had called both captains together and was conducting the coin toss. On its completion, Paul Power signalled to his players that they were changing ends. In the first half, we would be attacking towards our own supporters.

It was Spurs who kicked off. Considered to have the advantage in terms of their age and big-game experience, their players found it difficult to settle as a young Blues side, stiffened by some seasoned professionals, immediately took the game by the scruff of the neck. In the first five minutes the lads were rampant and forced four corners. The dominance continued as the creative threat of Hoddle and Ardiles was stifled by the aggression and hard tackling of midfield veteran Gerry Gow.

"That's the benefit of experience," said Dougie, enthusiastically applauding the ex-Bristol City man. "He's got nowhere near the talent of their midfielders but he knows how to stop 'em playing."

Yet rarely could a team continue to totally dominate a game and with the attacking talent at their disposal it was only a matter of time before our opponents began to put us under pressure. Fortunately, we had 'England's number one' and Big Joe Corrigan was soon called upon to prove his worth when Perryman crossed from the right and a Roberts header was smothered and held by the big man, so denying the opportunity of a tap-in. Then Tony Galvin ran at young Tommy Caton, moving him to left and right, before entering the area. As the goal opened up before him, he seemed odds-on to score, but Big Joe dived full-length to push his shot around the post and out for a corner.

"I thought that was it," said Ken, nervously sucking in the air and almost immediately expelling it again.

"So did I," said Bert. "What a keeper."

"It's what we pay him for," said Dougie. "It's all in a day's work for Joe."

It was true. We had depended on him for so many years but we never took his brilliance for granted and here at Wembley the fans constantly chanted their appreciation. Yet although he had kept us in the game, City had continued to threaten to take the lead themselves. A free-kick played down the left to Paul Power, saw the team captain twist and turn to get past his defender and play a ball into the area. Receiving it with his back to goal on the edge of the six yards box, young Dave Bennett swivelled and shot towards goal only to be denied by a last-ditch block from Roberts. With the fans' expectant, the ball was swung in from the resultant corner. Flicked on by Power at the near post, it ran agonisingly past the lunge of Bobby McDonald.

The Spurs goal seemed to be living a charmed life, yet City would not be denied. With almost half an hour gone Dave Bennett picked up the ball by the left touch line and played it inside. Blocked, the ball ran loose but Bennett, following up, immediately regained possession and chipped it to Kevin Reeves who headed it back and then dropped to the right edge of the area. Quickly, Bennett returned it and Reeves played a short pass back to Ray Ranson who whipped in a wicked cross that just invited Tommy Hutchison, the oldest player on the pitch, to dive full length and head the ball past Aleksic's despairing dive and into the left-hand side of the net.

It was unbelievable and it had unfolded right in front of us. And there was that magical moment, that millisecond when everything seemed to stop and every sound dissolved into an almost eerie silence and you were sure that you had heard the swish of the net as the ball nestled itself within it. Then the explosion. The crescendo of cheers, the surge down the terracing; friends and strangers hugging one another, dancing joyously together. We had scored and there was no question that we deserved it.

Taking a few deep breaths, I could feel my heart racing. Dougie looked at me and smiled. I must have reminded him of the time, almost fifty years ago, that he had first seen City score at Wembley.

"That was Bennett's goal," insisted Vic. "It was because he refused to give the ball up that Tommy Hutch got his chance."

"I still can't believe Hutch headed it," said Bert.

It was true. Hutch had never been renowned for his aerial ability but he had taken the chance like an accomplished centre-forward. It was Wembley and the headline writers were always looking for an unlikely hero. Perhaps it was going to be his day.

Having taken the lead there seemed no doubt that the general sense of euphoria meant that for the next few minutes the fear of failure seemed to have been temporarily lifted from the shoulders of our supporters. The players remained confident and eager to retain the initiative and on the occasions that our opponents attempted to break their shackles, a last-ditch tackle or the calm presence of Big Joe seemed able to keep them at bay. When referee Hackett finally blew the half-time whistle, the Blues cheered and clapped vociferously as they watched their heroes make their way towards the sanctuary of the changing room, to be replaced on the pitch by the Massed Bands of the Royal Marines. Hopefully the boss was preparing them for more of the same. If they were able to reproduce it, then I believed that we were well on our way to winning the Cup. Yet I was surrounded by older heads, men who had supported the club for over sixty years. They had experienced the setbacks of the past and knew that the footballing gods could abandon you on a whim. To such men, nothing was certain and you always had to brace yourself for heart-breaking disappointment. Never would they simply abandon themselves to the flights of fancy that were the prerogative of the optimism of youth.

"We're well on top, grandad. This game's ours."

Dougie smiled.

"Hear that, lads?" he asked, turning to his pals.

Vic and Bert grinned, whilst Ken shook his head.

"We are," I insisted. "We just need to keep it up."

"As long as Hoddle and Ardiles don't buck their ideas up," said Vic.

"They won't," I insisted. "We're controlling the midfield."

"Aren't you forgetting Joe's saves?" asked Bert. "If it wasn't for him, they'd be level at least."

"Well, they're bound to get some chances," I replied, somewhat defensively.

"It's alright to be excited kid," said Bert. "You may well be right but us old-timers have learned not to get too carried away."

The words of caution failed to dampen my enthusiasm. I was eager to feel the emotions that Dougie and his pals had experienced when they had seen us victorious at this stadium in the past. And when I considered it, I realised that today they could afford to be hesitant and circumspect, for if our opponents did take the game away from us, it would not deprive them of their victorious memories.

As the players emerged ready for the second half both sets of fans roared their appreciation. After we kicked off our opponents began to display more purpose and energy. It was then that the reality of a slender one goal lead began to undermine the confidence I'd felt when talking up our prospects of victory. It was natural to feel concerned, for the fear of every supporter is that everything can so easily go horribly wrong. Just one mistake by our defence or a flash of brilliance from one of them would put the result in the balance. Furthermore, it was clear that however well we played, at some stage they were bound to get opportunities to score. Yet our midfield and defence remained organised and strong. Leading the way was Gerry Gow who was sticking resolutely to Hoddle and Ardiles, closing them down, denying them space and hitting them with a series of crunching tackles, both fair and foul. And the Spurs boys were uncomfortable, unable to impose their silky passing game with its intricate attacks; forced to rely instead on hopeful long balls through to Archibald and Crooks who were being well marshalled by our defence. Yet the chances did come. The ball broke to Garth Crooks on the edge of the area and he fired it just wide of Joe's left-hand post. Then Ardiles wriggled through a couple of challenges, played a one-two with Crooks and entering the area, looked likely to score before a brilliant tackle by Bobby McDonald dispossessed him.

With almost an hour on the clock Steve Mackenzie pushed purposely through the centre of midfield. With forward momentum, he played a couple of return passes to Kevin Reeves. The ball looped up into the area and as it reached the floor Mackenzie pushed it deftly to the left of goal, taking it away from the hapless Aleksic, whose onrushing dive at his opponent's feet had left him sprawled out helpless on the Wembley turf, looking like a man prostrated before the Lord and praying with all his might for the miracle that would leave his goal intact. Mackenzie, faced with the tightest of angles, wrapped his foot around the ball, stretching to divert it into the net. Expectant, over thirty thousand Blues held their breath, eyes rivetted on the young midfielder. Yet hopes so agonisingly raised were all too cruelly dashed as the ball hit the outside of the post and rebounded out of play. At just nineteen years of age the young man had, for just the briefest of moments, the world at his feet. The opportunity to become the match winning hero, finally justifying the record fee that had made him football's most expensive teenager, when Malcolm Allison had signed him from Crystal Palace.

I looked at Dougie. He was shaking his head in disappointment.

"That was the game," I said. "If that had gone in, they could never have come back from two down."

"No. Probably not," he replied.

"Don't be hard on the lad," said Vic. "It was a difficult chance and he did well to create it."

"I know. I just wish it had gone in."

To their credit the Blues on the pitch, unlike those off it, were not thinking about what might have been. They were continuing to get after their opponents who, the longer the game went on, seemed to be running out of energy and ideas. Attempting to give fresh impetus to his team Spurs boss Burkinshaw substituted Argentinian Villa for the direct and industrious Garry Brooke. Still however, it was City who held sway and as we approached the final ten minutes, I became convinced that it was going to be our day. Then, with ten minutes to go, Gerry Gow, out on the right, dwelled on the ball giving Ardiles the chance to close in and dispossess him. Dribbling inside and advancing towards the edge of the area, Ardiles was finally taken down by Gow who had chased back hoping to rectify his mistake.

"What was he doing. Dawdling about like that?" asked Dougie.

"It's all right," I replied. "He's played well. He's allowed to make a mistake."

"You can't make mistakes in games like these," insisted Dougie. "There's too much riding on it."

"But he chased back and recovered it," I added, in the player's defence.

"Well, not exactly," said Vic. "We've still got a free-kick to face and it's in a perfect position for Hoddle."

"Big Joe will handle it. He's faced lots of Hoddle's free-kicks in the past and he's trained with him for England. He won't get caught out."

And there it was again. Surfacing every time adversity threatened. The desire to put on the brave face of optimism in the hope that if I believed things would turn out fine, then indeed they would. We'd got this far I thought, surely the footballing gods wouldn't desert us now.

Watching Joe lining up the wall, I remained confident. It would have to be a feat of extraordinary skill from Hoddle if he were to beat England's number one. Hoddle, flanked by Ardiles and Perryman stood ready. Everything was set. Standing over the ball Ardiles tapped it the short distance to Perryman who touched it back to Hoddle. As he did so, Tommy Hutchison suddenly peeled off the end of the wall and retreated towards Joe's left-hand post, his head diverting Hoddle's shot away from Corrigan and into the far side of the net. I had been right, but it gave me no sense of satisfaction. Hoddle had been unable to summon the touch of genius necessary to beat our keeper. Joe had the near post covered and it was pure luck and luck alone that had taken the ball into the back of our net.

A collective groan went up from the Blues whilst relief, delight and disbelief exploded at the opposite end of the ground. Almost resigned to defeat, Spurs had got out of jail and both their players and supporters knew it.

"What's he done?" asked Dougie, exasperated by Hutch's own goal. "Why didn't he just stay in the wall?"

"He was trying to cover back," I replied in his defence. "He knew what Hoddle was going to do and thought he could block the shot."

"But Joe was behind the shot. It was never going in," insisted Dougie.

"It didn't look to me like it was actually on target," added Bert. "I reckon it was going past the post anyway."

"Never mind," said Vic, "we've been here before. There's no reason we can't go on and win this."

He was alluding to the League Cup final of 'seventy-six when Newcastle had pulled it back to one-all before Dennis Tueart had won the game with a spectacular overhead kick. Remembering that final, one that I had watched on television, I smiled.

"Wouldn't it be great, Vic? If someone could score as spectacular a goal as that."

"Aye lad. It certainly would."

If Spurs thought that the equaliser had dampened our spirits, they were wrong. Quickly processing the fickle circumstances of fate, City's supporters had rallied before the ball had made its way out of Corrigan's net and back to the centre spot.

'Come on City!' 'Come on City!' roared out in unison; sung from the throats of over thirty thousand Blues. The equaliser was nothing short of a travesty of justice and every one of us was determined to show our dedication to the sterling efforts of our lads on the pitch and will them on to the victory they surely deserved. As play restarted it was obvious that the players had put their misfortune behind them. There was less than ten minutes to go; both sides determined to take the lead and avoid the gruelling punishment of thirty minutes of extra-time. But it was not to be. Neither side could break the deadlock and as referee Hackett blew the final whistle, although both sets of supporters continued to sing for their heroes, it seemed strangely calm as both sets of players made their way over to the touchline and their waiting managers. Watching them closely, I took heart, for even though they were a fair distance from us, it was clear that our young players looked ready to take on the burden of extra-time. The Spurs men seemed less so and there were more of their number who had sunk down on the pitch, desperate to gain respite from the battle.

"Do you see that Grandad?" I asked, pointing over to the half-way line.

"What?"

"There's more of their players on the floor and look at how many of them are getting treated for cramp."

"The lad's right," said Vic.

"Well, they're Southern softies, aren't they?" added Ken who, a model of quietly intense concentration for most of the game, now took the opportunity of the break in proceedings to extol the virtues of Northern superiority.

"Not all their players are Southerners," said Bert.

"Doesn't matter. Once they start playing for teams down here, they become just the same."

The rest of us laughed. Ken's reasoning was ridiculous, but it was good to have a little light relief given that it helped to dispel the nervous tension. Meanwhile, on the pitch both managers were going round their players, talking to each of them in turn.

"I wonder what John Bond is saying."

"He's just encouraging 'em, lad," said Vic.

"Probably asking 'em how they feel," added Bert. "He can still make a substitution but he'll want to wait as long as possible."

As the game restarted, there was a marked reduction in the intensity of the play. Wembley's lush turf was renowned for sapping the energy of even the most physically powerful. Aching muscles and limbs, the ever-present threat of cramp and tiring minds meant that players had to operate at a reduced pace, saving what energy they had to hold their opponents at bay and only racing forward for the most favourable of opportunities. By the end of the first fifteen minutes of extra-time neither side had made a breakthrough and the tension was becoming unbearable. I turned to Bert.

"I can't stand it. I wish I was out on the pitch, then I could do something about it."

"You are. You're getting behind them like the rest of us. That's our job."

"But we're so close and yet just one mistake and it's gone."

"Look lad, there's no point worrying. Whatever happens, you just accept it. They've given us their best. That's all we can ask."

"It looks like Tommy Hutch is coming off," said Vic.

The oldest player on the pitch, Hutch's departure from the game was to be expected. Although he seemed to have been coping with extra-time as well as anyone, perhaps he'd indicated to John Bond that he'd run his course. His replacement, midfielder Tony Henry, would certainly inject some fresh energy into the ranks and was well capable of finding the back of the net too. And as the final period of play unfolded it became apparent that we were by far the stronger, several of our opponents cramping up or exhausted as they fell to the ground, seeking respite as referee Hackett occasionally brought the game to a halt. It seemed that the opportunity must come but Spurs, digging deep and with the knowledge that the clock was ticking relentlessly towards the final whistle, were able to hold out. It was honours even and we would have to do it all again.

As the whole stadium cheered in appreciation of the phenomenal effort provided by both sets of players, I felt so proud to be a Blue. The object of ridicule following their disastrous start to the season, the players had recovered to a position where they had shown themselves equal, if not superior to, one of the country's most talented sides. As there had been no winner, both teams immediately dispersed to opposite ends of the ground so that they could acknowledge their supporters. Quickly however, they were rounded up by officialdom and directed towards the steps to the Royal Box. It was City who went up first.

Clapping the players enthusiastically as they climbed to the top, events had moved too quickly for Ken and consequently caught him out. Suddenly he realised that his show of appreciation could be misconstrued as being directed at the Quen Mother and immediately stopped. It was too late for the radical republican who having insisted that he would give short shrift to royalty, had now opened himself up to the jibes of his pals who had been watching him with amusement.

"Aren't you going to give the Queen Mum a cheer?" asked Vic, grinning. "After all you've just given her a good clap of appreciation."

"Get off with you, No, I haven't," growled Ken.

"Why the change of heart?" asked Bert. "I thought you would have been back down on the concourse once the final whistle had gone."

"He must love her after all," added Vic, laughing.

"You know I was only showing my appreciation for the lads. I'd forgotten all about her being here," replied Ken, almost apologetically.

"Well, if you say so."

Ken said no more. It was pointless and he knew it. Besides, the team was now gathered at the side of the pitch and about to set off around the ground to show their appreciation of the fans. Proceeding at a steady jog and led by Paul Power, the players recognised that despite their sterling efforts this was no lap of honour, the destination of the Cup had still to be decided. As they quickly passed us, before heading down the tunnel, we cheered and clapped loudly. Somewhat behind them Big Joe and Hutch, the latter now wearing a track suit top, had taken a different approach to their team mates and were walking slowly off the pitch together and taking more time to wave to the crowd. I was sure that as our two senior players they were more cognizant of the uncertainties of a footballer's career when compared to their younger colleagues. Both could appreciate the fact that for them, there may not be another occasion similar to today. As such, they were determined to take the fullest opportunity to soak up the special atmosphere created within the national stadium.

Still gathered behind our barrier, we waited for our section to empty. As we watched our fellow Blues slowly disappearing down the exit, no one spoke. It was a time to finally catch our breath and begin to process the events that we had just witnessed. For all of us there had to be conflicting emotions; relief that we had not been defeated but tinged with regret, knowing that we had been just ten minutes from victory. Nevertheless, we had a replay to look forward to and although I remained highly optimistic about our chances, I suspected that the others may see matters differently.

Finally, Dougie spoke.

"I think that might just have been our best chance to win it. I can't see us dominating the game like that again."

Bert and Vic murmured in agreement, whilst Ken nodded his head.

"Why not?" I asked.

"Hoddle and Ardiles are bound to play better next time."

"Only if we let them."

Vic smiled. He knew that since I had been going to Maine Road this was the first group of players that had brought glory within our grasp. As such, he recognised that they would always retain a special place in my affections, just as Sam Cowan's FA Cup winners of 1934 did for him.

"Perhaps," said Bert, "but you have to remember that we've got some older legs in the side; Hutch, Gow and McDonald. They've given a lot today. Especially with extra-time. They'll need time to recover."

"But we've got the young lads," I quickly replied. "They were brilliant today. All of them."

"Youthful vigour, hey Rick?" replied Bert, laughing.

"You're forgetting all the travelling as well Rick," added Dougie. "They've to traipse all the way home to Manchester and then come all the way back again. All that time on the coach, knowing that they should have won today, whilst Spurs are comfortable at home, feet up and no disruptions before Thursday. Nah, they've got all the advantages lad."

I looked at him. He seemed deadly serious and for a moment I panicked. If he was so pessimistic about our chances, perhaps he would not be attending the replay and if that was the case, I knew that in all probability neither would I.

"We are coming to the replay, aren't we Grandad?"

Immediately, the expression on his face changed to one of disbelief.

"Of course we are," he growled.

His pals looked at me. I could sense their disapproval. It was clear that I had done Dougie an injustice.

"Rick," said Ken. "We've all been following City a hell of a sight longer than you and by God we've been through some tough times; relegations and years going nowhere in Division Two. And we've been there through all of that; your grandad and all of us. Do you think that any of us wouldn't turn up for the replay, even if all our players were injured and we had to turn out a team of reserves and juniors?"

"No," I replied, quietly.

His words were chastening. Suddenly I felt guilty.

"I'm sorry. I didn't mean to upset any of you."

"It's alright Rick," said Bert. "We know you're just desperate to come back and support the lads."

The others nodded in agreement. Thankfully I had been forgiven for my foolish and thoughtless comment. And suddenly I recalled the thoughts of historian A.J.P. Taylor on the culture of sacrifice inherent in the collective character and conscience of the English Working Class. Taylor had noted how the solidarity of working-class men had seen them through two great sacrifices: the Battle of the Somme in 1916 and the General Strike in 1926 and that they had made these sacrifices even though they knew that eventually, they were destined to fail. And it seemed so obvious that for the working-class supporter, football was also a sacrifice. Dougie and his mates were die-hard Blues. For them City was not just a team, but a family that as members they would stand by through thick and thin, however adverse the situation may become. Their dedication not only required a significant commitment of their money and time but, most of all, a huge emotional investment that would only be relinquished once they had spent their final day on Earth.

"What's the ticket arrangements for the replay then?" asked Vic.

"It says here in the programme," I said, leafing through it until I found the relevant page.

"Ah, here it is. If a replay is necessary, it says, thirty thousand tickets will be given to each team plus an extra twenty thousand tickets will go on sale at Wembley Box Office from ten am on Sunday May 10th."

"Oh aye," said Bert "and who do they think will get the extra available at Wembley? Tomorrow morning all our lot are going to be back in Manchester. Spurs are going to get far more tickets than us."

"Typical," said Ken, in disgust. "Why should we be surprised? Everything for the benefit of the Southerners as usual."

Deep in conversation and somewhat oblivious to the fact that we were the only ones left in our section, we were approached by a couple of stewards who politely asked us to make our way out.

"Aye, no problem," said Dougie. "I suppose you lads want to get home."

The stewards smiled. No doubt they appreciated the positive response. I could imagine that when a team had taken a beating here, it would be difficult to communicate with shell-shocked fans, some of whom were all too ready to vent their frustrations on the nearest available target.

"I tell you what," said Bert, as we made our way down to the concourse. "The FA must love Tottenham."

"What, more than any other London club?" asked Vic.

"Of course. They made Chelsea play their replay at Old Trafford."

"It's all corrupt," said Ken. "Wouldn't surprise me if money was changing hands."

"I think they made the decision to play at Wembley again because of it being the centenary final," I suggested.

"Really?" asked Ken. "And there I was starting to think what an intelligent young man you are."

He and the others turned towards me and burst out laughing.

Chapter Nineteen

The journey back to Euston was one without incident. The game had proved physically and emotionally draining to both sets of supporters and so those younger elements who were most inclined towards confrontation, had less energy and inclination to follow it through. Furthermore, as there was neither victor nor vanquished, it meant that tempers could not easily be incited by the ridicule of the opposition. Bizarrely, mild-mannered as I normally am, I could not help but feel slightly irritated by the sight of so many contented Spurs fans as we walked away from the ground. It seemed to reinforce my conviction that we had deserved to win and only good fortune had saved our opponents. I was therefore convinced that they too understood this and so in a way, had come out of the game better than us.

Back on the tube, such negative thoughts were dispelled by the sight of a father and his two young children who were sat opposite. Proudly wearing their club colours, we could see that they were supporting our opponents. Dad looked in his early thirties, his daughter, no more than eight and his son, perhaps six. The girl was all eyes; looking everywhere. For her the day was an adventure; not just a football match. She was wearing a navy blue and white scarf over a pretty pink jumper. It showed her association with the club but was nothing like her younger brother who was wearing a Spurs shirt, scarf and a navy, white and yellow cap. His hands were clutching tightly on to his matchday programme, clearly afraid that he may lose it but consistently refusing his father's suggestion that he should hand it over for safe keeping. It seemed that the boy believed that if he did so, his magical day would disappear in a puff of smoke, almost as if it had never existed. Looking at him, I recognised my younger self. How magical it had been when, as a special present, my own father had taken me to Maine Road on my seventh birthday. Seeing me smile at his son, the Spurs fan nodded.

"Their first trip to Wembley," he said proudly. "Their first cup final."

"The same for me," I replied.

"This is Alex," he continued, indicating his son "and this is my daughter Stephanie."

Stephanie smiled and said hello but Alex was clearly shy and looked down towards the floor.

"It must be my scarf putting him off," I said, trying to make light of it.

"Perhaps you're right," said his dad, laughing.

"He must be tired out," I continued. "It's a long day for him, isn't it? Especially for one so young."

"Well, not as long as it is for you. You are from Manchester I take it?"

If he had been speaking to any of my companions then his question would have been unnecessary but unlike them, I lacked a recognisable accent. It was at moments like this that I felt myself to be something of a fraud. I knew of no logical reason why I should and Millie would have said that I was gormless for thinking it. After all, I wasn't the only Mancunian who, for one reason or another, didn't sound like they came from the city.

"Yes, Sale," I replied.

"Oh, the posh part."

His response surprised me. Noting my reaction he explained.

"I work in insurance and for a time I was based at the CIS offices in Manchester. Quite a few of the bosses lived in Sale."

"I suppose they did. My grandad lives in Chorlton-on-Medlock."

"Yes. I know it. Around Upper Brook Street near the university."

He smiled. It was if he recognised that I was eager to establish my working-class credentials; or at least those of my family. Perhaps, in his youth, he would have wanted to do the same but now he was older and with a family to support I suspect that he regarded such concerns as trivial.

"Are you coming down for the replay?" he asked.

"Yes. We all are. Grandad, his pals and I."

"Well, I'd say good luck but then we were the ones who needed it today."

Pleased to hear him acknowledge the fact, I felt no need to push the point any further.

"Anyway, nice to meet you," he said. "It's our stop now. Come on you two. Up you get."

Getting quickly to their feet, Alex and Stephanie followed him to the carriage doors, the latter turning to give me a wave as the train came to a halt. Raising my hand in acknowledgement, I watched as they disappeared on to the platform.

It had been a civilised conversation and yet for two hours in the cauldron of Wembley, wrapped up in an intense atmosphere of enthusiastic fervour, each of us had been desperate to see our own team completely rout the other's. Now it felt reassuring to know that most of us could gradually reign our emotions back in once the final whistle had been blown. Nevertheless, football is a passionate affair and the public-school ethos which holds that where sport is concerned, the taking part is more important than the winning, has little or no relevance to the professional game. For working-class Mancunians, whether from the older generation like Dougie or younger men like Dave, football offers hope; something in which they can believe. For life is tough for the working man. All week spent grafting hard, tolerating the capricious demands of foremen only too eager to ingratiate themselves with bosses who were all too willing to rationalize the workforce to maintain their profits. Manchester in 1981 was a city in industrial decline; heavy engineering and manufacturing rapidly disappearing and no sign of where economic re-generation would take place. Dave and his contemporaries were facing the prospects that had haunted Dougie and his mates throughout the depression of the 'thirties. Yet every Saturday afternoon at three o'clock that was all forgotten, for it was the one time of the week where, with the skill and commitment of their boys on the field, they too could be winners. It was why they were prepared to sacrifice so much to follow their team and backed them so ferociously from the terraces. And for the blue side of the city the highs of the last fifteen years had more than compensated for the vicissitudes of life. Supporting City had given them not only pride in the team, but pride in themselves and that is why winning would always remain so important.

Chapter Twenty

Having reached Euston, we only had a short time to wait until we boarded our train home. Once again, Dougie and I settled ourselves in the aisle seats on one side of the carriage, whilst Ken, Bert and Vic sat opposite. Unlike on the journey down, there were empty seats around us and thankfully no passengers that came close to matching the profile of Sergeant Wilson's party. At first, sinking back into our seats, my companions and I were relatively quiet. It was hardly surprising given that we had been on the go for quite some time now but once the buffet car was open and Bert and I had returned with some beers, the batteries were soon recharged and the conversation began to flow.

"Grandad, Millie was telling me that part of the Brunswick Estate is built on the old Rusholme Road cemetery and that people have reported seeing ghosts in some of the houses."

"Yes, that's right Rick."

"Why haven't you mentioned it?"

"What for. It's a load of nonsense. Have you seen any ghosts Vic?"

Only our Elsie when she's just woken up with her rollers in and a face pack on!"

The others burst out laughing.

"You'd better hope your Elsie never hears you saying that," said Bert.

"That's true," replied Vic.

"Anyway Rick, less of the Brunswick," continued Bert. "It's still Chorlton-on-Medlock whatever the Corporation tries to say."

"Ah, but they want everyone to be grateful for providing us with a brand spanking new place to live," observed Dougie, "which they claim is a damn sight better than it used to be."

"But it's not. Is it? It's not a patch on the old Chorlton-on-Medlock," insisted Vic.

"It was Roland Nicholas and his Manchester Plan that was to blame," said Ken, "along with greed and corruption."

"Allegedly," noted Vic, with a wry smile.

"Well, if you put it that way."

"Nothing's been proved."

"Or is likely to be," added Bert.

"Yeah, but you'd have to be gormless not to think it," said Dougie.

"Manchester Plan?" I asked.

"Yes, lad. Nineteen forty-five. Nicholas was the City Surveyor and he produced a plan for the redevelopment of Manchester at the end of the War."

"Oh, I didn't know."

"He said that one hundred and twenty thousand homes would need rebuilding; over sixty thousand immediately because the City Medical Officer said that they were unfit for human habitation."

"And that was a load of rubbish," added Dougie. "I'll show my arse on Ardwick Green if there was anything wrong with the houses on Cresswell Street."

"Or most of Manchester," said Bert. "A bit of renovation and an inside bathroom and toilet and most of the terraces would have been good for another fifty years."

"And beyond," said Vic. "Solid. Not like the rubbish that's thrown up now."

"Having an outside toilet and a tin bath in front of the fire never concerned us," said Bert.

"Really?" I asked.

"Well, you don't miss what you've never had," remarked Dougie.

"You see Rick, they never bothered to ask us what we wanted," explained Bert. "Planners, politicians and middle-class 'do-gooders.' They're all the same. Full of themselves and convinced that they know better than we do, even though we're the ones who have to live on their new estates."

"Aye lad," said Ken, "for all they claimed to be acting in our interests, in reality they were doing it for themselves."

"Not all of them, surely?"

"Yes lad. Beware the false prophets. The best you can say is that some of 'em wanted to gain a reputation for being public-spirited. Most were after an award in the honours list or trying to help their political aspirations. If you examine the costs of the clearance programme, building the new estates produced some hefty contracts. It's strange that the Corporation never went for modernising the existing homes. Lots of communities formed residents' groups and carried out detailed studies. They proved refurbishment was far cheaper than rebuilding. Yet the planners and the Corporation ignored them."

"And worst of all," added Vic, "they not only levelled the houses but by doing so they destroyed the communities that lived in 'em. Families who had known one another for decades. Everyone looking out for everyone else."

"It's not the same now," said Bert. "You don't know many of your neighbours. It makes it difficult to trust people."

"Aye, in the old Chorlton-on-Medlock there'd have been hell to pay if you were caught trying to rob one of your neighbours," said Dougie. "Now you worry about being robbed every time you go out."

"They couldn't have come up with a better way to undermine working-class solidarity if they'd tried," said Ken. "They broke the communities and the old camaraderie. Destroyed the experiences and values of the old terraced streets; the essence of the working-class heritage that they feared and despised."

It was a highly politicised statement but I would have expected no less from Red Ken. Shaking their heads, I could see that his pals were unprepared to see matters in quite the same way. There was no doubt that they had been unhappy to leave their old, familiar homes but they were unable to accept that it had been a planned conspiracy to destroy the working-class. Yet I had stayed long enough with Dougie and spent enough time with Millie and her friends to gain enough of an insight into life on the estate and recognised that there was merit in what Ken was saying. I had certainly not seen any evidence of a united front among its residents. On the contrary, there was much division. Instead of a community of interest and mutual concern, residents generally felt isolated and unsure as to whether, in times of difficulty, they would be able to fall back on the support of their neighbours. It was the younger generation who most reflected this changed situation. No longer reigned-in by the neighbourly precepts that underpinned the stable communities of the past, many young men were too easily drawn into crime and antisocial behaviour and far from reluctant to resort to violence and intimidation towards those who tried to stand against them.

"No Ken," said Vic. "It's not that complicated. It might be different with Thatcher's lot but you can't say that back then demolition was carried out to weaken the working-class. No, politicians only looked at housing in terms of how it could benefit themselves."

"Ken's right about one thing though," said Bert. "Governments, MPs, councillors, it doesn't matter what their politics are, because none of them understand us. You get them in the Labour Club, especially at election time. Local councillors after your vote. And it seems to me there's two types. You've got the trendy lecturers, teachers and professionals and they want to make themselves feel good by doing their bit for the poor and downtrodden. Then you've got your union men, keen to keep their attendance allowances and seats on the important council committees."

"Well soon there won't be any more working-class," said Dougie, "the way that factories are shutting down. Manufacturing, iron and steel and heavy engineering will all be things of the past."

"And under Thatcher it's only going to get worse," said Ken. "Rationalisation the Tories call it. Restructuring. Efficiency. Sustainable industries for the future. Oh yes. Brilliant for the bosses but it means nothing less than extinction for the workers and the prospects of families spending a lifetime living on unemployment benefits."

"Well at least they're not taking it lying down at Laurence Scott," said Bert. "I've got a pal who works there and when they got bought out the unions were promised that jobs would be protected. Then it turns out that the new owners had already decided to shut it down and sell off the assets. If you haven't worked there at least twelve years then you aren't entitled to any redundancy money. That's why they organised the sit-in and they're holding firm."

"I don't hold out much hope for them," said Ken. "He's a cunning beggar that Arthur Snipe."

"Arthur Snipe?" asked Bert.

"Yes, the head of Mining Supplies. The bloke who bought them out. A Master of the Yorkshire Hunt and darling of the Tories. He takes over a company with three thousand workers based in five locations and decides to rationalise; concentrate the business in Norwich and close the other sites. The government helped him fool the unions. He used their temporary compensation scheme to put the Manchester factory on short time. It covered up his real intentions for six months; made it appear as if he was trying to resolve some temporary difficulties and lulled every one into a false sense of security. After six months, once the government subsidies ended, he announced that the factory was closing."

"But can he do that?" I asked. "Surely the law offers some protection to the workers."

"It should Rick," explained Ken. "The Employment Protection Act says that employers have to consult the workforce before making decisions on closure and redundancies. The Manchester factory has been profitable for the last nine years and has a full order book for the next twelve months but this government won't intervene and with the Courts ruling against the occupation and Greater Manchester Police ready to throw them out, the workers have got no chance."

"Ken's right, said Dougie. "They won't win. It doesn't matter if the company has been around for over a century and hundreds of men will needlessly lose their jobs."

"B&S Massey have been around just as long," said Vic "and they've got full order books too. They were bought out just the same as Laurence Scott and their new owners, Davy Loewy, are closing them down to move the work to Sheffield. It's always the same. People don't count. The bosses save on the costs of labour and premises and then sell off the assets for an even greater profit."

"Over two million manufacturing jobs have gone since Thatcher's been in," noted Bert. "Just how many more is it going to be before we can get the Tories out."

"We could get them out now if Thursday's results are anything to go by, the only problem is that parliament has another three years to run."

Vic was referring to the recent local elections that had delivered a crushing blow to the Tories. Dissatisfaction with Thatcherism had led to her party being routed. Not only Greater Manchester had turned red but even in the shires, including Cheshire, the Conservatives had lost control and been condemned to opposition.

"Huh. I wouldn't get carried away. It won't make any difference. Foot and Healey will be just as eager to cosy up to the bosses," insisted Ken.

"You're right," said Dougie. "None of these politicians are offering any kind of future for youngsters. Where's the opportunities? The apprenticeships? Look at a kid like Dave. He's a sheet metal worker isn't he Rick?"

"Yes, that's right."

"Well, what's the betting that before he's qualified, his works will have been shut down?"

"Or they'll let him go once he's qualified," added Vic. "Then they won't have to pay a higher wage and can hire a kid on the cheap who's just left school."

"Aye, they've always done that," said Dougie.

"Of course, said Bert, "that's capitalism. The factories are there to make money for the bosses and not provide a livelihood for the workers."

"You can't blame kids for giving up," said Ken. "They can't see a future. They've lost hope. What can they do? Join the 'Great Peoples March for Jobs?' A damn lot of good that'll do 'em."

Ken was referring to the march of unemployed youngsters from Liverpool to London that on Tuesday had stopped off to hold a rally in Crown Square.

"Aye, they tried that in the Thirties," said Bert. "The Jarrow marchers never got anywhere either."

"But it was a lot worse for us in the Depression," said Vic. "There was even more unemployment back then and we couldn't sit back and rely on social like they can today."

"Yeah, that's right," said Bert. "Some of these young uns round me spend all day in bed. They do all right for themselves living on thieving and handouts. The last thing they'd want is to do a hard day's graft. Yes, I feel sorry for those who genuinely want work and can't get it, but there's too many scroungers out there now."

Vic and Dougie nodded in agreement, an audible sigh from the latter indicating his disapproval. Ken, looking slightly embarrassed, remained silent. Even though he knew of such individuals it was impossible for him to agree with his pals. In Ken's world there could be no shades of grey; every member of the working class was a victim of capitalism and their situation could never be through any fault of their own.

"You're right," said Vic. "Before the War no one wanted to be on public assistance. People felt ashamed and men never stopped looking for work. Now I see families happy to live on social. They've got no pride."

It was a brutal assessment and being more liberally minded, one that I found hard to subscribe to. Yet I could understand why Dougie and his pals could think it and after spending time on the estate, I could also identify those whose profiles seemed to fit their appraisal.

"Aye," said Bert, "you're not far wrong. My dad used to work at the Steel on the hammer. That wasn't half hard. It was back breaking work."

Bert shook his head and grimaced to reinforce the point.

"The Steel?" I asked.

"Yes Rick. English Steel Corporation in Openshaw. The North Street Works. My dad would come home from work with his trousers all burnt. The sparks used to fly down them whilst he held the hot metal in the tongs under the hammer. But he was a proud man. People respected him. I don't know what he'd make of these layabouts today."

"It's a disappearing world now all right," said Vic. "Everything's changing and not for the better."

His comment was greeted by silence. The mood had suddenly become quite sombre, the four old friends thinking quietly about happier times. Taking a last draw on a Woodbine, Vic slowly exhaled, the smoke rolling across the aisle. Stubbing it out on the top of an empty beer can, he dropped it inside and then picking up the can gave it a rattle.

"It's not just Thatcher's fault though, is it? asked Dougie. "Unemployment was a million and a half before she took over and what did Callaghan do about it? At least Maggie's got a pair."

"Well, yes. I suppose she has," agreed Bert. "She didn't take any rubbish over that Iranian Embassy siege."

"Tougher than most men, I'd say," replied Dougie.

"Ah, you're only saying that because you fancy her," said Ken, lightening the mood.

"Well, why not? You've got to say she's not bad for her age. I wouldn't say no," insisted Dougie.

"Yeah. Always well turned out, isn't she? Hairs always done and wears some smart outfits. There's no way Maggie would show you up if you took her out to the club on a Sunday night," said Vic.

It was strange to hear Vic and the others talking about the fabled 'iron lady' in such amorous terms. Noticing the look of surprise on my face, Grandad made an observation.

"Hey lads, our Rick doesn't seem that struck on the thought of spending a night with Maggie."

The comment was typical of Dougie and his pals roared with laughter at my expense. Although I could feel my face flush with embarrassment, I was pleased. I realised that Grandad's comment and his friends' reactions, indicated that I had undoubtedly been accepted as part of the group; someone they respected as being able to appreciate the banter.

"I don't know. These youngsters," said Ken. "They haven't a clue. All they think about is chasing after these young lasses. They never appreciate the value of experience that can only be found in an older woman."

"Dead right," said Vic, "It's like they say, there's some fine wines stored in old bottles."

"And there's many a good tune that's played on an old fiddle," added Ken.

Perhaps they were light-hearted comments and stereotypical in their way. Nevertheless, they seemed to have something of the quality of ancient wisdom in them and reminded me that these men would naturally regard a woman of more advanced years very differently to someone as young as myself.

"Well, I'm sorry to disappoint the pair of you," continued Bert, "but it's obvious that she's only got eyes for Denis."

"I'm not sure about that," said Ken. "I reckon she's got half the Cabinet dangling on a promise. That's why they all run about after her."

"No, these rich old Tories love it when she orders them about. She reminds them of their old nanny and the matron they used to have in their swanky boarding schools," insisted Vic. "All she has to do is tell them that they're naughty boys. They're desperate to do what she wants."

"You never know then. Perhaps she might fancy a real working man. Someone who can show her what's what."

"You mean like you Dougie?"

"Well, why not?

"And does Muriel know that you've got a thing for Maggie?" asked Vic.

"I never said I had."

"I suppose you didn't realise that she was at the game today," continued Vic. "If you had you could have waited outside the VIP entrance to see her before she came in."

His pals started laughing but as grandad was looking in my direction, I thought it best not to join in the general hilarity. It was yet another extraordinary, rambling conversation; one only possible between a group of such long-standing friends.

"Hey, perhaps Dougie's waiting for the offer to buy his council house," suggested Bert. "Maybe that's why he loves Maggie."

Although his comment was clearly tongue in cheek, Dougie took it seriously.

"Well maybe I am, seeing as I don't owe anything on the rent," he replied, "but why would I want to? I'd be responsible for repairs and maintenance. I bet it would cost me more than I pay in rent as well."

"And why would you want to buy it when we've got knocked-off cars racing round the estate?" asked Vic.

"Nor buy on Fort Beswick where I am," said Bert. "If it was the terrace me and Doris had on Oliver Street and they'd offered me the chance to buy that, I would have snapped their hand off. Good solid houses, not like the crumbling concrete monstrosities they've replaced 'em with. They're saying that the Corporation will be knocking the whole lot down soon and moving us out because the flats are beyond repair. Can you believe it? They've not been up ten years."

"It's that wall frame system they used to build 'em," said Vic. "Cheap pre-fabricated concrete. You can't cut corners when you're building houses. It's just money down the drain."

"That Bison Concrete have got a lot to answer for," said Bert. "They gave them the contract for Fort Ardwick too and that's in a similar state. No doubt they'll end up having to come down as well. The company have built new estates all over the country and they're falling apart. And what a surprise, just like with us no compensation has been paid to any council or tenants."

"Aye, what would you expect? Can't have big business suffer," remarked Ken, "but there's another important point here. It's not all like Beswick. In areas like Burnage, lots of tenants will want to buy their homes. It's nice there and they're solid houses with gardens. I'll bet in years to come no one will be bothered about them being ex-council and they'll pay a fair price for them. Some of those tenants will end up with a nice healthy profit. It's a damn disgrace that they're selling off council houses. We don't have enough as it is. There's always been a shortage of good homes for people and now there's even less. Thatcher's 'Right to Buy' is nothing less than a shameless attempt to turn Labour tenants into Tory property owners."

"Yes, she's picked up on Eden's idea of a property-owning democracy and is trying to make it a reality."

The words were out of my mouth before I could consider their effect. I suppose it was because I had been listening to Dougie and his pals for so long that I was desperate to make my own mark in the conversation. Always prepared to appreciate their greater knowledge and experience, this time it was a subject that I knew something about and Ken's nod of approval indicated that he was impressed.

"That's right Rick. It's individualism," said Ken, "the antithesis of socialism. Buying support through the privilege of property ownership rather than creating security and well-being for all through collective ownership and making provision for people relative to their needs."

"Yes," I replied, feeling brave enough to take the conversation further. "Yet Thomas Jefferson believed that the yeoman farmer through owning and working his land, gained the economic security necessary to be politically independent. Jefferson argued that a nation of yeoman farmers would be the best guarantee of liberty. Thatcher could never have a vision like that. She only wants to give tenants an asset that they don't want to lose. That way they'll never embrace socialism."

"Interesting," said Ken. "I didn't know they covered American history in school now."

"They don't," I replied. "I read up on Jefferson so I could talk about him when I went to my university interviews. I might choose to take American Studies instead of straight history."

"What you have to remember Rick, is that for a century after the Revolution America was defined by the frontier and the availability of land meant that social class and economic opportunity remained fluid. Back then, Americans had opportunities. Here, everything has always been set in stone. It's a capitalist world and buying your council house won't change the fact that you'll still be among the exploited at the bottom of the heap."

The others looked askance at us. They didn't mind talking about the real, practical issues that impacted on their everyday lives, but a discourse on political theory was a step too far. My enthusiasm had clearly got the better of me.

"Oh no," said Bert, "there's two of 'em at it now. We'll never see an end to the politics."

"Dougie. You didn't tell us that your Rick was just like Ken," observed Vic.

Offering them a sheepish smile, I was met by an outburst of laughter from Bert, Vic and Grandad.

"Take no notice of them lad," said Ken. "It's good to see that there's at least one youngster with a bit of political nous."

"Ah, you say that now Ken but when he gets to university and meets up with all those rich beggars, they'll offer him all sorts to get him over on their side. He'll probably end up as some rich stockbroker or banker and be driving past you waiting at the bus stop in his fancy Roller," suggested Bert.

"Yes, said Vic. "He'll end up joining the Young Conservatives and becoming Thatcher's protégé."

"And then he'll probably be running City alongside Swales," added Bert.

"He'd better not or he'll have me to answer to," said Dougie.

"Did you hear that, Rick. You'd best watch out," said Bert.

Unable to reply, I stared in disbelief at my good-natured tormentors. There seemed no limits to their imagination.

Knowing their pal's dislike of the chairman, Bert and Vic laughed merrily and even Ken found himself joining in before gradually regaining his composure and offering me some support.

"Ignore 'em kid. They don't know any better. Anyway lads, we'll be back at Piccadilly soon and we need to sort out who's going down to Maine Road for the tickets on Monday."

It was a question that focused minds immediately, given that no one wanted to miss out on attending the replay. It didn't matter that today's game had stretched most of our supporters' finances to the limit. We all knew that somehow, they would find the money to go again and if we did not secure our tickets promptly, we may risk missing out. Getting back to London on Thursday night would throw up a host of other problems too. Those in work would have to ask for a day off or, if likely to be denied, be absent ill hoping that they could hide their return to Wembley from the boss. For young Blues, there could be no days off. The law demanded that they went to school and headteachers weren't enlightened enough to recognise the emotional needs of their pupils and turn a blind eye to them following their team. And it was no good parents writing them a sick note, for young Reds would quickly let their teachers know where they had really been. Nevertheless, a detention, or worse, was far preferable to missing out on Wembley. Now on study leave, I would be spared all that.

Naturally, as the officially designated general dogsbody, I expected that four sets of eyes would quickly settle in my direction. Yet I was wrong.

"Well, we can't expect Rick to do it," said Bert. "It's a lot of money for him to carry and there's bound to be muggers hanging around outside the ground, knowing people will have lots of cash on them. No criticism of the lad intended, but he does look an easy target. Doesn't he?"

"Oh aye. You're not wrong there," said Grandad.

"It's probably best that me and you go Dougie," suggested Vic.

"Yes, I suppose so."

Best give us your money and vouchers lads," said Vic, turning to the others.

Bert and Ken removed them from their wallets and handed them over. The club had already released details through the Evening News of the relevant vouchers in the event of a replay, so they had both come prepared.

The tickets having been dealt with, the next crucial question was would they make last orders? Looking at his watch, Vic gave them the bad news.

"Nah, it's ten to eleven, that delay outside Stockport has put paid to it."

"Typical British Rail," said Bert. "Too much to expect that they can manage to run the trains on time."

The sense of disappointment was unmistakable. Even though they had all downed a fair few cans over the course of the day, not being in their local on a Saturday night at last orders was highly unusual for them. It seemed nothing less than a break with tradition.

Chapter Twenty-One

Stepping off the train and deprived of the chance of getting one final drink, we made our way slowly along the platform, eventually greeted by the elderly ticket collector who had been watching our approach with interest.

"Lucky beggars Spurs," he said, shaking his head in sympathy. I thought we'd won it. Hoddle's shot was going nowhere. What was Hutch thinking?"

"Just one of those things," said Vic.

"Are you going back for the replay?"

"Got to, haven't we?" replied Ken.

"I have to say I admire you lads. Must be costing you a fair bit. As usual, it's everything for the Southerners. They should play it up here."

"Some chance," said Bert.

"Aye," replied the old man with a sigh of resignation. Like all of us he knew that as far as the great and the good were concerned, living north of Watford you simply didn't exist.

Walking out on to the concourse we noticed that there was still a significant police presence at the station.

"Probably the best result for them," said Bert, nodding over towards some uniformed officers. "No excited Blues celebrating to annoy any Reds in town and as we didn't lose, their lot wouldn't come to the station to rub it in."

It was clear that he had spoken too soon for after walking out of the station entrance and making our way down the approach to London Road, a group of youngsters shouted up to us.

"Come on Spurs!"

"You've no chance now."

It was obvious they were Reds and seeing our scarves were eager to dismiss our prospects in the replay. Hoddle's deflected shot had been catastrophic for the City faithful yet when it hit the back of the net, the Red half of Manchester jumped excitedly to their feet. Such is the intensity and fervour of football rivalry; the cruelty of so many wishing to savour the misery and failure of their closest competitors.

Immediately I was reminded of Dave's encounter with the Everton fans and smiled as I imagined Dougie and his mates charging down to sort them out. There was little chance of that however and absolutely no need for the kids to scarper off to safety in the direction of Whitworth Street.

Reaching the bus station on Parker Street we said farewell to Bert who went to catch the bus home to Beswick. The rest of us boarded the 192, Ken remaining on board after we had alighted at Ardwick Green, to travel on to Longsight.

"I'll see you tomorrow dinner in the King Billy," said Vic, as we stopped at the entrance to Hanworth Close.

"Aye. All right," replied Dougie.

"It's been a good day hasn't it, lad?" asked Vic. "Even with the disappointment of having it snatched away from us."

"Yes, it has."

"It'll always be special you know. That first final at Wembley."

I nodded in agreement before Vic continued on his short walk home.

"Rick," said Grandad, "I'd like a chance to sit down and have a chat with Muriel. If you don't mind, when we get in and you've had a brew, can you go up to bed?"

Coming from Dougie, it was an unusual request. I realised that whatever he wanted to talk to Muriel about, it must be of some importance.

"Yes, of course. I was going to anyway because I need to be up early to see Millie."

"You're getting quite serious, aren't you, lad?"

His question was asked without a hint of insincerity or ridicule. Dougie understood that I had deep feelings of affection for Millie and had no intention of upsetting me. Quiet for a moment, I suddenly realised how proud I was of my girlfriend and that I should not be reticent about our relationship.

"Yes, Grandad. I am."

Dougie smiled. It seemed that somewhere underneath his rough exterior he had a sensitive side after all.

"Come on then," said Dougie.

Making our way to the back gate, we went into the garden. The back door was unlocked and as we entered the kitchen Dougie shouted through to the front room.

"Muriel. We're back."

Almost before the words were out Shep was in the kitchen overjoyed to see his master. His tail wagging furiously, his body wiggling and waggling across the floor on its uncertain legs.

"Stop it Shep! Don't be daft."

It was a softer rebuke than usual but not wanting to be sent to his basket, Shep thought it best to transfer his attention to me. It was hard not to reward his enthusiasm and soon I was patting his head and rubbing his ears. It was a small price to pay for the unconditional love that he was so ready to give.

"You see Rick, dogs are much better than people," Dougie had once said. "All they want is some care and attention and they'll be your friend for life. People are different. They usually want something out of you and there's so few of 'em you can trust."

And where Shep was concerned it was true. He was always genuinely pleased to see me.

Walking through to the front room Muriel greeted us warmly. Dougie and I took off our coats and scarves and I took them out into the hallway to hang them up. Returning, I could see that Dougie had sat next to Muriel on the settee and that they were watching the end of 'Saturday Night at the Mill.' It was not a programme I often watched and Kenny Ball and his Jazzmen, who were blowing through their final number, were certainly not my choice of music. However, having regularly watched 'Magpie' on children's ITV, it was pleasing to see that Jenny Hanley was now co-presenting the show. It made me smile to remember that Jenny had been a regular object of desire for so many of us young teenage boys as we moved through adolescence.

"You must be disappointed love," said Muriel, as I sat down on the chair opposite. "It's a shame they didn't manage to win but never mind, they've got another chance."

It was the kind of blandly optimistic comment that only someone who had no emotional investment in the outcome of the result could make. But it was all right, for Muriel meant well and

Dougie and I appreciated the fact that she understood how much pleasure a victory would bring us.

"Yes, that's right," I replied.

"I suppose you'll want to be going to the replay. When is it?"

"Thursday," replied Dougie.

"You haven't got any exams on love, have you?" asked Muriel.

"No, it's another couple of weeks before my first one."

"That's good."

"Yes," I replied.

"I suppose you'll be wanting me to mind Shep again then?" she continued, turning to Dougie.

"Well, I can always ask Cyril," he suggested.

"Don't be daft. You know I'll do it."

Dougie grunted his agreement. When it suited him, he was quite content for Muriel to organise matters for him.

"Anyway, are you two hungry? Do you want me to make you a sandwich?" asked Muriel.

"No, I'm fine," replied Dougie.

"Yes, we've been eating all day," I added.

"Well, you must fancy a brew."

"Yes, go on then," said Dougie, looking as if he were doing her a favour.

"No, I'm all right," I replied.

"Oh no, love. You've got to have one," insisted Muriel.

"Yes, Rick. You've not had a hot drink since dinner."

At first, I suspected that Dougie thought that I had taken his request to get to bed early too literally but then wondered if he was merely trying to impress Muriel with his concern for his grandson.

"All right. Thank you."

Going to the kitchen, Muriel returned shortly after with a tray of hot drinks and a plate of biscuits. There was an assortment of chocolate digestives, custard creams, jammie dodgers and ginger nuts. It was clear that she had been out to the shops, for there were no packets of biscuits in the cupboard when we had left that morning. It was Muriel all over; considerate and generous to a fault. As Dougie's pals had told him, he was fortunate indeed to have the love of such a woman. As I got stuck into the biscuits and started dunking them into my tea, Muriel smiled. It was obvious that she was taking great pleasure in watching my enjoyment of them.

"I thought you weren't hungry," she remarked with a chuckle.

"I can't resist these biscuits. Thank you. They're lovely."

Muriel gave another satisfied smile, a sign that it pleased her to feel appreciated.

Having finished my drink, I put my mug down on the tray with the others. I was about to carry it through to the kitchen when Muriel stopped me.

"It's alright Michael, I'll see to them."

"Thank you. I'll be getting off to bed then."

"Yes. You must be tired love, going all that way."

"He wants to be up early so that he can see Millie," said Dougie.

"Ah, that's nice," observed Muriel, in soothing tones that signified her approval. "Millie's a decent girl, love. Not like a lot of 'em round here. You won't go wrong with her."

Yes, everyone liked Millie. I hadn't met anyone on the estate who had anything but a good word for her.

"Good night," I said, heading out into the hallway.

"God bless, love. See you in the morning."

"Aye, 'night lad," added Dougie.

Closing the front room door behind me, I made my way upstairs to bed.

Chapter Twenty-Two

Sunday morning.

I'd set the alarm for seven but it must have been my anticipation of spending the day with Millie, that had woken me in terror thinking that the alarm had not gone off and that I had overslept. Checking the clock, it was only twenty past five. I tried to get back to sleep but almost as soon as I nodded off, I would wake once more to check that the alarm was still turned on. When it finally rang, I threw back the sheets and dived out of bed before quickly getting washed and changed. Making my way downstairs, I opened the door to the front room. Almost immediately I felt a pair of front paws thudding into my chest, Shep panting in excitement after spending the night alone in his basket.

"Down Shep!"

It was no good. Shep was anxious for human company. Every time I tried to remove his paws and lower him to the ground he simply leapt back up again, his tail wagging furiously.

"Come on boy. Shall I take you out?"

Shep immediately bounded towards the kitchen and the back door. That simple word, take, had again worked its magic. It was the verbal trigger telling him that it was time for a walk and not having been out since last night, he waited patiently whilst I fetched my shoes and put on his lead. Soon we were outside heading towards the park. Given that it was still early, there was no one else around, so I took out a tennis ball from my pocket to throw for my little pal. At first, he chased the ball and returned it, dropping it on the ground for me to throw again. Then he reverted to type, changing the rules of the game by dropping the ball behind some bushes and refusing to go in and collect it, looking expectantly at me to do it instead. Although I knew his intentions, I still fell into the trap. Clambering awkwardly into the almost inaccessible foliage, I peered into the debris of leaves and branches, trying to find exactly where the ball had landed and then at the precise moment of its location, I felt Shep's nose push past my outstretched hand to grasp it away from me.

Ha! Outsmarted by a dog!

Pulling myself carefully out of the bushes, trying hard to minimise the cuts and scratches that always came when Shep played his usual trick, I looked down at him. Tennis ball clamped tightly between his teeth, his tongue protruding from his mouth, he panted softly. There was a gleam in his eye as he returned my disapproving stare and for a moment, I could swear that he was grinning back at me.

"You think you're clever Shep," I heard myself saying, "but if you do that again then I'll just leave it there."

Of course, he and I knew that I probably would not and putting on his lead once more, I followed him as he trotted home. Shep was tired now and when we were back in the house he went straight to his basket.

Making some toast and marmalade and a cup of tea I took it into the middle room and sat down at the table. The silence was soon broken by the sound of footsteps coming down the stairs and the opening of the door to the front room. Looking up, I was greeted by Muriel's smiling face. As she had stayed the night, I assumed that she and Dougie must have kissed and made-up.

"Morning Muriel. Would you like a drink of tea?"

"You're all right Michael. Finish your breakfast. I'll do it."

"Are you sure?"

"Of course, I am."

Muriel walked over to the table and put her hand on my shoulder and squeezed it gently. Looking up at her I could see her soft, gentle eyes smiling down on me.

"Do you know? You're a good lad Michael. You've been brought up well, haven't you?"

"Have I?" I asked, somewhat uncertainly.

"Yes, you have," she replied, with a chuckle "and you've no reason to feel embarrassed about it."

Not knowing what to say, I stared blankly into space.

"There's nothing wrong with being polite and considerate. You're not like your grandad. Him offering to make me a cup of tea. That'll be the day!"

"Oh," I said, surprised. "He's made me one now and again."

"Well, that's different. He doesn't mind you knowing that he can do it. No, your grandad wouldn't want me thinking that he's capable of looking after himself. He'd be afraid that I might go on strike."

I smiled. There was no doubt that Muriel had Dougie all worked out.

"Is that your scarf hanging out in the hallway?" she asked.

"Which one?"

"The one with the blood on of course."

"Yes."

You're all right, aren't you? You do look all right," she noted.

"Yes, I'm fine."

"Well how did you get that blood on it?"

I explained what had happened to us outside Euston after we had arrived.

"It's a good job your grandad and his pals were with you, wasn't it? I suppose he can do some things right."

"Yes. I suppose so."

"Well, I'll wash it for you."

"No, it's fine. You don't have to put yourself to any trouble."

"It's no trouble and if I don't do it, what's going to happen when you get home and your mam sees it?"

It was something I had not thought of but Muriel had. She was well-aware that my mother had not allowed me go to Maine Road before reluctantly, she had allowed Dougie to take me.

"She can't stop me going now, I'm too old."

"I'm not just thinking about you, there's your mam to consider. I don't want her seeing it and then worrying about you every time you go to a match."

"Of course."

"And we don't want her thinking bad of your grandad, do we Michael? She might blame him if she thinks you got caught up in any trouble. He won't admit it and I know that he can moan on about her, but he loves your mam and he'd be upset if she wasn't speaking to him again."

I nodded in acknowledgement of the fact that she was far more worldly-wise than I. Muriel had the kind of wisdom that comes only from a long, hard life full of tough experiences. She valued kindness and decency and she treated everyone with generosity, whether they deserved it or not. The victim of a loveless marriage, she had no children or family of her own and over the past few months that she had been living with Dougie, Muriel had gradually taken it upon herself to love, help and guide me. In effect she had adopted me as the grandson she had never had and in return, I offered her my full respect and affection.

Finishing off my breakfast, I took my cup and plate into the kitchen and put them in the sink.

"Leave those, love. I'll do them. You get off to see Millie."

"Are you sure?"

"Yes and don't keep asking me if I'm sure. I know I'm old but I've not lost my mind… yet," she added with a smile.

"You're not old."

"Oh, thank you. You are a little charmer, aren't you?"

My face was flushed with embarrassment and she laughed gently at my display of youthful innocence.

"I've not seen Millie for a while," continued Muriel. "Have the pair of you got anything special on today?"

"No. I don't think so."

"Why don't you bring her round for a cup of tea. I'll be in all day."

"All right."

Fetching my coat and shoes, I put them on and set off for Millie's.

Chapter Twenty-Three

I'd arranged to be at Millie's for nine o'clock and when I arrived, the kids were already standing at the back door putting on their pumps ready to go out. Seeing me, their faces lit up and I knew what was coming.

"That Glenn Hoddle's dead good, isn't he Michael?" said Craig, with a smirk.

"Yeah, Dad says he's brilliant," added Gary.

They were only kids and of a tender age but the loyalty to the Reds that Terry had instilled into them almost as soon as they could walk, meant that they were already veterans at winding-up their rivals.

"He doesn't mean it," I replied. "He's just pleased his shot deflected in. Mark my words, I'll guarantee that your dad's bound to say he's rubbish when he comes to Old Trafford next season."

"No, he won't," said Craig. "Dad said he was the best player on the pitch by a mile and City didn't have a player anywhere near as good."

I knew that I should have cut my losses and kept quiet. There was no way that I could win but that did not seem to matter, for we genuine fans are so easily sucked in by the banter. Call it loyalty or just plain stubbornness, the Blues were being ridiculed and it didn't matter who was doing it. There was no alternative but to defend the club's honour.

"Hoddle never got a look-in yesterday. Gerry Gow had him in his pocket."

"Huh, he's rubbish," replied Gary.

"Dad says he's an old man now and should have been pensioned off," added Craig. "Anyway, you're going to lose now."

"Yeah, you won't win the replay," insisted Gary.

They were like a double act; a pair of aspiring young comedians. I was sure that Terry, knowing that I would be coming to see Millie, had been priming his boys, feeding them the lines that would enable them to ridicule our prospects in the replay.

"You're not going, are you?" asked Gary.

"Of course I am," I replied, trying to sound as confident as possible.

"Dad said most of the Spurs team didn't turn up and City can't play as well again. There's no point having a replay. You should save your money," suggested Craig.

The pair of them began to laugh.

"Hey, quieten down you two!"

The tone was clipped; the words precise. The kids and I looked round. Millie had entered the kitchen.

"Your mam and dad are having a lie-in. They don't want the pair of you disturbing them, do they?"

Silent, Craig and Gary shook their heads.

"And whilst we're at it, that wasn't nice what you said to Michael. He spent a lot of time and money to go to Wembley and it's not clever to take pleasure in his disappointment. Now, is it?"

"No, Auntie Millie," said Craig quietly, lowering his eyes to the floor.

Feeling sorry for the lads and a little guilty that they were being told off because I had chosen to participate in the verbal jousting, I attempted to come to their defence.

"It's all right," I said, "they didn't mean any harm. They were only having a laugh."

"No, it's not all right," insisted Millie firmly. "Is it boys?"

She gave them that stare, the one that rooted them to the spot and from which there would be no escape unless they acknowledged the merits of her advice.

"No, Auntie Millie," said the boys, quietly together.

"And you can think again if you're planning on going out looking like that. The pair of you need a good wash. Don't forget your necks and behind your ears and do it quietly. Don't you dare wake your mam and dad."

As the kids went upstairs to the bathroom, Millie turned her attention to me. I could tell that she was far from impressed.

"Arguing with a couple of kids. You're supposed to be grown up."

"They're not all sweet and innocent," I replied. "I'm sure they were planning with Terry how to make fun of City when I turned up this morning."

I had little expectation that Millie would accept such a feeble attempt to justify myself and I was right.

"Do you realise how daft you sound?" asked Millie.

"Well, I'm only saying."

"Are you indeed?"

Unable to reply, almost unconsciously my eyes dropped to the floor.

Millie started laughing. Stood there in silence, like a naughty schoolboy, I must have cut a forlorn figure.

"You're puddled Michael Taylor. What on earth do I see in you?"

"I don't know."

"Never mind."

Shaking her head as if to emphasise the 'lost cause' stood before her, Millie began to smile. Gently pulling me towards her she kissed me gently on the cheek. Unexpected, it sent a tingle of excitement running though my body, a fact that did not go unnoticed.

"That's it for now," said Millie, as she stepped away.

Seeing the look of frustration and disappointment on my face, she laughed gently.

"Have you got the key for the shed Auntie Millie?" asked Craig, who had just entered the kitchen. "I need to get the ball out."

"Come here. Show me your neck."

Craig bowed his head so that Millie could check that he had washed it. She knew that if they were in a hurry they would quickly wet their hair at the back to convince her that they had done it. Fortunately for Craig, Millie's close inspection showed that he had but when Gary returned, Millie sent him back to the bathroom.

"Get it done properly. You're not going out until you do."

Gary pulled his face in disappointment.

"Aw, do I have to."

"Yes, you do."

Turning slowly, he laboured out of the kitchen in silent protest.

"Gary!"

Millie didn't need to say any more. It was clear that she meant business. Straightening up, her nephew made his way quickly upstairs.

"I told him she'd check," whispered Craig. "Now I've got to wait to go out."

I nodded in sympathy but thought better of saying anything in reply, concerned that Millie may hear me.

Returning, Gary offered himself for inspection and Millie finally declared that she was satisfied that he was in a fit state to go out. Getting the key to the shed Millie walked out of the kitchen followed by the rest of us. Opening it, Craig went inside and came out with the football which he immediately threw to Gary. Clutching it to his chest, as carefully as if he was collecting the ball in the most important of games, the young lad then stretched out his arms, rotating the football between the palms of his hands. Bouncing the ball on the grass he looked forward, scanning to left and right, imagining that he was getting ready to throw it out to one of his forwards who had found space out on the wing. Yes, I had watched this kid for a while now and it was plain to see that he lived and breathed the game. Young as he was, he seemed to have the attributes that could well take him on to follow in the footsteps of his namesake and hero, goalkeeper Gary Bailey.

"Craig, make sure that you don't wander off from the park," said Millie. "We don't want to worry your mam, do we?"

"We won't," said Craig.

"And keep an eye on our Gary."

"I always do."

Stepping through the gate, the boys suddenly stopped. Craning their necks, heads tilted to one side, they listened intently. A dull pounding could be heard in the distance and gradually it began to get louder, echoing and reverberating around the houses.

"The 'Sally Army' are on the way," observed Millie.

Her words were confirmed as the faint sounds of brass began to drift towards us, increasing in volume with every passing moment. Craig and Gary looked expectantly along the road as Millie and I joined them on the pavement. Finally, marching into view, the men and women of the band of the Salvation Army

Citadel on Grosvenor Street made their entry. Passing by us they were followed eagerly by a motley assortment of young girls and boys, fascinated and excited by the spectacle they provided on the estate every Sunday morning. As they stopped at the end of the road, close to the green in front of the maisonettes, there were kids running from all directions to join the others that had congregated around them. Among them were Craig and Gary, all thoughts of football temporarily forgotten. Once the music had stopped there was silence; the onlookers, mainly children, listening with respect to the prayers and sermon given by a female officer.

"It's fascinating, isn't it?"

"What's fascinating?" asked Millie.

"Well, all these kids running after the Salvation Army. I doubt any of them are from religious families and the staunch Catholics on the estate will have their kids at morning Mass."

"I think they like listening to the brass band," replied Millie. "It's so different to the music on the radio and the boys like to march after them and pretend they're in a real army."

The sermon at an end the band launched into 'Who is on the Lord's side?' one of their most popular hymns. It was clear that few of the assembled kids knew the words, or felt inclined to sing it. I looked towards Craig and Gary and noticed that the latter was starting to lose interest, turning the football over in his hands and throwing it up in the air. Finally jamming it between his arm and side, he pulled at Craig's sleeve. His brother looked at him, nodded and the two of them set off for the park.

"Well, that is disappointing," I observed, my voice laced with sarcasm. "It doesn't look like your Craig and Gary will be converting any time soon."

"Don't be daft," said Millie "and what have you got against the Sally Army anyway?"

"I haven't."

"Yes, you have. It's obvious."

I suppose it was and fixing me with that curious stare, I knew that Millie expected an answer.

"Well, doesn't it annoy you? The arrogance of them. They march round the estate every Sunday morning, banging their drums and making a racket when people like Terry and Jeanette, who've been working all week, are trying to have a lie-in."

"No. People sleep through it anyway. They mean well and they do good work helping the homeless and the down-and-outs. If they want to spread their message, then that's fine by me. They're not forcing you to listen."

"Perhaps, but why don't they march where I live? Wake my parents up? No, they assume that people living in the leafy suburbs aren't sinners. If they're such good Christians then they would know that's not true They say they want to help the poor and the needy but they look down on people here."

"You're wrong Michael. The Sally Army always has its members on the estate. They're genuine, not like social services or the police; only coming out when they have to. They visit the pubs late on Saturday night and the Citadel's there for the local community. People round here respect them; no one ever says a bad word about them. All the blokes in the pub buy a copy of 'War Cry,' even though they don't want to read it. And why? Because they know that every penny goes to helping the needy. But you are right about one thing, Michael. They do concentrate on areas like ours. That's because here they will find the poor and unfortunate and the kids who go hungry. They won't find many where you are, will they?"

"Fair enough but if it's their mission to save souls, then they shouldn't be confining their efforts to the council estates. Vanity, prejudice and selfishness can be found in abundance where I am."

"I don't know Michael," said Millie, with a sigh. "For you everything is so complicated. Why can't you just accept that even if you think members of the Sally Army are misguided, their intentions are good?"

"Or that they just want to feel good about themselves."

"Good about themselves?"

"Yes, they can impress their middle-class friends and neighbours with all the good work they're doing for the poor and downtrodden."

"I don't think you're being fair," said Millie. "Do you really believe that they'd be up early every Sunday morning when they've spent Saturday night in the roughest pubs in Manchester, just to impress the neighbours? They wouldn't be able to do that for very long, would they now?"

Her words were without a hint of reproach. Millie spoke calmly, delivering sound factual arguments that were difficult to counter. As I peered into her gentle green eyes, I could feel her drawing the goodness out of me. She was right. So much of my reasoning was at best foolish and at worst absurd. Perhaps I was showing my prejudice, feeling resentful that whereas I talked endlessly about the need for change, these respectable, mild-mannered, middle-class Christians were out in the poorest communities trying to do something about it.

"No, Millie," I finally replied. "I suppose you have a point there."

Millie smiled, then pulled my face down towards her and kissed me tenderly on the lips. Pulling away from me, she chuckled softly as she saw the flush on my cheeks.

"What was that for?"

"Because it takes a man to admit that he's wrong."

I thought I understood her, but with Millie I could never be entirely sure. Looking at her expectantly, waiting for her to elaborate, she was silent. That was Millie, so often exercising what she called her 'woman's prerogative' and telling me as little or as much about her feelings as she wanted.

"Anyway Michael," she continued. "You're far too serious. It's hard to remember that you're only eighteen. Sometimes you strike me as the oldest person I know."

"Oh."

Hearing the uncertainty in my voice, Millie was quick to reassure me.

"It's good to have a sense of responsibility but you are allowed to relax sometimes. There'll be plenty enough to worry about as you get older."

"Yes, I suppose there will."

"Come on then, let's go back in," said Millie. "I want to sort out the kids' clothes for school tomorrow. It'll save our Jeanette a job and whilst I'm doing it, you can make a brew. All right?"

"Of course."

Chapter Twenty-Four

Back inside we were alone, Terry and Jeanette still enjoying a lie-in. Whilst Millie took the basket full of dry washing into the middle room and set up the ironing board, I got on with making a brew. Bringing the drinks and placing them on the table, I offered to help her with the ironing.

"We need to get the creases out, not put them in," observed Millie.

"I can iron. I often do my shirts."

"And I can always tell when you have."

"Oh?"

"Of course. They always look a right mess. Especially the collars. It's obvious when your mam or Muriel have done them. That's when you look smart."

"Right," I said, unable to hide my disappointment.

Millie put down the iron, looked at me and laughed.

"Look Michael, it's good that you can cook and make a brew and tidy up, there's not many men that can, but ironing clothes is beyond you and I don't see any point in pretending otherwise. Don't you agree?"

"Well, if I don't get any chance to practice, how can I get any better?"

"Well, you can't but then again, you have to admit that you are cack-handed. What chance is there that you'd ever get good at it? And I can't afford to let you practice on the kids' clothes."

"Huh, I suppose I'm not practical, am I? I should stick to what I'm good at, like reading books."

"And what's wrong with that?"

"Well, quite a lot according to some people."

"And they're the type of people you should ignore."

"It's not always easy though. Studying isn't always regarded as being useful, is it?"

"And does that bother you?"

"Sometimes, especially when I sense it from people on the estate."

"Can't you see it's because most of them are jealous? They'd love to have your qualifications. They were the same with me too. I just ignored them."

"Yes, but now that you're working they look at you differently."

"Anyway Michael, there are those of us who do respect you for wanting to go to university. Look at Dawn and Dave for instance."

"Yes. I suppose you're right."

"Of course, I am."

"Since I've got to know Dave, he's been a really good friend but when I stop to think about it, it surprises me."

"Why?"

"Well, I know that we share a love of the Blues but otherwise we're so different and so I find it hard to understand why he's always prepared to put himself out for me. I'm not daft, I know very well what it means to have Dave's seal of approval. I'm sure that I'd have to watch out for myself a lot more if I didn't."

"Don't forget that I look out for you too."

"I know you do Millie but you understand what I mean, don't you?"

"Yes, of course."

"And it was Dave who had a word with Scott."

Millie nodded.

"So why is Dave so friendly towards me?"

Millie straightened up, lifted the iron from the board and placed it in the tray at its end. Examining me closely, she sighed.

"I don't know Michael, you're beyond me. You really shouldn't be so negative. I can't believe that you ever give a second thought to what people think about you in Sale."

"Well, I suppose I don't but I'd still like to know why Dave's so friendly."

"Because unlike a lot of people, Dave's open-minded and he looks beneath the surface. He doesn't care about where you come from or the fact that you don't sound like us, he judges you by your character. Like me, he appreciates you for the fact that you're genuine and that you don't look down on people round here."

"Of course I don't. Why on earth would I do that?"

"That's the point. You never would. But do you think that everyone from your background's the same; your friends at the cricket and tennis clubs? Most of them wouldn't be seen dead around here."

"I'm not sure that's true."

"That's you all over Michael, wanting to see the best in them. Sometimes people aren't very nice."

At that moment the door opened and Jeanette skipped in from the front room. Wearing a broad smile her face was glowing.

"Morning you two."

"You seem full of the joys of spring," observed Millie.

"Yes, I suppose I do."

Millie smiled, a tacit acknowledgement of the fact that Jeanette and Terry had made the most of their weekly lie-in. Confronted by the fact, I felt slightly uncomfortable. Turning away, I picked up a jumper from the table, pretending that it hadn't been properly folded. Noticing my awkwardness Jeannette chuckled softly.

"What have you two been up to?" she asked.

"We've been ironing the kid's clothes," I quickly replied.

"I can see that," observed Jeanette, "but wouldn't you rather have been doing something else?"

The question was posed in such a way as to appear quite innocent, yet clearly carried the implication that I would have rather shared an intimate moment with Millie. In her particularly playful manner, Jeanette wished to explore the possibility of teasing me further and Millie was not averse to joining in.

"Yes, I'm sure he would, wouldn't you Michael?"

Millie looked at me with those beautiful sparkling eyes, her soft lips parting slowly into a deliciously impish smile, while she waited patiently for a reply.

"Erm…"

"What's the matter?" asked Millie. "Cat got your tongue?"

"It must be all that ironing. It's got him all hot and bothered," suggested Jeanette.

"Yes, it can get pretty steamy, can't it?"

"And then it's easy to start getting carried away."

"And feeling like you're going to lose control."

Unable to speak, I could only stare blankly into space hoping that the pair of them would desist.

"Oh dear, he seems lost for words, doesn't he?" suggested Jeanette.

"Too busy thinking about other things, I shouldn't wonder," said Millie, shaking her head and tutting.

I looked at the floor. I had nothing to say. All too often I was the target of the sisters' good-natured humour and I still hadn't found a way to respond. Without the ability to engage in quick-witted repartee and too self-conscious to simply laugh along with them, there seemed little that I could do. Thankfully, they were always gracious enough to recognise the point at which I had suffered enough.

"Aw, Michael. Aren't we terrible?" asked Millie.

"The poor lad doesn't know whether he's coming or going," said Jeanette.

The two of them, realising the potential for innuendo that lay in her words, burst out laughing. As I appeared even more uncomfortable, Millie decided to change the subject.

"I've finished ironing the lads' clothes."

"Yes, I can see. Thanks, Millie. It's good of you but you shouldn't have bothered. I could have done them later."

"Well, it saves you a job."

As Jeanette went into the kitchen to make a brew, I suddenly remembered Muriel's invitation.

"Muriel asked if you wanted to come round as she's not seen you for a while."

"Yes, I'd like to. I'll just change my top and we'll get off."

I couldn't see any reason why she needed to but I knew better than to ask. Going upstairs she returned wearing a crisp, light green blouse. Tucked tightly into her beige pants, it accentuated her wonderful figure.

Saying farewell to Jeanette, we set off to see Muriel. On the way, Millie asked me why I had been so embarrassed when her sister had come down the stairs.

"I wasn't," I replied.

"Don't be daft, you know you were."

I was silent.

"Did it embarrass you because you knew that they'd been making love?"

That was Millie. She would always tell it how it was; plainly and directly. The fact was that when we were on our own her words would never make me feel uncomfortable. I could discuss the most intimate of matters without any inhibitions. Yet with others present I could never talk about such subjects without feeling distinctly uneasy.

"I suppose it did."

"But why? It's natural. They are married and it wouldn't matter if they weren't, as long as they loved one another. Dougie and Muriel sleep together, don't they?"

"Of course."

"So, there was no need to get embarrassed in front of Jeanette, was there?"

"It's just that I didn't want her to think that I was aware of what she and Terry had been doing."

"She wouldn't be bothered."

"I suppose so but I wanted to respect her privacy."

"I don't know, there's only you who could think like that," replied Millie. "Do you know what Michael Taylor? You're completely doolally."

Chapter Twenty-Five

It was almost ten-thirty when we arrived at Dougie's. Opening the back door, we entered the kitchen, where Muriel was peeling the potatoes as part of her preparations for Sunday dinner. Seeing us, she put the knife down on the top, ran her hands under the cold tap and quickly dried them. Throwing her arms around Millie, she gave her a hug.

"Hello, love. I've not seen you for ages. How are you?"

"I'm fine and you?"

"Oh, I'm all right love. Us women can't afford to be any other, can we?

"That's right," said Millie, "chance would be a fine thing."

"Yes, if we decided to be ill, then everything would grind to a halt."

Hearing our voices, Shep had left Dougie and wandered in from the front room. Seeing Millie, his tail began to wag furiously, his body waggling from side to side. About to jump up, a terse command rooted him to the spot.

"No!"

Shep slowly sat down on his haunches, his eyes looked pleadingly up towards his mistress.

"Aw. Isn't he sweet?" observed Millie.

"Sometimes love," said Muriel.

Sensing the affection in Millie's voice, Shep offered his paw. When Muriel nodded her head to signal that it was all right, Millie bent down and took it in her hand. Stroking it gently, she slowly stood up and patted him lovingly on the head.

"You have to remember love, dogs are just like men. You have to keep on top of 'em or there's no telling how much of a merry dance they'll lead you."

I suppose she was right but although she clearly had Shep reigned in and under control, in Dougie's case it was somewhat different.

"If it was left to him in there," she observed, contemptuously referring to Grandad who was quietly reading the News of the World in the front room, "our Shep would run riot."

"Yes, I suppose he would," agreed Millie.

"Well, look at you," said Muriel. "Don't you look nice. She does, doesn't she, Michael?"

There was no need to ask me but I was happy to confirm her opinion.

"Yes, I think so."

"The prettiest girl on the estate I don't wonder. I keep telling our Michael how lucky he is," she continued. "Don't I cock?"

"That's true, you do," I mumbled, somewhat uncertainly.

Noticing my reaction, Muriel smiled.

"Oh dear, I've not gone and embarrassed you, have I?"

"No," I replied, somewhat awkwardly.

"There's nothing wrong in talking about your feelings for Millie, now is there? It isn't something to be ashamed of."

Muriel's voice was quiet and soothing, her face gentle and caring. She was trying hard to smooth the course of true love, even though there was no reason to suggest that where Millie and I were concerned, she needed to. I could appreciate that Muriel only wanted what she felt was best for me but it didn't make it any easier to respond. Millie, finding amusement in my awkwardness, looked at me mischievously.

"Yes, Michael. We should all be able to express our feelings to one another, shouldn't we?"

I looked at Millie and then at Muriel and could see them both smiling, eagerly waiting for my reply. Silent, I could only hope that they would relent and that one or the other would change the conversation. I thought of Shep and how often he would be sent to his basket. Right now, I wished that I could go and quietly curl up with him inside it. Unfortunately, there was to be no respite. A puzzled expression on her face, Millie gently shook her head and addressed Muriel.

"He seems to have gone all shy, doesn't he?"

Muriel looked at me. I felt like an obscure exhibit in a dusty old museum where visitors stopped briefly to satisfy their curiosity, only to turn away in disappointment. Unsurprisingly, I began to feel a little awkward.

"You're right love. He has, hasn't he?"

Muriel started to chuckle and Millie soon joined in. It was the second time that morning that I had found myself unceremoniously cast as a figure of fun. It may have been in the nicest of ways but there was no escaping the fact that the two of them were ganging up on me. Young or old, it didn't seem to matter. Women took great pleasure in making light of their menfolk.

Finally, in an attempt to change the subject, I suggested to Muriel that I could finish off peeling the potatoes for her.

"Oh no, cock. You're not doing that. You can make a brew instead."

"No, it's alright," I replied. "I don't mind doing the spuds."

"Now Michael, you should know that I won't let you do them. It's a sharp knife and you'll only go and cut yourself."

Her response was quiet and firm. I ought to have known that it was pointless to appeal but I was determined to challenge her decision.

"No, Muriel. I won't. I'm not daft," I insisted. "I'll be careful."

"You said that last time, didn't you? And look what happened."

Muriel had spoken in that superior tone that she sometimes used to correct those younger and less experienced than herself. In effect, it told me that I was gormless.

"What did happen? asked Millie, her curiosity aroused.

The question landed with a crash. How foolish I had been. I should have just kept quiet and accepted Muriel's invitation to make a brew. Now I was going to look even more ridiculous.

"It was shocking," recounted Muriel. "He offered to help peel the vegetables for tea. I said he could whilst I tidied the front room. Next thing, I hear a shout and lots of cursing. I went in the kitchen and there's blood all over his hand and it's dripping on the tops and the floor. I grabbed a tea towel, soaked it in cold water and pressed it round his hand. I wiped away the blood and could see that the silly beggar had only gone and sliced his finger."

"Eugh," said Millie, with a shudder.

"Yes. It wasn't a pretty sight. At one point I thought we were going to have to rush him down to the MRI. But I kept pressing on it and slowly it stopped bleeding."

"How did he manage to do it?" asked Millie, her voiced laced with incredulity.

"Lord knows," replied Muriel, with a sigh. "Head in the clouds no doubt. They're like that these studious types, aren't they?" she insisted, confident in her assessment of character and temperament. "They're just not practical."

"Is that right Michael? Was it because you had your mind on other things?" asked Millie. "Is that why you nearly chopped your finger off?"

Millie was clearly amused by my discomfiture and of course, it only confirmed her previous assertion that I was 'cack-handed.'

"It's not funny," I replied.

"I didn't say it was. I just asked you how it happened."

"Well. It was just one of those things. Bad luck," I insisted.

"Now come on cock, you know that's not true," said Muriel. "Why, I could tell Millie about lots of your other little mishaps, now couldn't I?"

I looked at Muriel, silently pleading with her to save me from further embarrassment. Millie felt differently however and was enjoying watching me being put in my place.

"Nothing you could say would surprise me, Muriel. He's nothing but a calamity, isn't he?"

"There was never a truer word spoken. Sometimes I think that he's just like that daft old beggar in there. Lord help the poor lad if he turns out like him."

The two of them burst out laughing. They could hardly stop until finally, Millie put her arm around me and gave me a gentle squeeze.

"Aw, poor Michael. You know we love you really."

Picking up the kettle, I filled it at the sink and turned it on. Whilst I got busy sorting out the tray for the drinks, Millie helped Muriel as they quickly finished preparing the vegetables. Their task completed, I poured the boiling water into the teapot and took the tray and placed it on the table in the middle room.

"Michael," said Muriel, "tell your grandad to come and sit with us, we've something we want to tell you."

Whilst she and Millie sat at the table I walked into the front room and told Dougie that I had made him a brew.

"Oh, right lad."

Glancing up from his paper, he appeared confused.

"Well, where is it?"

"It's on the table."

"Fetch it me then."

"No, Grandad. Muriel says that you've to go and sit in there."

"Why's that?"

"She said that there's something you want to tell Millie and I."

Dougie's face dropped.

"Oh hell," he mumbled. "Not that."

As usual, Dougie wasn't wearing his hearing aid. Nevertheless, he had heard every word I had said, even whilst he had been reading his paper.

"All right Rick," he continued. "I'm coming."

Back at the table, I was about to sit down.

"Where's the biscuits, Michael?" asked Muriel.

"Oh."

"Never mind 'Oh,' go and get them."

As I went back into the kitchen I could hear her tutting.

"He'd forget his head if it wasn't screwed on."

"Probably," replied Millie, with a chuckle.

Bringing them back in, I tried to justify my error.

"I didn't think anyone would want a biscuit," I observed.

"That doesn't matter, we've got a visitor."

"But Millie doesn't mind, do you?" I asked.

"That's not the point," replied Muriel. "Do you want me being called for being mean?"

"Nobody could ever say that about you," said Millie. "Everyone knows you've got a heart of gold. Why, Dougie and Michael would be lost without you."

"Oh, I don't know about that," observed Muriel.

Praise did not necessarily sit comfortably with Muriel, given the fact that for much of her life she had been unappreciated. It was therefore unsurprising that she had become naturally self-effacing and somewhat dismissive of her own kindness and generosity. Quickly she changed the subject.

"Michael. I've washed your scarf and hung it out on the line. It'll be dry in no time. Don't forget it when you go home."

"Thank you. I won't."

Coming in from the front room, Dougie pulled out a chair and sat next to Muriel at the table. Turning to look at him, Muriel let out a sigh.

"Where's your hearing aid?"

Dougie stared blankly ahead.

"He can't hear me, can he? The daft beggar."

Looking across at Millie and I she shook her head and sighed once more. Tapping Dougie, he gave a start and turned towards her, a surprised look on his face.

"Where's … your … hearing … aid?" she asked, slowly and loudly.

Dougie's face was covered by the mists of confusion. He gave the impression that he was struggling hard but he couldn't quite understand her.

Pointing to her lips, Muriel mouthed the words slowly so that he could read them. This seemed to do the trick.

"In …the … front … room… love," he replied, slowly and loudly, mouthing the words just as she had done.

I felt Millie grab my hand tightly under the table. Her body was tense. She was desperate not to burst out laughing. I turned towards her and with a hardly perceptible shake of the head indicated that she must not.

"Well go and get it," said Muriel

"Eh?"

"I'll get it," I said.

I went into the front room and saw that Dougie had left it on the arm of the chair. I suspected that he was half-hoping that Shep would fancy chewing it. It was a forlorn hope. Fearing Muriel, Shep wouldn't have dared. Bringing it back, I handed it to Dougie who took an age to fit it back into his ear. Having finished, he turned to Muriel.

"Are you switched on?" she asked.

"Eh? Eh?"

"Switch the damn thing on!"

Her voice was sharp but its penetrative qualities left much to be desired, for Dougie showed no signs of understanding.

"Eh? What love?" he asked, cocking his head to one side and rolling his eyes to show that he was trying hard to understand.

It was a solid act. Just like having Colin Crompton in the house fresh over from the Wheeltappers and Shunters Social Club. The only difference was that Dougie provided his laughs for free. Of course, that made little impression on Muriel and Dougie's deaf act was now driving her to distraction. Whatever it was she wanted to tell Millie and I, Grandad seemed to be trying his hardest to stop her. Not wanting to witness another fallout between them, I stepped into the breach. Looking directly at him, I spoke slowly and precisely.

"Grandad, you need to turn your hearing aid on."

Returning my gaze, a momentary smile flickered across his face. It told me that he knew that I had understood and that now, he would stop playing the game.

"Oh, right!"

It was as if the scales had suddenly fallen from his eyes. Pretending to adjust the control attached to his ear-piece, he finally nodded.

"That's better," he declared with no little sense of satisfaction.

"About time. Thank the Lord for that," declared Muriel.

"Well, love. What did you want to talk about? What did you want to tell our Rick?"

His face was a picture of innocence.

"Don't tell me that you've forgotten already?"

"Eh?"

"The wedding."

"What about it?"

"Michael needs to know that we're getting married."

"Oh, that," said Dougie, as if it were a matter of no consequence.

I can't say that the news was that surprising, given that the two of them had been living together, more on than off, for some considerable time. Yet it was a significant step to take and I was impressed by the fact that Muriel was prepared to commit her future to such a challenging character as Dougie. He of course, had everything to gain. Muriel would wait on him hand and foot and take care of him if he were ill. I suppose Muriel wanted him to make an honest woman of her and marriage would provide some sense of stability in the later years of her life. Nevertheless, the announcement of their marriage was still important to her and although she didn't show it, Dougie's nonchalant attitude towards it must have upset her. Neither did it impress me. It was one of the few occasions where Grandad had left me feeling disappointed.

"That's great news," I said, smiling at Muriel.

"Congratulations," said Millie. "I hope you're going to keep him in line, Muriel."

Millie walked around the table and when Muriel stood up, kissed her on the cheek and gave her a hug. Understanding that I was naturally reticent when it came to displays of public affection, it was a reminder that I should do the same. One of Millie's many endearing qualities was that she understood the emotional needs of others. As I gave Muriel a kiss, she threw her arms around me, hugging me tightly. It was clear how much she valued my support.

"I'll soon be your grandma, love."

"I think you already are," I replied.

"Aw. Aren't you a good un."

"Show 'em the form love," said Muriel, turning to Dougie.

"The form?"

"Yes, the one we're taking to the Register Office on Tuesday morning."

Dougie went over to the wall unit opposite, took a large envelope from the pull-down and having sat back down, placed it on the table for us to examine. Millie and I read through the details confirming that the two of them were applying to get married.

"Oh," remarked Millie, surprised. "That's an unusual spelling, isn't it?"

"What is?" I asked.

She placed her finger on Dougie's name. Fraser had suddenly been transformed into Fraizer.

"I've never seen it spelt F-R-A-I-Z-E-R. Do you come from a special clan, Dougie?" she asked, quite innocently.

Dougie looked at her blankly. Muriel tapped him on the shoulder.

"She's asking about your name, love."

"Eh?"

Muriel shook her head and sighed as Dougie started to adjust the volume on his hearing aid. Soon it had begun to shriek and whistle but his countenance didn't alter, it looked for all the world as if he couldn't hear it.

"Turn it down!" shrieked Muriel.

"Eh. Eh?"

"Your hearing aid Grandad," I said, mouthing the words slowly. "Turn it down."

"Oh. Yes."

Turning the control, silence returned.

"Ah that's better," he declared with satisfaction. "This'll have to go back. It's always playing up," he added, shaking his head in disappointment.

I knew immediately what Grandad was up to. He hadn't counted on Millie's natural interest when he had shown us the form. Assuming that she would give it just a cursory glance, he was surprised when his unusual surname had piqued her curiosity. It had created a difficult situation, for he didn't want Muriel to suspect that he had filled in the form incorrectly. Dougie knew that I would know the spelling was wrong but he was confident that I would accept that he had his reasons and so could be relied upon to remain silent. The commotion created by the shrieking earpiece had created the distraction he needed to be able to change the conversation. Picking up the form, he placed it back in the envelope.

"Best keep this safe for Tuesday love," he said to Muriel, before putting it back in the pull-down.

"Now then Rick," he continued. "There's a skip at the back of Ardwick Green. They're doing one of the big houses up and they've thrown some empty Dulux cans in there. We could do with going over and fetching 'em back."

"You can't go wearing your decent clothes," said Muriel.

"Who can't?" asked Dougie.

"Michael, of course."

"Oh?"

"I wouldn't mean you now, would I?" replied Muriel. "It'll be the lad who'll be expected to rummage around for them."

"Well, of course. He's younger than me. He's still got a spring in his step."

Millie chuckled whilst Muriel shook her head.

"Still, he can put a pair of your old overalls on."

"There's no need. The paint'll be dry by now."

"And what about all the other rubbish? He'll end up getting filthy. What do you think your Anne will say if his clothes get ruined?"

"Yes," I said. "It's probably best that I go and get changed."

"They're in the bottom drawer," shouted Muriel, as I disappeared up the stairs.

It was the logical thing to do for I could see that Muriel was not going to let the matter drop. It was better to do as she asked so that we could save time and get on our way. When I got back downstairs, suitably attired, Dougie had already made his way outside. Before I could join him, Muriel asked me to wait. The women were ganging up on me again.

"Millie, do you mind going as well to keep an eye on them love? Make sure that Dougie doesn't get our Michael into any mischief."

"No, of course not."

"The lad can't afford to be getting into any trouble. He's got university to think of."

"Oh, I'm sure he'll be alright."

"I wouldn't be so certain about that," replied Muriel, "for all he's supposed to be clever, our Michael's too keen to do whatever that daft beggar tells him."

"Yes, he is gormless at times, isn't he?"

Millie turned to me, a broad smile on her face. She found it amusing to listen to Muriel's assessment of my limitations, appreciating that it was only a reflection of the latter's concern for my welfare.

"Come on then Michael, let's get off," continued Millie. "Don't worry Muriel, I'll keep my eye on the pair of them."

"I know you will. But remember, if they do try to step out of line, you just tell them straight. Dougie thinks a lot of you love and you'll get no arguments from him."

"No, I wouldn't expect to."

And she was right.

Chapter Twenty-Six

Dougie was getting impatient at the back gate.

"There you are. What took you so long?"

"I had trouble putting these overalls on," I replied, not wanting to tell him that Muriel had delayed me.

Dougie gave me a withering look and shook his head.

"Hasn't your mam taught you how to get dressed?"

Millie laughed.

"Don't worry love," said Dougie. "We won't be long. He'll be back before you know it."

"No. Millie's coming with us Grandad."

"Coming with us?"

"Yes. I thought she could help."

"Oh aye?"

Dougie looked at Millie who stared straight back. There was a gleam in his eyes and the flicker of a smile. He knew that Muriel had sent her to make sure that we didn't get into trouble.

"That's all right, isn't it Dougie?" asked Millie.

"Of course, love."

"Couldn't put your overalls on. Humph!" mumbled Dougie.

Walking across to the block of garages, Dougie opened the door to the one he rented and took out his old green Austin mini-van. Registered in 1966 he had bought it five years ago and had cared for it with love and attention. The body work was still as good as new and the chrome trim, bumpers, head lights and mirrors, gleamed in the sunlight.

"Here you are love, come and sit in the front," said Dougie, holding the passenger door open for Millie. "You'll have to get in the back Rick," he added, somewhat dismissively.

"Of course," I replied.

Opening the back doors, I clambered inside the van and closed them behind me. There wasn't a great deal of room, even though Dougie emptied it of materials and equipment every night and the floor was hard. There was the lingering aroma of turps and oil-based paint but it was neat and tidy, something that Dougie always put great store by. Every night he returned from work he would remove his materials and equipment and put them safely away in the small brick built shed in the back garden. That was only after he had religiously cleaned his brushes and rollers ensuring that they would have a long life of usefulness. Dougie had little time for many of the younger generation of painters and decorators bemoaning the fact that so many of them would only use a brush once, simply throwing it away and buying a new one.

"They're bone idle," he had remarked. "They'd rather throw their money away, then spend time cleaning 'em. Years ago, they wouldn't have been able to afford to do that. Remember, if you take care of your tools, then they'll look after you."

"But I suppose if you're employed by the Direct Works Department you don't have to buy your own, so you won't feel the need to bother," I suggested.

"Direct Works," he replied, with disdain. "A bunch of cowboys. Get there at eight, don't start till nine and then they're in the pub for two hours at dinner. The only time those lads do a proper job is when they're on a foreigner."

Dougie didn't have much time for tradesmen who worked for the Corporation. He thought that they had it easy; working on public contracts where there was no specific accountability for the quality of the work.

"You see Rick I have to do a proper job. If not, I don't get paid. All my work comes from recommendations. I wouldn't get very far if I took their slap-happy approach to everything."

Dougie was doing himself something of a disservice for everyone knew that he was a perfectionist who took an enormous pride in his work. Grandad would always do the best possible job whatever the circumstances. He was probably correct in suggesting that most of those employed by Direct Works did not, nevertheless I also suspected that he was envious of their job security; the regular hours and guaranteed wages. That he lacked the same opportunity was his own fault, for it was his decision not to work on the books and pay tax and national insurance. Ultimately though, Dougie was his own man. He could never tolerate a boss telling him what to do. He was the same with his customers too and if any became too demanding he would simply walk away, his customary parting shot ringing in their ears: "You can stick your job up your arse!"

Pulling out of Hanworth Close, Dougie drove us down Wadeson Road then left at the junction with Brunswick Street. Going across the roundabout, we travelled a short distance up Higher Ardwick before turning left along the park and Ardwick Green North. Towards its end, close to the barracks, were a couple of large, three-storied Regency town houses. The buildings were obviously undergoing some degree of renovation with scaffolding erected against them. A couple of skips were on the road outside, Dougie parking the van a short distance before them. Getting out we surveyed the buildings.

"They'll look nice when they've finished," said Millie. "They're a lot grander than the houses on the estate."

"Ardwick used to be a wealthy suburb of Manchester," said Dougie. "Ardwick Green was a private park and these were grand houses for the wealthy. They're grade two listed now."

Pointing to the series of ladders attached to the scaffolding, Grandad asked a question.

"Can you climb up them, Rick?"

"The ladders?"

"Yes. To the top."

"Why?"

"Oh, I'm just curious."

As I walked over and placed my hands on the rungs ready to start climbing, I felt a hand on my shoulder. It was Millie and she had a concerned look on her face.

"What do you think you're doing?" she asked.

"I'm just going to climb to the top."

"Are you completely gormless? You don't know if it's safe."

"Oh, I'm sure it is," said Dougie, reassuringly. "They've been up there a while now, so we'd have heard if there was a problem with them."

"Oh, you mean that no dead bodies have been reported in the Evening News," observed Millie, with more than a hint of sarcasm.

"It's all right. I'll be fine," I said, reassuringly.

The ladders had suddenly become a challenge and I wanted the satisfaction of being able to reach the top. Millie however, was having none of it.

"You've never been up ladders before, have you?"

"No."

"So, you've got no idea how to climb up them safely."

"I'll be careful," I insisted. "I'm not stupid."

"Oh, really?"

Millie gave me one of her withering looks. I tried hard not to flinch, but it was impossible. Her angry, blazing eyes forced me into submission and bowing my head I waited for the inevitable reprimand.

"I wonder how many scaffolders have said that when they're encased in plaster in the MRI. And how do you know that you won't get dizzy and let go? You've no idea whether or not you've got a head for heights, have you?"

It was Dougie who responded and he seemed to have a logical suggestion.

"Well, love. That's right, he doesn't know but there's a chance for him to find out. If Rick takes it steady and climbs up slowly, if he starts to feel dizzy, he can stop and come back down. That's what I do."

Grandad may have thought that he could win her over but Millie was naturally suspicious where his intentions were concerned. Alert as ever, she pounced on his reply.

"That's what you do?"

"Oh, yes love."

"You must suffer from vertigo then?"

"Well," he replied, somewhat hesitantly. "Not all the time."

"Ah, I see," said Millie. "You're not thinking of getting Michael to help you on some outsides, are you?"

Dougie was shocked. Whilst I was keen to prove that I could race up the ladders to the top of the building, Millie had quickly realised his intentions. She was right, I certainly looked foolish now. Aware that he may appear selfish and lacking in concern for my welfare, Grandad attempted to justify himself.

"It's not like that love, I'm thinking of the lad. When he goes off to university he wants a bit of money behind him. You're right, there is a chance of some outside work and it pays well; a lot more than he'd get elsewhere. There's other lads I've used before, so I don't need him but I'd rather give Rick the chance. That's why I wanted to find out if he'd be all right up a ladder."

"Don't worry, I'm sure Michael won't have a problem earning himself some money over the summer. Once he's finished his exams, he'll soon be able to pick up a vacation job."

"Will he?"

"Of course, lots of firms take on students to cover the staff that they've got going on holiday. We take them on at the bank. In fact, I might be able to get him a job with us."

"Oh, I see. Well, that's settled then."

Dougie had signed off with an air of quiet resignation. It was an acknowledgement that Millie, for all her relative youth, could be just as forthright and strong-willed as he. And that only increased the respect he had for her. Furthermore, I no longer had any intention of trying to climb the ladder and upset Millie by placing myself in unnecessary danger. The matter now closed, Dougie turned his attention to the skips.

"Come on then Rick, let's find these cans of Dulux."

Walking over to the skips, I could see that Muriel had been correct in insisting that I should wear overalls. Both were piled to the top with all kinds of debris. Rooms had been completely gutted and there were old fireplaces, tiles, bits of coving, old lathe and plaster and lots of dust and soot. In addition, there were ripped and empty bags of sand, cement and plaster and the odd pieces of broken glass.

"Get up there," said Dougie as he saw me hesitating.

"Watch out. There's some sharp edges," warned Millie.

"Oh, he'll be alright if he watches his step love."

As I clambered on top and looked at the chaos around me, I was hard pressed to see any evidence of empty Dulux cans.

"There don't seem to be any cans here."

"That's because they'll be underneath Rick. I saw them at the beginning of the week and they've thrown more stuff on top since then."

The idea of rooting down through all the debris was hardly appealing.

"Well, I suppose they've got crushed and damaged with all this weight on top of them. Is there any point looking now?" I asked.

"Get off with you. You don't give up just like that. Dig round a bit."

I glanced at Millie but this time in vain. Shaking her head, she gave a slight sigh, the expression on her face devoid of any kind of sympathy. She may as well have said it: "You agreed to come, so it's your own fault."

As I rooted through the debris Dougie, safe on the pavement, was keenly directing operations.

"You need to start at one end and work down carefully."

"I'm trying grandad."

"But you're covering it up again as you go along. Move everything behind you and then you can get to the bottom and see what you're doing."

"What do you think I'm trying to do?"

"Well, you're not doing it very well lad."

I heard Millie laughing. I could imagine that I looked a complete clown, or worse still like a down-and-out searching through the bins for food outside a city centre restaurant. Either way, it did little for my self-esteem. Finally, I happened upon the holy grail but there was a problem.

"Here you are," I announced triumphantly, pulling out the can and passing it to Dougie. Much to my surprise, he looked at it with disappointment.

"It's no good without the lid."

After all my exertions, his response was anything but welcome.

"Well, that's not my fault, is it?"

"No, but you can keep looking. They've probably not bothered putting it back on with it being empty. I'm sure it'll be there and the rest of the cans too."

If I had been one of Dougie's pals, I would have told him exactly what I thought of his idea but I was the posh kid from Sale and good manners had been hammered into me for as long as I could remember. And he was my grandad too and as I stood there fuming, I suddenly burst out laughing.

"What's up with you, you daft beggar?" asked Dougie.

His response only increased my laughter and it wasn't long before I was joined by Millie. She too could only admire the audacity of the man, demanding I sweat and toil in the filth and rubble of the Skip whilst he remained fresh as the proverbial daisy. He'd made a complete fool of me and we both knew that I would end up doing as he asked. What else was there but to acknowledge the latent humour in the situation.

Calming down, I turned my attention back to the skip and continued the search.

"Here you are, is this it?" I asked, handing a lid to Dougie.

Taking it, he placed it on top of the can.

"Yes, that's it. It's in good nick too."

"Good."

"Go on then," said Dougie, impatiently. "Keep looking. The others are bound to be in there somewhere too."

I didn't wait for a thank you. Why would I? For this was Dougie and he was never one to show his appreciation. Just like with Muriel, whatever I did for him, however arduous the task, he simply expected it. I therefore continued burrowing through the debris and when I had finished, I had recovered eight empty cans of Dulux brilliant white emulsion along with their lids and some re-sealed smaller tins of coloured gloss.

"Well, they're all fine," said Dougie, placing the lids loosely on the cans. "I can make good use of this gloss too. There's some popular colours here and still a good bit in most of 'em."

I could almost hear Dougie's mind ticking over, calculating how much extra he would make on materials from this hoard of 'treasure' that the skip had offered up to him.

"You might have a bit of a job cleaning the dried gloss off the outside of the tins," I suggested.

"No, that'll come off and anyway Rick, I'll let you have that pleasure."

Millie chuckled, tickled by his comment.

"It seems a lot of work Dougie. How do you know that you won't be wasting Michael's time? Your customers might not ask for any of these colours."

"Well love, I'll show them on the colour cards I take round with me and suggest the ones I think would look nice. A lot of customers do take my advice, you know. I'm a good decorator, not a cowboy," remarked grandad, proudly.

"I'm sure you are Dougie, but don't you feel a bit guilty charging them for paint that you got out of a skip for free?" asked Millie.

"No. Of course not. We've had to graft to recover these. Customers can't expect something for nothing. That's not the way of the world, is it?"

"But Michael did all the work."

"Well, that doesn't make any difference …"

For a moment, Dougie hesitated. I suspect he was contemplating whether Millie was suggesting that I should get something for my efforts. It didn't take him long to dismiss the idea.

"He doesn't begrudge helping his old grandad. Do you lad?"

He turned towards me with that mischievous look on his face. What could I say?

"No. Of course not."

"I don't know Fraser. It seems to me that you're nothing but a rogue," observed Millie.

"Well, I suppose some might say that," he replied. "Others might think that I'm just creative. Artists, like us painters and decorators, have to be."

Millie burst out laughing. Dougie. What to do with him? He could so easily drive you to distraction but it was almost impossible to remain annoyed long enough to take offence. And of course, he knew it. Smiling, he reminded us that there was still work to be done.

"Come on then. Let's get this lot in the van and then there's the other skip to go through. We need to get weaving. I'm supposed to be seeing Vic in the King Billy."

Whilst he and Millie started moving the cans, I prepared to clamber out of the skip. Looking along the road to make sure that it was safe to get out, I noticed a police patrol car approaching. As I waited for it to pass, the car slowed down and came to a halt on the opposite side of the road. The passenger door on the far side opened and a policeman jumped out, putting his cap on his head as he did so. He was middle-aged. A sergeant and stalwart of the force. Now it was safe to get down, I jumped to the ground.

"Oi! You! Stay there!"

"What?"

"I said, stay there!"

There was menace in his voice, a warning of unpleasant consequences should I fail to respond. His colleague, a young PC, who had now exited the vehicle, reinforced the message.

"Is he giving you any trouble Sarge?"

"Only tried to make a run for it."

"Oh dear. That is unfortunate."

I remained rooted to the spot, whilst the officers walked towards me. Ordering me on to the pavement, I did as I was told.

"What's your name?" asked the sergeant.

"Michael."

"Michael who?" asked his partner, sharply.

"Michael Taylor."

"Are you from round here?"

"Well, yes and no I suppose."

"Don't try getting smart with us."

"I'm not officer. If you'll just allow me to explain."

The sergeant slowly looked me up and down, the scowl on his face indicating that he wasn't impressed. He could best be described as portly; the days of pounding the beat which had kept him in shape, now well behind him. Pulling in his stomach, he raised himself to his full height and responded to my request with disdain.

"Oh, he's not from round here, all right. Not with that la-di-da accent."

"Yes, what we have here is another clever little sod. Isn't it Sarge?"

The constable gave me an evil smile. He could only have been a few years older than myself but was unsympathetic. It was hardly surprising, for he was nothing but a snivelling sycophant whose progress in the force required him to acquire the goodwill of his colleague who insisted that suspects were guilty until proven innocent.

"Yes," replied the sergeant, "I bet 'College' here knows all his rights, but he'll soon find out that it won't get him very far with us."

I had learned that if you were black or lived on the council estates, there was no guarantee of even-handed treatment by officers of the Greater Manchester force. Now it became apparent that some of its members were not exactly fair and impartial when it came to dealing with members of the educated middle-class.

"What's the matter officer?"

It was Dougie. He and Millie had been behind the van loading the cans when they had been alerted by the shouts of the sergeant. As they were a distance from the skips, the latter didn't seem to have registered their presence. Somewhat disorientated, I had forgotten that they were there. It was fortunate because Dougie had the good sense to move the tins of gloss just behind the seats and cover them with a couple of dust sheets, whilst leaving the empty Dulux cans next to the back doors. Although it was obvious that the gloss had been thrown away, Dougie didn't want its discovery to create any further problems.

"And who are you, sir?" asked the sergeant.

"Dougie Fraser," replied grandad brightly. "This is my grandson, Michael."

It was strange not to hear him call me Rick but it made me aware that we could not take the situation lightly.

"Make a note of that constable."

With a flourish, the latter took out his notebook, flipped over the pages, took up a pen and proceeded to record our names and Dougie's address.

"What about you lad? Where do you live?"

"Oh, he's living with me at the moment. Family difficulties you know."

It was quick thinking and the officer accepted his response. In fact, since Dougie's appearance their attitude hadn't been quite so hostile. I was grateful that I had avoided giving my mother's address.

"Now then, just what have you been up to?" asked the sergeant. "The lad was behaving very suspiciously."

"All they've done is to search through the rubbish to find some empty cans that have obviously been thrown away," said Millie, who had joined us.

Surprised by the lilting sound of Millie's soft, feminine voice they looked round and were greeted by the sight of her radiant, smiling face. It seemed incongruent to see such a beautiful young woman against a background of dirt and debris. Visibly stunned, they seemed unable to respond. Dougie smiled, aware that with Millie's presence matters were likely to become much easier.

"I can show you, if you like," continued Millie. "We've put the cans in the van."

The officers stared at Millie, captivated by her charm. The young constable surreptitiously running his eyes all over her.

"Should I go and have a look, Sarge?" he asked.

"Yes, all right, whilst I talk to these two."

As Millie and her escort walked back to the van, the sergeant continued his interrogation but it was notable that he now seemed more prepared to listen.

"You see," said Dougie, "a lot of my customers are never satisfied, especially them rich beggars out in Cheshire. The normal colours aren't good enough for them, so I have to make up some unusual ones. When I find one they like I have to mix up a load of it and I need some empty cans to keep it in. None of the paint companies will sell you new ones so I have to look out for old empty ones that have been thrown away in skips."

It was a brilliant explanation and it had me convinced, even though I knew it wasn't true. He could hardly tell the sergeant about tricking his customers over Johnstone's paint.

"I see, sir," said the sergeant, "but you should still have waited until the morning to check with the builders that it was all right for you to take them. The cans are still their property you know."

Typical. The sergeant had already decided that there was nothing for him here but he still had to exert his authority and let us know that he could charge us on a technicality. What he wanted was an expression of gratitude from us for not doing so. That wasn't exactly what Dougie provided. Shaking his head he looked at the sergeant with a pair of sorrowful eyes.

"I appreciate that officer," he said with quiet resignation, "but aren't things in a bad way when an old soldier like me who fought for the freedom of his country from Hitler and the Nazis, could find himself behind bars for something like this?"

"Well, sir. I'm sorry, but it's the law."

The sergeant looked a little uncomfortable. It wasn't as easy to dismiss Dougie as he had me. I could tell that he was eager to get away. The return of Millie and his colleague provided the opportunity.

"Everything in order?" he asked.

"Yes," confirmed the constable. "There's a few empty cans in the van but nothing else. It's just as the young lady said."

"Well then, we can be getting off."

"Excuse me sergeant," I said. "What happens to the notes the constable made in his book?"

"What do you mean?"

I could see Millie looking at me intently and shaking her head. She was willing me to say no more but it was too late, for I had to reply.

"Well, do you keep them to hold on record, or do you destroy them?"

"Why do you want to know?" asked the sergeant, his tone suddenly menacing.

"In case my name and details are kept with the criminal records when I haven't done anything wrong and if that might affect me in the future if I apply for jobs like teaching."

"Oh, clever bugger, eh?" snapped the sergeant, struggling to contain himself. "You students are all the same, aren't you? Don't trust the police; they're all fascists determined to put you away. You believe any nonsense about us, don't you? You and your socialist friends."

There was clearly no point in answering his questions for he had no wish to hear a reply. I was young and educated and so in his mind was a natural enemy of law and order. I looked at Millie and nodded, an indication that this time, I would hold my tongue.

"You just keep your nose clean 'College' and then you won't have anything to worry about, will you?"

"No, sergeant," I replied, quietly.

I hated doing it but I had to recognise that he had the power. Best to let him think that he had won.

"Right," he said, sounding satisfied. "I think we can get off now."

Walking across to the patrol car, the sergeant was first to get in. Hesitating, his colleague turned to look back at Millie.

"Don't forget what I said Miss."

Millie nodded politely as we watched him settle into the driver's seat and start the engine. Moving off, the car turned right and disappeared towards Manor Street.

"That's a relief," said Millie. "You were daft there Michael. You can't give a policeman the impression that you're criticising them."

"I'm pleased you charmed that young copper Millie," observed Dougie. "I bet he wasn't that bothered about searching the van."

"No, he wasn't and you two should be thankful that I was able to jolly him along."

"Oh, aye?"

"Yes. I'd have normally told the cheeky beggar to get lost if it wasn't for having to protect you two. He was mithering me to go out with him."

"He's not allowed to do that," I said.

Dougie laughed whilst Millie stared in disbelief.

"Michael Taylor are you completely gormless?"

"Of course he is love," said Dougie. "Haven't you realised that by now?"

Feeling foolish, I remained silent.

"Do you think coppers are any different, Rick? They see a pretty girl and try to chat her up, whether they're on duty or not."

"He wouldn't take no for an answer," said Millie.

"What did you say?" asked Dougie.

"He was so full of himself. I wanted to tell him that he had a face only a mother could love but I could hardly do that, could I? Instead, I told him that I wasn't able to. The neighbours would make my life hell if they discovered I was going out with a copper. He couldn't argue with that and it still allowed the arrogant so-and-so to believe that I fancied him."

"You didn't tell him where you lived, did you?" I asked.

"Of course not."

"Oh, good. I was worried he might harass you."

Millie smiled, pleased by my concern.

"Round here," noted Dougie, "you soon learn not to tell the police anything unless you have to."

"Obviously," I replied.

"Well, I think we'll have to leave the other skip," continued Dougie. "We've wasted too much time talking to those coppers."

"Yes, we should be getting back," agreed Millie.

Pleased that I no longer had to burrow my way through another packed and dirty skip, I followed them to the van. Getting into the back I could see Grandad watching me like a hawk, making sure that I didn't damage any of his precious cans. Closing the back doors, I could finally relax as we set off on the short drive home.

Chapter Twenty-Seven

Arriving at Dougie's we put the cans and tins of gloss neatly on the shelves of the back garden shed. As we approached the kitchen door Muriel opened it and greeted us.

"Oh good, you're back. I was starting to get worried."

"There was no need to," said Dougie. "Mind out love, I need to get changed."

Brushing past her he walked through the kitchen to make his way upstairs. Their relationship had none of the romance of youth; there were few tender kisses or words of endearment. Yet Muriel wasn't concerned, accepting that she had reached the age where to Dougie she expected to be more mother than wife.

"Yes, everything's all right," confirmed Millie. "A police car stopped to ask what we were doing but they could see we were only searching through stuff that had already been thrown out."

"And we've Millie to thank for pointing it out to them," I added.

"That's why I wanted her to go with you," remarked Muriel, satisfied that her decision had been vindicated.

Millie stepped past her into the kitchen and I was about to follow when I was ordered to stop.

"You can just stay there," said Muriel. "Look at the state of those overalls. Don't think that you're bringing that muck in here."

I stared back at her, not sure what she wanted me to do about it. Then, using my hands, I tried knocking the dust off my overalls.

"That's no good. You need to take them off."

"What, out here?"

"Of course."

"But people can see me."

"You've got your underpants on, haven't you?"

"That's not the point."

"Don't be silly. There's only me and Millie who can see you and do you think we haven't seen lads in their underpants before?"

Tutting and shaking her head, Muriel rolled her eyes and let out a sigh. Behind her Millie began to chuckle. Joining Muriel at the door she was eager to embarrass me further.

"Yes, don't be daft Michael. You haven't got anything special to see, have you?"

As she and Muriel burst out laughing, I felt increasingly self-conscious.

"Aww, poor Michael, you've gone beetroot. Are you getting all embarrassed?" asked Millie.

"No."

It was an unconvincing answer and thankfully Millie took mercy on me.

"Have you a clothes brush, Muriel?"

"Yes, love. In the cupboard under the sink."

Popping back into the kitchen, Millie quickly returned and joined me outside.

"Right, stand still and put your arms out."

Doing as she asked, Millie then set about brushing me down from front to back and top to bottom.

"There you are. It was mainly dust. He'll be fine now."

"All right Michael. You can come in now," said Muriel.

Grateful to get inside, I was off to get washed and changed.

"Make sure you put those overalls in the wash basket."

"I will."

When I reached the hallway, Dougie had put on his jacket and was about to slip out of the front door. He was eager not to lose any drinking time through being waylaid by Muriel in the kitchen.

"Right lad, I'm off. I'll be back for dinner."

When I came downstairs, Muriel and Millie were sat in the middle room. A pot of tea, three mugs, milk and sugar were on a tray in the centre of the table. The welcoming aroma of roast beef was beginning to waft its way through the house; Sunday dinner well on course to be delivered on Dougie's return from the pub.

"Sit down, love. Me and Millie are having a natter."

Pouring out the tea, she added the milk and sugar and set the mugs down on the mats next to us.

"Muriel was telling me Michael, that the reason she went home on Friday night, was because Dougie hadn't taken the forms to the register office to arrange a date for the marriage as he'd promised."

"Yes," said Muriel, "but last night, after you'd gone to bed, we sorted everything out."

"Oh, I see. He told me that it was because he'd forgotten your birthday."

"That's true as well," she replied, "but that didn't bother me so much."

"I didn't know it was your birthday, otherwise I would have got you a card."

"I know you would cock. You're not like your grandad."

"Dougie doesn't realise how lucky he is," said Millie.

"He's just inconsiderate, the same as most men. They're just like big kids."

"I suppose so," agreed Millie.

"Yes but at least things are starting to change," observed Muriel. "Young Michael and there's others like him, are a bit more thoughtful. You've still got be on top of 'em though."

"That's true enough," replied Millie, smiling across at me. "It's not a good idea to let them get ideas above their station."

"That's right," said Muriel.

"How did you meet Dougie?" asked Millie.

"I've known him and Vic since before the War but I didn't see much of them after I got married. A couple of years ago, after I lost my husband, some of my friends took me out to the King Billy. He saw me, came over to talk and we started meeting regularly. He was a cheeky beggar though."

"Oh?"

"Yes. When he first asked me out, we went to a fancy restaurant in town. He brought me home in a taxi, I asked him in and we sat talking for a while. Well, it got past midnight and so I suggested that he should think about getting off home and do you know what he said?"

"Well, no," replied Millie, eager to hear the rest of the story.

"He said, 'What? You want me to go home?' Well, yes, I replied. It's getting late. 'You mean to say that I've paid for an expensive night out, a taxi and everything and I'm not getting anything in return?' Well, I was shocked. I thought, you cheeky so-and-so."

It was Dougie all over. Was there anything that he wasn't capable of? I looked at Millie. She too was struggling to contain her laughter, unsure as to whether Muriel would be upset if she could not.

"It's all right. You can laugh," said Muriel. "I had to."

"You had to?"

"Yes. He's such a lovable rogue. What can you do?"

"So, you did then?" asked Millie, quietly.

Muriel nodded, turned her head away from me and silently mouthed the words of confirmation to Millie.

Her actions seemed bizarre, for she had been sharing Dougie's bed for most of the weekends that I had been staying. Yet that traditional sense of decorum, the hallmark of older working-class women, had suddenly reasserted itself as she tried to protect my innocence by concealing Grandad's amorous antics. Quickly she changed the subject.

"Michael, me and your grandad are planning a bit of a celebration for after we get married. Do you think your mam will want to come?"

"Yes, I don't see why not."

"Oh, good. Your grandad told me she was devoted to her mam so I thought that she might not be keen on the idea."

"She's grateful that you try to keep Grandad on the straight and narrow and anyway, it doesn't matter what she thinks. Your only concern should be about doing what's right for you."

"Things are never that simple. You'll understand when you're older. Families are important. Your grandad would be upset if he lost touch with your mam again."

"Well, I'm sure that's not going to happen."

"Don't rush back for dinner Michael, I'll put it in the oven" said Muriel, changing the subject. "You two need to spend some time together. You've not seen so much of one another this weekend, have you?"

"No, we haven't," replied Millie, "but it was all in a good cause, except for the fact that City didn't win."

"Ah, but they've still got the replay love."

"Yes, I suppose so."

"Well, I'd best be getting on with the Yorkshire pudding," said Muriel, getting up from the table. "It's your grandad's favourite. He'd have me make one every day if I let him."

It was our cue to leave.

"We'd best be getting back to Jeanette's," I said.

"All right then cock."

"Bye Muriel," said Millie.

"It was nice to see you love. Don't leave it so long before you come again."

"I won't."

Millie threw her arms around Muriel, gave her a hug and then we were on our way.

Chapter Twenty-Eight

When we arrived back, Jeanette was also getting on with the dinner but her approach was far more relaxed. For Muriel's generation, it was a practice set in stone that Sunday dinner would be ready on the table on their husband's return from the pub at just after two o'clock. For many young wives and mothers, the timetable had become something of an anachronism. It was indicative of the fact that older conventions had been slowly breaking down. For Jeanette, who enjoyed a lie-in, dinner would be served when she was good and ready. After all she knew that there were cereals, bread and jam in the cupboards and milk and butter in the fridge. If Terry or the kids were hungry, they could help themselves. Yet not all children on the estate were as fortunate as Craig and Gary and for many the cupboards were almost bare and sugar butties the nearest that they would get to a Sunday roast.

"Do you need any help?" asked Millie, noticing that her sister had only just started peeling the potatoes.

"No, I'll be fine. Terry's just nipped out. He'll be back soon to give me a lift."

"I don't mind," said Millie "and Michael can help too."

"No. Don't be daft," replied Jeanette. "You two need to spend some time together and if Michael's here when Terry gets back, they'll be arguing over the match won't they? Then you'll never get out."

"Yes, no doubt," replied Millie, looking accusingly at me.

"No, we wouldn't argue," I objected.

"Oh, of course not," observed Jeanette. "Men!"

Millie sighed in agreement. My objection rejected.

"You could just go and check on the kids in the park," Jeanette suggested.

"Of course. We're going there anyway. When do you want them back in?"

"Well, dinner's going to be about an hour and a half."

"Right, we'll bring them back if they're still out there."

"Oh, you know the kids. They will be. Once they start playing football they haven't a thought for anything else."

"Well at least they're fit and healthy and it keeps them out of trouble," I suggested.

"Yes, hopefully. Anyway Michael, would you like me to put some dinner out for you?"

"Thanks, that's very kind. I'd love to but I'd better not. Muriel's keeping some in the oven for me. I'll struggle to eat it if I have any more."

"Aw, he's always so polite, isn't he?"

"Yes, that's our Michael," agreed Millie.

Had we been led blindfold to the park and then abandoned on its edge, the shouts of excitement or the groans of despair that greeted every goal or missed opportunity would have soon directed us towards Craig and Gary. The game, which was now into its third hour, was still as intense and fascinating as ever. Artistry and chaos produced by a hotchpotch of talent. Against the backdrop of the towering maisonettes, the playing field was levelled and the hoofer competed with the prodigy and players from all points in between. Lads seven to seventeen, the youngest keen to impress. Jumpers for goalposts and a wide-open pitch. Around twelve-a-side and sometimes more, as kids wandered off whilst others joined in. And here there was no need of referees for the spirit of fair play always prevailed. Disputes over goals quickly settled; handball and clumsy tackles soon acknowledged. Rascals many of these kids could be but cheating on the pitch they didn't want to see.

"Jeanette was right. I don't think there's any danger of the kids giving up any time soon," said Millie.

"Of course not," I replied. "Football's everything to them and all these other lads too."

"Let's go and sit on the swings," suggested Millie. "There'll be no one there now and we can sit and talk."

Slowly we made our way over. There were two sets, one of them consisting of safety seats for toddlers, as well as a seesaw and a roundabout. The equipment had been put in when the estate was first built but it was now looking tired. The tarmacked floor was crumbling and uneven, yet the playground was well used by children in the day and was a place for teenagers to hang around at dusk. Sitting side by side we began to swing gently back and forth before Millie placed her feet on the ground and asked me about Dougie.

"It's a very unusual spelling, your grandad's surname, isn't it? At work we have quite a few customers called Fraser, but it's always with an s or a z. There are people called Frazier but I've never come across the spelling f-r-a-i-z-e-r."

"That's because it's not right."

"What?"

"He's made it up."

"But why? He's written it on an official document."

"Because he's always evasive when it comes to the authorities. He doesn't pay tax or insurance so he thinks it makes it harder for them to track him down."

"But surely he knows that the register office will ask him for his birth certificate."

"I suspect Grandad believes that they'll accept his army discharge certificate and on it his name is spelled f-r-a-i-z-e-r."

"That's not very likely though, is it?"

"No, it isn't. I can't imagine how Muriel's going to react if he has to produce a birth certificate and she realises that he's using two different names."

"From what I've learned about Dougie," said Millie, "he'll find a way out of it. Anyway, Muriel's not daft, she knows what he's like. She's happy enough to put up with him."

"Still, I wish I hadn't found out about the form. Perhaps I should have a word with Muriel. I'll probably feel guilty if I don't."

"No, Michael. You mustn't. It's not your responsibility. They have to sort it out for themselves. Neither of them will thank you for getting involved."

"Yes. I suppose so."

"Anyway, it's your future that's most important. Have you decided on your choices for UCCA?"

"Yes. I'm putting Manchester down first."

"What about Birmingham?"

Millie's question came as a surprise for my decision could not have been unexpected. I had fallen in love with her and she knew it. There was no chance that I would be going anywhere else.

"Birmingham's my second choice but as the offer's the same, it's a bit pointless putting it down."

"But I thought you wanted new experiences; to go somewhere different."

"I only said that when we first met and if you remember, at the time you told me that I just needed to find something that would make me want to stay in Manchester and I have."

"Oh. And that's City is it?"

"Don't be daft. You know what I mean."

"Do I?"

Millie, her eyelashes fluttering ever so slightly, observed me with her curious green eyes. Her cheeks were aglow; her lips soft and inviting, drawing me irresistibly towards them. Kissing her tenderly, I took her hand gently in mine.

"Well. Michael Taylor. It's not like you to be so bold."

"Back then," I continued, encouraged by her smile, "you also told me that it would have to be something I couldn't find anywhere else."

"And you've remembered that all this time, have you? I am impressed."

"Yes. And it's not something that I've found, it's someone. I love you Millie Arkwright and I want us to be together."

"That may well be but you also spoke of going elsewhere. You said you wanted new experiences. Are you sure that you won't regret giving them up by staying here?"

I could see that Millie was determined not to make it easy for me. Hers was a caring nature; a concern for others rather than herself. Although pleased by my declaration of love, she still had to be convinced that my best interests would be served in Manchester.

"There's nothing to give up," I explained. "I've already found those new experiences. And they're right here. All around me. Being with Dougie and his pals, spending time with Dave and Dawn, staying here on the estate. It's been an education. I've seen so much. And most of all, because of you, I've learned that love is everything."

"So, you're like a man transformed?"

"I believe I am."

"Are you sure? Perhaps its infatuation. It does happen."

"Do you think I'm too inexperienced to know the difference?"
Millie waited, looking at me closely before replying.
"No, Michael, but I had to ask. I don't want to see you give up good opportunities because of me. I need to feel sure that you are doing the right thing."
"I am Millie. I've given it a great deal of thought. I was well-aware that you'd expect nothing less."
Millie laughed gently, a sign that she was now satisfied with my decision. Feeling relieved, I felt confident enough to ask her a question that had been on my mind for quite some time.
"Millie?"
"Yes."
"Once I start university, can we get engaged?"
"Engaged?"
"Yes."
"Why? What's wrong with things as they are?"
"Well, nothing but I'd like to make a formal commitment to you."
"And have me do the same?"
"Well yes, I suppose so."
Millie laughed.
"You don't have to worry, Michael. I'm not having second thoughts about you."
"Oh no, I didn't mean to …."
I was silent. I had no idea how to continue. I was deadly serious about getting engaged for I knew that I wanted us to get married and spend the rest of our lives together. Yet I also knew that what Millie had said was partly true. I did at times feel insecure. After all, I still struggled to understand why a young woman as beautiful and wonderful as Millie, would choose to go out with someone like me.
"It's all right Michael, I understand but we've got plenty of time. I want to wait until Christmas and if we still feel the same about one another then you can buy me a ring, we'll get engaged and find ourselves a house together."
"Before we get married?"
"Of course."
"But that means we'd be living over the brush."

"So what?" asked Millie, with a chuckle. "You are old-fashioned Michael. Isn't it what Dougie and Muriel have been doing? And haven't you been happy enough to stay with them at weekends?"

"Yes, but they're older. Wouldn't people criticise you for doing it?"

"Not many would round here, but perhaps they would where you live. Then again, the middle classes are supposed to be more liberal, aren't they? Jeanette's always telling me about the stories in the News of the World and the antics that go on behind the closed doors of suburbia."

"Hmm. I'm not sure about that."

"Really? No wife swapping going on at the tennis and cricket clubs then?"

"Not that I know of."

"Or is there something you're not telling me?"

"What do you mean?"

I should have known that Millie was pulling my leg but her ability to keep a straight face whilst asking questions in serious and measured tones had me completely fooled.

"Well, do I know everything about you Michael? After all, you belong to those clubs, don't you? I wonder if any of those bored and frustrated wives have taken a fancy to you?"

"No, of course not."

"It's all right. You can tell me."

"There's nothing to tell. Nothing like that has ever happened."

"Oh, hasn't it? You do sound disappointed."

Millie observed me closely. I could feel my face starting to burn. It was an open invitation for her to tease me further.

"Well, I can see that just the thought of it is enough to get you all hot and bothered. It's obvious that you must have been tempted."

"Tempted?"

"Yes. All those experienced older women wandering around in their short, frilly tennis skirts. Don't tell me that it didn't get you all excited."

Surprised by her comment I was unable to respond.

"You're thinking about it now, aren't you? That's why you've gone all quiet."

"No, I'm not."

"Really?"

Millie paused. Her eyes sparkled as her lips parted slowly into the most beautiful of smiles. I shook my head and sighed, realising that she had been having me on. Or had she? With Millie it was difficult to tell where the teasing ended and flirtation began. And she did it on purpose, taking pleasure from the fact that she could so easily excite my emotions.

"Anyway," she continued, changing the subject, "if we do end up living together you must think of it as part of your transformation; just one more of those fascinating new experiences."

Millie smiled and hearing her light-hearted repetition of my own words, I found myself joining in with her gentle laughter.

"Attitudes are changing Michael and for the better. Our Jeanette and Terry are very happy but my mam and dad's marriage was a disaster. It's better to live together first and find out if you can get along with one another twenty-four hours a day before getting trapped in an unhappy marriage."

"I suppose it is."

"And more to the point, you'll be able to find out if you really do enjoy having your wicked way with me. In a place of our own, we can do what we like, when we like."

It was a wonderful thought. How awkward it was for us to be alone. Terry and Jeanette rarely went out and if they did, then we had to babysit the boys. Muriel too, preferred to stay in, only infrequently accompanying Dougie to the pub. Millie had offered a vision of the future where all my pent-up frustrations would be consigned to the past. As I let slip an involuntary sigh, Millie took my hand and squeezed it gently.

"I'm sorry Michael. I'm not being fair. I really shouldn't tease you like this. But you do like it, don't you?"

Wearing a coquettish smile, Millie knew how easy it was to arouse me. Seductive and suggestive, her words had the power to electrify. She was the most gorgeous woman I had ever seen and as I looked pleadingly into her eyes, my heart was pounding, my pulse racing. It seemed so unfair. I wanted her so badly and now all I could think about was being alone together in our own little house. And I'm sure that she knew what I was thinking, her soothing voice a signal that it was time for to me dampen the flames of desire.

"What you have to remember Michael, is that it will be worth the wait."

"Will it?" I mumbled.

"Of course it will. Don't you think that something you want is so much better when you have to wait for it?"

Taking a deep breath, I reluctantly nodded in agreement.

"I suppose so. It certainly gives me something to look forward to."

Yet I did not tell her how much the waiting could hurt. The battle to suppress the insatiable desire that erupted without warning from the simplest of triggers. A toss of the head that made her soft, light brown hair dance across her cheeks. The unbuttoned top of her blouse that revealed the smooth white skin of her graceful, elegant neck. And always that stunning figure which I was so eager to embrace. Of course, ours was a relationship in which Millie was in charge. It had been that way from the start and I admit that it suited and excited me. Perhaps the pain excited me too and I knew that when I was around Millie my feelings and senses were truly alive.

"Right, come on," said Millie. "Stop thinking about rude things. It's almost time for dinner so we'd best get the kids."

Chapter Twenty-Nine

Back at the game the non-stop action had started to take its toll. The teams were down to around seven-a-side as exhausted youngsters lay resting behind the goals. Even Craig was taking a breather but Gary was still in goal, watching the action carefully from his position between the posts. An outfield player, Craig expended far more energy around the pitch, yet Gary's role required intense concentration and was mentally tiring in a way Craig's position was not. Of the two it was Gary who impressed the most. He had already gained the respect of the older boys who wanted him on their side. He was brave and agile and rarely made a mistake. If Gary retained his enthusiasm and continued to develop his skills, who knows how far he could go. What a pity he supported the other lot.

Walking behind the goal Millie told the boys that it was time to come in. Too tired to protest, Craig got to his feet whilst Gary told his teammates that he needed replacing. Unwilling to risk ridicule by comparison to the young keeper, no one stepped forward. The game had ground to a halt.

"Were you watching us?" asked Gary, as we set off home.

"Yes. Earlier on and for the last few minutes," replied Millie.

"What did you think?"

"Auntie Millie's a girl," said Craig. "She won't know."

"Oh, yeah and what about Helen then?" asked Gary. "She's a girl right and goes to all City's games and she knows what makes a good player."

"Well, she's different," replied Craig.

"There are lots of women and girls who go to watch both City and United," I said.

"When Georgie Best was playing for United," said Millie, "loads of girls used to go and watch."

"They went to his boutiques as well," I replied.

"So?"

"Well, a lot of young women fancied him. I suspect a fair number of them weren't that interested in football. When he and Mike Summerbee opened their boutique in Sale, hordes of

teenage girls and young women skipped off school and work to
go and see him."

"Yes, I can understand that," said Millie. "He's lovely."

"To be fair, a lot of lads were there too. I hate to admit it but
you can only admire a special talent like George. Anyway Millie,
you haven't told the boys what you think of their performance."

"But I'm only a girl. What do I know?"

Millie turned to look at Craig who, believing that he had upset
her, appeared very guilty.

"I'm sorry Auntie Millie. I didn't mean it. Please tell us what
you think."

"I thought you were both brilliant. How you can keep playing
for so long amazes me. And you're both so skilful. You never
know, in years to come the scouts from Old Trafford might offer
you both a trial."

"Oh yeah," said Gary. "That would be great."

"And if you're really good," I added, "then you might get one
at Maine Road."

"Huh, we wouldn't want to play for them," said Gary.

"Yeah, we'd rather turn out for Accrington Stanley," added
Craig.

"That's you put in your place," said Millie, laughing.

"I suppose I asked for that. These boys will never see sense."

Leaving the park, I noticed a large mound of blackened
carpets, furniture and appliances that had been left in front of the
maisonettes on Hursthead Walk.

"What's that doing there," I asked?

"It's Bob and Ian's. They had a fire," said Craig.

"When was that?"

"In the night."

"I must have been fast asleep. I didn't hear any fire engines."

"Neither did I," said Millie.

"Our friend Tommy lives in the block," continued Craig "and
everyone had to get up and go outside until they'd put it out."

"No one was hurt, were they?" I asked.

"I don't think so," replied Craig.

"That's not surprising," noted Millie. "Bob and Ian are getting
to be experts at it."

"What do you mean?" I asked.

"What do you think?"

I shrugged my shoulders.

"I don't know, you are slow on the uptake."

Suddenly the penny dropped.

"You mean they started it themselves?"

"Yes. Of course."

"But why would they do that?"

"For the insurance money."

"What's that?" asked Craig

"Nothing for you to worry about. Stop being nosey."

The boys walked on a few yards ahead kicking the ball backwards and forwards to one another.

"But surely they'll have to spend it on replacements for the damaged items, won't they?"

"No. The insurance company will give them the cash. Bob told me that they were after the tenancy of a pub in town. It's going cheap because it's rundown and they intend to make it a venue for the gay community. They probably want the money to do it up."

"The gay community?"

"Yes. There aren't many places where they're safe in Manchester and they know that Bob and Ian will make them welcome."

"Why?"

"Because, if you haven't noticed, Bob and Ian are gay."

"Oh. I see."

Millie laughed softly and shook her head at my naïvety.

"Anyway," I continued, "what they did was dangerous. They could have set the whole block on fire. Surely the neighbours aren't very pleased."

"They won't be bothered. When it happened before Bob called the fire brigade right away. He claimed that Ian had fallen asleep on the settee with a lit cig. The fire hardly got going but it didn't matter. The firemen still had to hose everything down so Bob claimed for smoke and water damage. None of the other maisonettes were affected and it looks the same this time. Ian will be full of apologies and insist that it was an accident. And of course, no one has any sympathy for the insurance company."

"But from what you've told me, the neighbours know it wasn't an accident. Surely someone will be angry and tell the insurance company."

"I don't know," said Millie, "you still haven't learned that much about people round here, have you?"

"I know. You're going to say that no one's going to grass on their neighbours, but Bob and Ian have put people in danger and they could do it anonymously."

"If they don't get their money anyone even slightly suspected of informing will get their windows put in."

"What. Bob and Ian would do that?"

"No, they wouldn't, but any number of lads would."

"Why would they get involved?"

"Because it lets everyone on the estate know what happens to informers. They see it as protecting their own interests."

The conversation ending, we reached Jeanette's. As we entered by the kitchen door, she was taking the plates out of the cupboard and placing them on the top ready for dinner.

"I know Muriel's saved you some dinner Michael but you can have that later. I've got loads here so you might as well have some with us and then you and Millie can spend more time together."

"Oh, all right. Thank you."

Walking into the kitchen, Terry was immediately on the offensive.

"Huh, I just watched the highlights of your lot on telly. You know you've blown it, don't you?"

"No. We just fancied another day out in London, that's all."

"You can stop right there!" said Jeanette, sharply. "If you think I'm listening to you two arguing about football, then you've got another thing coming. Terry, watch those pans don't boil over and you Michael. Well," she paused and took a deep breath, "you're supposed to be intelligent, so act like it and ignore him. I don't know. The pair of you. Just like a couple of kids."

Craig looked at me with a self-satisfied smirk, a costly error as Jeanette quickly rounded on him.

"And you've got nothing to laugh about. Look at the state of you. Get upstairs and get washed. You're not sitting at the table like that. And you can get up there with him," she continued, giving Gary the sternest of stares.

Jeanette had spoken and none of us were prepared to defy her.

"What can I do to help?" I asked.

"You can set the table, if you would."

"Yes, of course."

Jeanette gave me a smile. Like Millie she was never angry for long. Once she had made her point then it was all forgotten. Terry, standing behind her, raised his eyebrows and shook his head as if to register disapproval at my abject surrender. Yet for a man dutifully attending to the boiling spuds and cabbage, his criticism was hardly convincing.

Once ready, the meal was something to savour. Jeanette was an excellent cook and eager to see her meals enjoyed. Sunday dinner, although a relaxed affair, was still important to her. After all, it was the only time that she knew the family could eat together. Having brought healthy appetites to the table we were rewarded with roast leg of pork, crackling and apple sauce. Individual Yorkshire puddings. Mash and roasties, cabbage, peas and carrots and to top it all, lashings of marmite gravy. There was no talk of football at the table for it had been forbidden. The spotlight turned instead on Craig and Gary and their time at school, whilst Terry told us about the families and companies he had worked for and the far-flung places to where he had removed them.

With dinner over, the boys were eager to be back out. It was late afternoon and school tomorrow. Bath time would soon be upon them and so every minute was vital. Under strict orders to be back by half-past six, Craig and Gary escaped. Volunteering to do the washing up, Millie and I went into the kitchen whilst Terry and Jeanette snuggled up on the settee and watched television together.

The pots put away and the tops washed down, Millie and I went up to her bedroom where we could sit, chat and cuddle whilst listening to music. The weekend was nearing its end. Soon I would have to leave to see Dougie before he left for the pub and then it would be time to set off home.

"I can come back and see you tomorrow night," I suggested.

"No."

Millie's firm response came as a shock. For a moment I wondered if I had somehow upset her. Seeing my concern she smiled.

"It's all right, Michael. You'll be back at Dougie's on Wednesday. You can see me then. You need to get on with your revision. Don't leave anything to chance."

"Don't worry. Getting into Owens and staying with you is the only incentive I need. I've revised solidly for the last six weeks. I won't be unprepared."

"That's good. I know you're clever but you can't be complacent. There's no substitute for hard work. I know that from my 'O' levels and it certainly paid off for me."

"Yes, it's just like drawing a lower league side in the Cup. If you're overconfident, don't prepare properly and underestimate the opposition, then a shock is on the cards and out you go."

Millie laughed.

"Are you sure that you want to stay in Manchester because of me? It does sound like City are the ones holding you here."

"Of course, I am. I just like making football analogies."

"All right then. I'll let you off."

Millie looked closely into my eyes before kissing me unexpectedly on the lips. As she moved away, I could still sense the lingering pressure of her soft, full lips on mine and I tingled with excitement.

"I don't know," she said, shaking her head.

"What?"

"Can't I kiss you without you getting fruity?"

"I'm not."

"Really?"

Millie gave me a look of stern disapproval. Excited by the fleeting fancy that I was about to be sternly punished, I began to blush.

"It's not my fault that you affect me so."

I could tell by her sparkling eyes that my response had pleased her but she was determined to play the game a little bit longer maintaining a serious air.

"It's no good getting amorous. We're not on our own and anyway we don't have the time. It's back home for you and on with the revision."

"Oh," I replied, sighing in frustration.

Millie laughed softly, her hair dancing gracefully across her cheeks.

"Poor Michael. Never mind. These things are sent to try us."

Once again, she burst into laughter. Oh, how she loved to tease me but then, how much I enjoyed it. After all, I had learned long ago that she would always leave me wanting more.

Outside the bedroom door, we could hear the boys coming up the stairs. The time had crept around to half past six and it was time for me to leave. Making our way downstairs, we popped into the front room so that I could say farewell to Terry and Jeanette before Millie and I shared a long, lingering kiss at the front door. Setting off down the path to the road beyond, I kept looking back and waving at Millie. Halting at the corner, she waved in return, before slowly closing the door and right away I was missing her. I would return to see her on Wednesday night and it couldn't come soon enough.

Chapter Thirty

At Grandad's all was quiet. Shep lay asleep in his basket whilst Dougie had nodded off in the front room. Muriel though was full of energy and almost as soon as I had entered the kitchen, she was fussing around me in that endearing way of hers; kindness and affection in equal measure.

"I said to your grandad that Jeanette must have given you some dinner or you'd have been back earlier."

"Yes, I'm sorry."

"That's all right cock. I told you to spend your time with Millie. Your dinner's fine. I can still warm it up."

"Well, if it's not too much trouble."

"Trouble? Nothing's too much trouble for my grandson. You're a growing lad. You need feeding up. Especially for those exams."

"Yes, I can't slip up if I want to spend the next three years here with Millie."

"You've decided to stay in Manchester then?"

"Yes."

"I knew you would. I told your grandad. I said to him, our Michael's not going to Birmingham or anywhere else, he thinks far too much of Millie. He loves the girl. And you do. Don't you Michael?"

"Yes, I do."

Muriel threw her arms around me and gave me a squeeze.

"Your grandad won't say it but he'll be pleased you're staying. He wouldn't want to lose one of his best pals now, would he?"

"I hope not."

Having put my dinner to warm through in the oven, Muriel suggested that we go into the front room as 'Hart to Hart,' one of her favourite programmes, was just about to begin.

"Do you like it cock?"

"I've not really watched it."

I had and thought it was rubbish, but I couldn't tell Muriel that.

"Oh, I never miss it. That Robert Wagner. He's lovely."

Fortunately, I didn't have to watch it all, for at the second break Muriel went to check on my dinner and declared that it was ready. Setting a place at the table, I sat down to eat whilst Muriel returned to Robert Wagner and the lovely Stephanie Powers.

"You're back then?"

I looked up from the table as Dougie entered the room.

"Yes."

"You'll be off home soon?"

"Yes, once I've finished my dinner."

"And you'll be here on Wednesday night? We'll need to get off early on Thursday."

"I certainly will."

"Good."

Dougie nodded his head.

"It's been a good weekend Rick, hasn't it?"

"Yes. Except for Hoddle's jammy equaliser."

Dougie laughed.

"Never mind. Perhaps it'll be our turn to be lucky on Thursday."

I nodded but wasn't convinced. Grandad had a lifetime of memories to look back on but during the time that I had attended matches, we never seemed to have our share of good fortune.

"Well Rick, I best go up and get washed. I've to meet Vic at the King Billy."

As I finished eating, I could hear the theme tune from Hart to Hart playing in the background. It was the cue for Muriel to come in from the front room.

"Did you enjoy it cock?"

"Yes, it was lovely."

"Well, you must have. I can see you've cleaned the plate."

Muriel had a smile on her face. She loved to be appreciated and I suppose the fact that she could see I was genuinely grateful for all she did, endeared me to her. In a sense, my presence at weekends compensated for the fact that with Dougie she could rarely feel treasured. After all, any gratitude he felt towards her was grudging at best. It was a legacy of her generation. She was just one of the millions of wives and mothers who had given their all to their husbands and children and were all too often simply taken for granted.

About to clear the table, Muriel beat me to it.

"I'll see to these. You need to be getting off. Go and get your coat and scarf and then you can shout up to your grandad."

Going out to the hallway, I tried to put on my shoes whilst Shep, eager to slow my departure, grabbed at my laces.

"Shep!"

Startled by Muriel's reprimand, Shep went scurrying for his basket, whilst I took a sharp intake of breath.

"I'm sorry cock. I didn't make you jump, did I?"

"Just a bit."

The two of us started laughing as I put on my coat.

"Right Grandad. I'm off," I shouted up the stairs.

I heard the bathroom door open and Dougie reply.

"All right then lad."

Opening the front door, I turned to Muriel.

"We love having you here Michael."

"I love coming and not only because of Millie."

"We know that. Come here, give us a kiss before you go."

As Muriel put her arms around me, I bent forward but she still had to stand on her tiptoes to kiss me on the cheek. As she stood back, we said our farewells and I was gone.

Catching the 192 I soon reached Piccadilly and boarded the bus back to Sale. It had been an eventful weekend and one that I would long remember. The moment when I had committed myself to remaining in Manchester. It was the only decision possible given my desire to share a life with Millie, yet there were other benefits too. Travelling with Dougie and his pals I had learned that real life experience was as important to education as reading and lectures. And for a privileged young man from the suburbs, there could be no better classroom than the Brunswick Estate. Yet there was still a matter that lay unresolved; the destination of the Cup. The shared loyalty to the Blues would draw me back to Grandad and his pals and together we would journey south once more and hope that this time, fate would be on our side. But whatever the result, however despondent we may become, at the start of August a new season would begin and for football fans everywhere, hope always springs eternal.